"You won't be free of your nightmares until you face them head-on."

Lacey looked determined. "I won't go." She leaned back against the corral's fence.

Scully's voice softened. "You don't have to be afraid. I'll be there. You have to face the shadows in your dreams sooner or later."

The sudden fear in Lacey's expression stopped Scully cold.

"It's just...I don't know if I want to face them. The shadows scare me, Scully. I don't want to remember anything about them."

"Shadows can't hurt you."

"I know, but—"

"But what?"

Lacey's eyes filled. "You won't always be there for me, Scully. What will I do then?"

The question suddenly more than he could bear, Scully drew Lacey close. She trembled as he stroked her hair and said, "Who said I wouldn't always be there for you? I expect to be around as long as you need me."

Books by Elaine Barbieri

Love Inspired Historical

The Redemption of Jake Scully #10

ELAINE BARBIERI

was born in a historic New Jersey city. She has written more than forty novels and has been published by Berkley/Jove, Leisure, Harlequin, Harper, Avon, and Zebra Books. Her titles have hit *USA TODAY*, the *New York Times* extended list and other major bestseller lists across the country, and are published worldwide. Ms. Barbieri has received many awards for her work, including Storyteller of the Year, Awards of Excellence, and Best Saga Awards from *Romantic Times BOOKreviews*. Her novels have been Doubleday and Rhapsody Book Club selections, and her book *More Precious Than Gold* was a launch novel for Romance Alive Audio. Ms. Barbieri lives in West Milford, New Jersey, with her husband and family.

THE
REDEMPTION
OF JAKE SCULLY

ELAINE BARBIERI

Steeple
Hill®

Published by Steeple Hill Books™

STEEPLE HILL BOOKS

Steeple
Hill®

ISBN-13: 978-0-373-82790-9
ISBN-10:   0-373-82790-3

THE REDEMPTION OF JAKE SCULLY

www.SteepleHill.com

Printed in U.S.A.

Rise up and help us;
redeem us because of your unfailing love.
—*Psalm* 44:26

To my brother, Andrew Favati,
whose life was a celebration of God's love,
and who left us with the memory of his smile.

Prologue

$\backsim\!\!\bullet$

Weaver, Arizona
1872

The heat of midafternoon scorched Weaver's main street as Lacey Stewart walked wearily toward the Gold Nugget Saloon, pulling a limping burro behind her. Her platinum pigtails were in disarray, her face and clothes smoke-stained and the wound on her forehead was grotesquely swollen. She was feverish and more tired than she had ever been in her eight years of life, but she forced herself on.

Dizzy and disoriented, unaware of the sudden silence her appearance elicited, she pushed open the saloon doors and started toward the bar. Fragmented sounds and images raced across her mind. She heard again the gunshot that had awakened her at dawn in her grandfather's isolated cabin. She heard the crackle and hiss of fire, felt the intense heat and choking smoke of the blaze suddenly surrounding her. She saw her grandfather appear beside her bunk to guide their frantic escape through the flames and falling beams.

Flashing even more brightly before her eyes was the image of her grandfather slumping to the ground when she thought they were safe at last, the same moment when she noticed the bloody wound on his chest.

Her grandfather's final words resounded in her ears as Lacey reached the saloon bar—words he had spoken as he pressed the small, family Bible he had also saved from the flames into her hand...

Go to town...to the saloon. Ask for Jake Scully. Tell him who you are. He'll take care of you, Lacey. Take the Bible. Depend on it. Let it guide your way. It's yours now, darlin'. Go...hurry...

Lacey nodded in response to the voice so vividly real in her mind. She had been too numb to cry when she covered her grandfather's still body with Careful's blanket and placed a bunch of drooping wildflowers beside it. His instructions had reverberated in her mind as she left the charred remains of the cabin behind her and turned the burro toward town.

She couldn't remember when Careful started limping, or when she started walking.

The sound of her name penetrated Lacey's confused haze. She turned and looked at the big man standing behind her in the silent saloon.

The big man reached for her as darkness abruptly consumed her.

Lacey came slowly awake in a large, shadowed bedroom. Her head hurt, and her limbs felt too heavy to lift. She shifted in bed and moaned slightly at the pain. She became belatedly aware that the tall man was sitting close by.

She strained to focus as he moved closer. She heard him say, "My name is Jake Scully, Lacey."

She rasped in response, "My grandpa's d-dead."

"I know."

"The cabin burned down."

"I know that, too."

"My grandpa said—"

"I know what he said." Interrupting her, the gentleness in his deep voice a comfort despite his emotionless demeanor, Scully continued softly, "Charlie Pratt was a good man. He staked me when I needed help. He did right when he told you to come to me. Don't think about anything but getting well, Lacey. I'll take care of the rest."

The single tear that slipped out the corner of Lacey's eye somehow scorched her skin as it slid across her temple, but Scully brushed it away with his hand.

His deep voice soothed her fears as her consciousness began slipping away and he repeated, "Don't worry. I'll take care of everything."

A bright afternoon sun lit the large, masculine bedroom as Lacey slowly awakened. She glanced at the unfamiliar surroundings, gradually recalling the numbing events of the past few days: long, confused hours as she lay in bed recuperating from her wounds; the doctor's gentle words; encouraging female voices; Jake Scully's reassuring presence.

Lacey's throat choked tight and she threw back her coverlet. She stood up slowly, hardly aware of the oversize man's shirt and rolled-up trousers that hung loosely on her childish frame as her attention was caught by the muted notes of a song coming from the saloon below.

She stepped down onto the barroom floor and walked

toward the piano, where a gray-haired, heavily mustached fellow continued his enthusiastic playing.

Unconscious of the attention she drew from the saloon patrons, Lacey joined in, singing hoarsely, "Oh, Susannah, don't you cry for me…"

So intense was her recollection of the many times she had sung that song to raise her grandfather's spirits after another day's fruitless prospecting, that she did not notice the two men at the end of the bar who exchanged anxious glances at the sight of her. She did not see them slip out the doorway into the alley, nor did she see them meet up with the fellow obviously waiting for them there. She had no way of knowing that fellow harangued the two men for their ineptitude before slapping money into their hands and giving them new orders that they dared not ignore.

Lacey remained beside the piano as the old fellow banged out another boisterous tune. She was unaware of the danger that still threatened her until Scully slid a protective arm around her shoulders and turned her back toward the safety of the upstairs room.

Chapter One

New York City
1882

Yes, her hands *were* trembling.

Lacey stared at her hands, at the long slender fingers with well-tended nails, and at the smooth skin and soft palms reflecting the total absence of physical labor. They were "a lady's hands," which she realized was part of the reason for their shaking.

Lacey did not need to look at her reflection in the dressing table mirror to know that the image there further perpetuated that description of herself. She was no longer eight years old. The neat pigtails she had worn when she first arrived at Mrs. Grivens's Finishing School had given way to a graceful upsweep of hair that was still a brilliant platinum in color; her childish features had matured into a finely sculpted countenance in which clear, blue eyes hid uncertainty behind a downward sweep of surprisingly dark lashes; and her slender, adolescent proportions had developed feminine curves that went undisguised by the ladylike cut of her simple, gray traveling dress.

Lacey glanced toward the hallway door at the sound of a soft knocking. It opened at her response to reveal a small, dark-haired girl who rushed sobbing into her arms.

"I don't want you to go, Lacey." Tears streamed from her eyes as fourteen-year-old Marjorie Parsons drew back and rasped, "I'll be so lonesome here when you're gone."

Her reassuring smile aimed as much at boosting her own confidence as it did comforting the motherless girl who had become almost a sister to her, Lacey replied, "I can't stay in school forever, Marjorie. Everyone graduates when they're eighteen years old—even me."

"Maybe so." Marjorie brushed away her tears and continued almost pleadingly, "But Mrs. Grivens would gladly let you stay on as an instructor if you wanted to. Everybody knows that."

An instructor.

Lacey was almost amused by those words. She could read, write and cipher. She could "play the piano with considerable finesse," "embroider beautifully," was well versed in the rules of etiquette, knew the proper protocol and manner to address any member of a titled aristocracy and had committed to memory the correct placement of every piece of silverware that could possibly be needed at a formal dinner party. Those accomplishments aside, she was at a complete loss when it came to cooking or maintaining a household without a battery of servants. She was also totally ignorant as to how a "young lady" was supposed to earn a decent living in a society where the only choices open to her were a good marriage or sensible spinsterhood.

Yes, she'd be good at teaching young women to be as clueless as she.

"Please tell Mrs. Grivens you'll stay."

"I can't do that. Uncle Scully sent me tickets for my transportation home. He's expecting me, and I owe him that."

She did not bother to tell Marjorie she had decided that the chaperone Uncle Scully had arranged to accompany her was unnecessary, or that she had cancelled the arrangements he had made and cashed in the extra ticket he had provided so she might return the funds to him when she arrived. Yes, she owed him that…and so much more.

Lacey blinked back unexpected tears, then continued kindly, "I'm not like you, Marjorie. I have…obligations. I don't have a wealthy father ready to introduce me to society so I can get properly married after I graduate."

"Pooh! Papa would introduce you to society, too, if you wanted. I'd make him do it. And you're so pretty that you'd find a husband in no time."

"That wouldn't work for me, Marjorie."

Marjorie stared at her, uncomprehending.

"It's time for me to pay Uncle Scully back for financing my schooling and supporting me all these years." She smiled sadly. "He must be pretty old by now. I know he never married. He probably needs somebody to take care of him."

"But he never came out to see you—not once!"

"He wrote to me faithfully and made sure I always had whatever I needed." Lacey felt no need to explain that Uncle Scully's letters had rarely arrived more often than six months apart, or that while being friendly and expressing concern that her needs were met when he wrote, Uncle Scully had shared little of the private information that would have made him seem more like family.

"He didn't visit you on your birthday, or at Christmas."

"But he never forgot me." Lacey did not feel she needed to add that she would have preferred a visit to the sometimes elaborate presents that had arrived without exception on the holidays.

"He didn't even send you a likeness of him to remember him by!"

"That's because I didn't need a likeness." She did not choose to clarify that her actual memory of Jake Scully had dimmed over the years—that all she could truly remember was that he had been tall and well dressed, and that with a single glance of his sober, gray eyes, he had made her feel safe from the gunshots that had robbed her of the life she had known.

Lacey added solemnly, "I owe Uncle Scully more than I can ever repay."

"But you shouldn't waste your life caring for an old man when you're so young."

"I owe it to him, Marjorie." Lacey silently added that she owed her grandfather a debt, too—to return to the place that gentle, decent man had loved so she could clarify memories that had become confused and distorted by the violence of that night long ago and put an end to the nightmares that still haunted her.

Lacey turned at the sound of a summons at the door. She pulled it open to see little Amy Harding standing solemnly in the hallway.

"The carriage is here, Lacey." Amy's eyes were moist. "Mrs. Grivens said to hurry or you'll miss your train."

Lacey was conscious of the footsteps following her as she carried her suitcase down the staircase toward the front doorway.

Tears, hugs and sincere, loving words behind her, Lacey stepped up into the waiting carriage. She looked back as the conveyance jerked into motion and she waved at the solemn group gathered in the doorway of the boarding school.

The carriage turned the street corner, and Lacey took a breath, wiped away a tear and determinedly faced forward. She had told Marjorie the truth. She needed to go "home" because she had obligations she could not ignore.

Lacey withdrew her grandfather's worn Bible from her reticule. She scanned the text, taking comfort from the familiar passages and the small illustrations her grandfather had drawn on the page corners when they had read together.

Her attention shifted back to her well-tended hands.

Yes, her hands were trembling—because she had no idea what the future held in store.

Weaver, Arizona
1882

Lacey looked out the window of the stagecoach as it bumped and swayed along the rutted trail. She glanced at the harsh, dry land bordering both sides of the narrow expanse, then at the rise of mountains in the distance outlined against a brilliant blue sky devoid of a single cloud. She breathed deeply, aware the heat of the day was climbing.

She recalled the carriage ride to the train station in New York, through streets that were neatly cobbled, where well-dressed pedestrians hurried to meet their needs in a city that bustled with activity. Somehow, she had not expected that that uneventful ride would initiate an endless, uncomfortable journey that had not yet come to an end.

Lacey did not choose to recall the countless times along the way that she had doubted the wisdom of making the journey alone. She had not taken into consideration that the passing years would have dimmed the memory of a wild country where civilization was held partially at bay by long-haired, thickly bearded and heavily armed men—a place where she stirred surprised attention and whispered comments wherever she went.

Despite the tedium and discomfort of the journey, however, Lacey found herself somehow shaken at the thought of her arrival in Weaver, where she would meet up with a past she suddenly realized she hardly remembered.

Lacey looked at the unpaved trail ahead, then glanced up at the shadowed mountain peaks in the distance. Why was it that everything looked so unfamiliar to her? Why had the ten years she had been away dimmed all clear memory of this place?

The sound of a crackling blaze echoed unexpectedly in her ears. She felt the heat…the flames…the smoke…*the fear.* She saw the faded image of her grandfather's body.

Yes, all clear memories had dimmed…except one.

Lacey closed her eyes. She clutched her small Bible tightly in her hand.

"Are you all right, ma'am?"

Lacey looked up, focusing for the first time on the disreputable-looking fellow seated across from her. Like the two other rough-and-tumble male passengers presently sleeping, his hat was stained, his beard was overly long, his clothes were worn and the gun at his side was *exceptionally* large—but the concern in his bloodshot eyes was obviously sincere.

She replied, "I'm fine. I'm just tired, I guess."

"We'll be getting to Weaver, soon." The fellow frowned and added, "If you don't mind my saying so, ma'am, Weaver is a fine little town, but it's not accustomed to ladies like you."

Lacey almost smiled. "I was born in Weaver—or thereabouts."

"Oh."

"I'm going home."

The fellow nodded. "Been gone long, ma'am?"

"Awhile."

He nodded again. He looked at the Bible in her hand. "Going to join Reverend Sykes, are you?"

"Reverend Sykes?"

"I hear he's a fine man and real dedicated to his work in the church."

"I'm sure he is, but I don't know him."

The fellow's frown deepened. "You'll be having somebody meet you in Weaver, I hope." He stammered, "I mean, it's a fine little town, but...well..."

Lacey stared at the unkempt fellow more closely. Because of his questionable appearance, she had done her best to ignore him and the other two occupants of their coach when she boarded. Now, glimpsing the man inside his unappealing exterior, she was oddly warmed by what she saw.

Lacey replied with a smile, "Someone will be meeting me. His name is Jake Scully. Do you know him?"

"Jake Scully." The fellow blinked. "He's...you...I..."

He took a breath, then continued with a tip of his soiled hat meant as an introduction, "My name's Pete Loughlin, ma'am. I'll be spending some time in Weaver, and I want you to know I'll be at your disposal if things don't turn out the way you expected." He paused, adding, "I hope you'll remember that, ma'am."

"I'm pleased to meet you, Mr. Loughlin. My name is Lacey Stewart, and I thank you for your concern."

"Everybody calls me Pete, ma'am."

"Thank you. I'll certainly remember your offer, Pete."

His face reddening unexpectedly, Pete averted his gaze toward the window and ended the conversation as abruptly as it had begun. With no recourse but to follow his lead, Lacey turned to the Bible in her hand, silently embarrassed that she had been so harsh in her first assessment of the dear fellow. She looked down at the page to which she had inadvertently turned.

Judge not, lest ye be judged.

Somehow startled by the familiar passage, Lacey glanced back up at Pete Loughlin, whose bloodshot eyes had fallen closed.

A timely lesson, gently served.

Lacey's spirits lightened.

The stagecoach rounded a turn in the trail and Weaver came into view. Lacey reached up nervously to adjust her hat and smooth back a few pale wisps that had strayed from her upswept coiffure. She then slipped her Bible into her reticule and gripped the handle anxiously. Her three fellow passengers had somehow awakened the moment Weaver appeared on the horizon. They appeared as eager as she to see the end of their journey.

Lacey did her best to ignore Pete's frown as they entered town and she searched the street in vain for a familiar face. She struggled against an expanding anxiety as the conveyance rumbled farther down the dusty main thoroughfare, passing a livery stable, a blacksmith's shop, a bank, a hotel. She scanned the street more closely, seeing what appeared to be a jail, a barber shop and several other stores. Her gaze halted. Memory stirred when she viewed the establishment that took up the major portion of the street at the far end.

The Gold Nugget Saloon.

Lacey took a shaky breath, then searched the street again. She was expecting too much, she knew, to expect Uncle Scully to be waiting for the stage as she had hoped. The exact date of her arrival had been uncertain when they had last communicated. She certainly couldn't expect that he would meet every stage the week she was expected to arrive.

The stage shuddered to a halt in front of the mercantile store and Lacey's heart began pounding. She silently scolded herself for her rising apprehension as she waited for her fellow passengers to alight. She reminded herself that she had just traveled hundreds of miles alone, that she had walked through the Gold Nugget's swinging doors by herself once before, and she certainly could do it again.

"Ma'am…" Lacey took the hand Pete offered her. She stepped down onto the street as he continued politely, "If you're needing any help…"

Lacey skimmed the street again with her gaze. She saw a tall, gray-haired gentleman step out onto the boardwalk a distance away. Her heart leaped when he turned in her direction.

"Lacey?"

She went still at the sound of the deep, familiar male voice behind her. She turned toward the big man who started toward her from the shadow of a store's overhang.

Lacey's throat went dry as the well-dressed, dark-haired

man approached. This fellow wasn't old at all. Actually, he appeared to be a man in his prime, with strongly cut features and dark brows over eyes that were a soft, sober gray.

Lacey caught her breath. She remembered those eyes.

The man stopped in front of her. He said, "Welcome home, Lacey."

"U-Uncle Scully?"

"If that's what you want to call me."

Lacey looked over at Pete, who remained stiffly solemn beside her. Uncertain why he stood rooted to the spot, she said, "I'd like you to meet one of my fellow passengers on the stage, Uncle Scully. His name is Mr. Pete Loughlin, and he's been very kind."

Scully's expression remained unchanged as he replied, "Pete and I are old acquaintances." He addressed Pete directly, adding, "I appreciate your looking after Lacey, Pete, but she's in good hands now."

Scully turned again to Lacey. "I'll get your bag."

Dismissing the introduction and Pete with that statement, Scully strode toward the rear of the wagon to catch Lacey's suitcase as it was tossed down from the stage.

"Ma'am…"

Lacey's attention jumped back to Pete.

His voice lowered, Pete whispered, "I hope you'll remember what I said."

"Thank you, but you don't have to worry about me. As Uncle Scully told you, I'm in good hands now."

"Like I said, if things don't turn out the way you expected and you're needing any help, I'll be around."

"Well, thank you again, Pete."

Glancing back at Scully as he approached, Pete added, "I

guess that's all I got to say." He walked away without waiting for her response.

Scully was frowning when he reached her side. "What did Pete say?"

"Pete just offered me his support. It was very kind of him."

"Kind...right." Scully's frown deepened. "Let's get going. I told Helen to make up a room for you upstairs from the saloon."

"Helen?"

"Helen's the woman who cleans the second floor for me at the Gold Nugget. She's a nice old lady whose husband died a while back. She agreed to move into the spare room and serve as a chaperone while you're living there."

"Living there...like before." Lacey's throat choked tight as memories began flooding back. "I'm glad."

"I'll find a more suitable place for you as soon as I can."

Struggling to keep up with Scully's long-legged stride as they started across the street, Lacey was not able to reply.

This was going to be harder than he thought.

Intensely aware of Lacey as she walked beside him, Jake Scully shoved open the swinging door and stepped back to allow her entrance into the saloon. His jaw ticked at the silence that came over the barroom as she walked in.

Well, what had he expected? Did he think Lacey would return the same little girl in pigtails that he had sent away to school years earlier?

Scully remembered that little girl clearly. Lost and alone, and so brave...Charlie's granddaughter. She had looked up at him with total trust in her eyes, and he had lost his heart to her the moment he saw her. He hadn't doubted for a moment what he would do.

Memories of Charlie were vivid. Scully had been in his teens when he met the old man. He'd been out on his own after the deaths of his parents—jobless, homeless, without funds and unsure where his next meal was coming from. He couldn't remember exactly how he met Charlie and struck up a conversation with him, but he did remember that Charlie bought him the first good meal he'd had in days, and that he'd never tasted anything better. He had ending up working with Charlie at his claim for almost a year before starting back out on his own with a stake that Charlie had insisted on providing. He had made good use of that stake, and he had never gone hungry again.

Nor had he forgotten Charlie. Years passed, however, before the old man walked into Scully's saloon one day and told him he was prospecting in the area, then mentioned during their extended conversation that he had taken in his granddaughter after his daughter's death.

The next time he saw Charlie, the affable old man was lying dead outside his burned-out cabin.

There hadn't been a moment during the years following that Scully had doubted providing for Lacey, the poor, wounded little girl in pigtails who had needed him. But the child in pigtails was now a woman—and everything had changed.

Scully remembered the look in Pete's eyes as he had stood protectively at Lacey's side. He recalled the stunned silence when Lacey and he had walked through the saloon doors moments earlier.

It had started already.

The truth was, he hadn't been ready for Lacey Stewart, the beautiful woman who had stepped down from the stagecoach, and the shock of it was with him still. Charlie Pratt had been a rare man, indeed: sincere, generous, God-fearing and God-loving, and the truest friend he'd ever had. But he had also been a scrawny little fella with a crooked smile and bowed legs. Somehow, Scully hadn't considered for a moment that Charlie's granddaughter would turn out to be a beauty.

And not only was Lacey beautiful, but she was also a lady, and the combination of the two had set his mind spinning.

His hand on her elbow, Scully ushered Lacey directly toward the staircase to the second floor. Barely acknowledging the greetings of a few customers in passing, he urged her up the stairs. He introduced Lacey briefly to Helen when the old woman appeared at the top of the stairs, then pushed open the door of her room to allow Lacey to enter and followed her inside, making certain to leave the door open behind them. He deposited her case on the bed and turned to face her expectant expression fully.

Lacey looked up at him, waiting for him to speak, and Scully went suddenly still. There she was…the child he had seen ten years earlier. She was visible in the trusting blue eyes Lacey turned up to his, in the shadows of uncertainty he saw there, in the faint glaze of tears gradually overwhelming them. On the outside, Lacey was a mature, beautiful woman, but on the inside she was still the little lost girl who had looked up to him…to whom she had come "home."

And she was waiting.

His slow smile sincere, Scully said again, "Welcome home, Lacey."

With a single, spontaneous step, Lacey stepped into his welcoming hug. With that step, the past dropped away. Lacey was again his brave little girl, and he was her protector, provider and guide for her future.

And he was glad.

* * *

The hum of curious conversation and leering snickers following Scully and Lacey's entrance into the Gold Nugget had gradually faded. No one noticed that the swarthy fellow at the bar glanced back surreptitiously over his shoulder to scan the upstairs landing where the couple had disappeared from sight. Nor did anyone hear the angry curse he muttered under his breath before exiting the saloon as inconspicuously as he could manage.

Chapter Two

"I like the Gold Nugget. I don't want to 'find a more suitable place to stay.'"

Scully looked at Lacey, who sat across the small table from him in Sadie Wilson's restaurant, the town's only eating establishment. They had taken to having breakfast together there each morning, and in the few days since her return, an indefinable bond had developed between them that somehow erased their years of separation and dismissed the reality that they were virtual strangers. Lacey had grown into a woman whose stunning beauty left Scully a bit breathless—yet she was still the determined little girl who had walked miles in a deadening heat, injured and feverish, in order to follow through on her grandfather's last wishes.

"Scully…"

Lacey had automatically dropped the "uncle" prefix from his name when she saw it was turning heads, and Scully was glad. He didn't need it to remember he was still responsible for her safety and for the direction of her future.

"Scully…"

Responding with an unconscious furrowing of his brow, Scully said, "The Gold Nugget isn't the right place for you to live."

"*You* live there."

"That's different."

"Why?"

"I own the place."

"So?"

He could not believe she could be so dense. As determined as she, Scully asserted, "Helen can't stay indefinitely. She'll want to go home, and your grandfather wouldn't approve."

"Grandpa sent me to the Gold Nugget."

"He sent you to me, not to the Gold Nugget."

"He sent me to the Gold Nugget to see you because he knew I'd be safe with you. I *am* safe with you there."

Scully took an impatient breath. "You're a respectable young woman, Lacey."

"You're respectable, too."

"No, I'm not."

"Yes, you are!"

Scully stared at Lacey. He had angered her by refuting her statement, but he couldn't let her dodge the truth. "I own a saloon, Lacey," he explained. "You saw Pete Loughlin's reaction when I met you at the stage. Even he didn't think I'd be a good influence on you."

"He doesn't know you like I do."

"He probably knows me better."

The startling blue of Lacey's eyes linked with his. "I don't believe that."

"Lacey…things get pretty wild in the saloon at times. Drinking, gambling…and more."

"Oh…"

Scully remained conspicuously silent.

She shrugged. "I've read the Bible, you know. I know about those things. But Jewel and Rosie both told me you don't allow that kind of activity on your premises. They said they respect you for it, too."

Scully's frown darkened. How had Lacey become so friendly with the girls at the Gold Nugget in so short a time? And when had they begun talking so frankly? He didn't like it. He needed to get her out of there as soon as possible.

He replied, "Whatever the girls said is beside the point."

"No, it isn't."

"A room just became available in Mary McInnes's boarding house this morning. It's a fine place—clean and respectable."

"The Gold Nugget is clean."

"But not respectable."

"It's respectable enough for me."

"No, it isn't."

Lacey was beginning to smart at his insistence. She countered, "Besides, I don't have an income yet and I can't afford to pay the board at Mary McInnes's."

"Pay the board…"

"That's right. I don't intend to let you support me forever, you know. It won't cost you as much to keep me at the Gold Nugget until I find a position and can start paying my own way."

"A position…?"

Lacey's lips tightened.

"No."

"No what?"

"No *position*. And I'm not supporting you. I'm only returning a favor to your grandfather."

"Grandpa may have helped you, but in time, you went out on your own."

"In time. It's not time for you yet."

"When will it be time then?"

"I'll let you know."

"No."

"Yes."

Lacey continued resolutely, "I'm not going to move into the boarding house right now. The Gold Nugget is fine."

Scully didn't agree. Choosing to conclude the discussion for the present, he said, "Are you finished?"

"I'm not moving out of the Gold Nugget."

"With your breakfast."

"Oh…yes."

He stood up. "Let's go."

Lacey drew herself to her feet as Scully dropped a few coins on the table and nodded at Sadie. She felt the firm pressure of his hand on her elbow as she smiled a quick goodbye at the hardworking woman and Scully guided her toward the door. She knew she had made him angry, but she refused to let him say harsh things about himself in an effort to protect her.

Lacey raised her chin as they walked toward the restaurant doorway. A familiar passage rang in her mind.

Man looketh at the outward appearance, but the Lord looketh at the heart.

She didn't need anyone to tell her that Scully's heart was good. No matter how he looked, she knew the Lord could see that as well as her grandpa obviously had—and she had only to look into Scully's eyes to see that he wanted only the best for her. As for the *outward appearance* part…well, maybe it needed work, but she believed the hand of the Lord had played a part in directing her to Scully, she hoped for both their sakes.

Lacey glanced at Scully where he walked beside her. Whether he chose to accept it or not, he had proved to her in so many ways that he was a better man than he considered himself to be. Also, she *trusted* him. She felt *safe* with him. Those truths had become more desperately important to her since she had arrived back in Weaver and the vague shadows surrounding her past had begun shifting in her mind.

She was determined not to burden Scully with the lingering fears that haunted her. It was up to her to resolve them. She would, too, but she needed to assume responsibility for her future first.

However, Scully did not agree.

That thought in mind, Lacey stood stock-still as they emerged onto the boardwalk. Scully was still frowning when he looked down at her, and she asked simply, "Are you angry with me, Scully?"

"Angry? No."

"You look angry."

His gray eyes searched her face. His gaze softened. "The Gold Nugget isn't the place for you, Lacey. You know it, and I know it."

"No, I don't know that."

"All right." He was angry again. "Whatever you say."

She supposed there would never be a better time.

Dislodging her arm gently from Scully's grip, Lacey said, "I'm going to stop in at the mercantile store to see if they received any mail for me there. The girls back at the boarding school said they'd write to me the same day I left. They're very dear. I know they'll follow through with their promise."

The anger in Scully's eyes mellowed. "All right. I'll be in my office. Come back there as soon as you're done. I have something to show you."

Scully did not see Lacey turn back to watch his departure after starting toward the mercantile store. Nor did he see her frown as the thought struck her that perhaps she was being unfair. Scully was a mature, powerfully masculine man. He might not consider himself respectable, but she had seen the way the *respectable* women in town looked at him. It wasn't much different from the way the girls at the Gold Nugget looked at him. Maybe she should give him the space he needed.

That thought somehow difficult to accept, Lacey shook her head. Maybe…but not now.

She raised her chin and quickened her step.

Definitely not yet.

Things weren't getting any easier.

Scully nodded automatically at the heads turning his way as he crossed Weaver's main street. Taller than most at a height well over six feet, and with broad muscular proportions that belied his supposedly sedentary lifestyle, he was aware that he stood out in a crowd. Dressed as he was in a well-tailored dark suit and fine linen shirt, with a brocaded vest and the dark Stetson he wore pulled low on his forehead, he was also unmistakable as the owner and operator of the Gold Nugget Saloon, the most successful business in town. He had always been proud of his success. He had dressed appropriately and behaved as suited him best, uncaring of fluctuating public opinion.

Scully paused to glance back at Lacey as she walked toward the mercantile store. His jaw tightened at the assessing looks she drew from passing matrons. Those busybodies were already beginning to talk. Given a few more weeks, they would paint Lacey a scarlet woman simply because she lived in a room upstairs from the town's only saloon—two doors down the hallway from him, the town's most notorious bachelor.

Illustrating his concerns, Scully watched as a bearded cowboy turned with a sly remark to his friend when Lacey passed them on the street. Scully took an angry step in the man's direction, then checked himself in time. He'd just make matters worse by defending Lacey's honor when it needed no defense at all.

Galling him was the reality that Lacey seemed oblivious to the implications that living at the Gold Nugget raised. He was living proof that rumors—sometimes without a speck of truth—spread fast and functioned as gospel. He also knew that once damaged, a woman's reputation was never fully regained. Charlie had trusted him with both Lacey's reputation and her future. He owed it to the old man and to Lacey to see that she found a man who was worthy of her—a respectable man who would marry her and give her the good life she deserved.

Scully watched as Lacey neared the store entrance. It occurred to him not for the first time that Lacey dismissed her beauty as playing any part in the person she was, just as she dismissed her own purity of heart with the belief that everyone had the same spark of goodness inside them—including him. He knew that wasn't true. He had been on the wrong side of that equation for too many years as a youngster not to realize that the spark—if it ever existed in him—had long since been extinguished. He was determined Lacey would never experience that difficult truth firsthand. He was dedicated to that resolve…more than he had ever believed he could be.

Lacey disappeared through the mercantile store entrance, and Scully took a shaken breath. Whoever that *respectable* man who eventually won Lacey's hand turned out to be, he'd be lucky, indeed.

Still frowning, Scully pushed his way through the Gold Nugget's doors. He had started toward his office at the rear when a familiar, throaty voice turned him to the sultry redhead who stepped into his path.

"You don't have time for a good morning today, Scully?"

Scully's gaze swept over Charlotte briefly. He remembered the first time he saw her, when she came into the saloon looking for a job a year earlier. He had known at a glance she'd be an asset in his establishment.

Scully's smile softened. He and Charlotte had both been on their own long enough to be well versed in what the world had to offer people like them.

He responded, "You're in early today, aren't you?"

"Maybe." Charlotte smiled with a quirk of her arched brows. "I've got a lot of energy stored up, I guess."

"Charlotte…"

She said unexpectedly, "I like her, Scully. Lacey's a real nice girl…innocent, you know? Not like you and me, who've seen it all and made our choices." Charlotte took a step closer. "I expect she'll make some rancher a real good wife someday. She's suited to that life. She'll take to it like a duck to water."

Charlotte's heady perfume filled his nostrils as she added, "I'll see you around, Scully." She winked. "You know where to find me."

Charlotte walked back out through the saloon doors, disappearing as quickly as she had appeared, and Scully looked up to the expressive wiggling of Bill's hairy eyebrows as the rotund bartender stood behind the bar. Bill had the keenest eye in town, but Scully resented having it turned in his direction. He made a mental note to tell him so, too.

That thought firmly fixed, Scully turned toward his office, and within seconds he had slammed the door behind him.

"You're sure you don't know of any positions that might be open for a young woman in town…anything at all?"

Wilson Parker stared at Lacey Stewart from his customary position behind the mercantile store counter. He had been standing in this same spot ten years earlier when a bedraggled little girl walked down the town's main street dragging a scrawny burro behind her. Nobody had been more shocked than he to see how that pale little girl had turned out.

"Mr. Parker…?"

And no one was more incredulous than he as he responded, "Do you mean to say Scully thinks that you should…that he expects…"

"Scully has nothing to do with what I'm intending." Lacey's gaze pinned him as her smooth cheeks colored. "Is there something wrong with supporting oneself, may I ask? If I were a man, everyone would expect it of me. Certainly being a woman doesn't change things that much."

"But you're not a woman. You're a *lady*." Lacey snatched back her well-groomed hands as Mr. Parker said, "Scully wouldn't have to support you forever, just until the right fella comes along."

The right fella, Lacey thought. There it was again.

Lacey controlled a spark of impatience as she responded, "I have plans for the future that don't include waiting for the 'right fella' to turn up, and I'll need to earn some money in the meantime."

"Still, I don't think—"

"That's the trouble." Lacey turned toward Sadie Wilson as the matronly restaurant owner interrupted their conversation. Sadie continued, "You *don't* think, Parker. You just react, and this lady here is the kind who chooses to use the abilities God gave her to support herself instead of depending on others. I'd say that's admirable, wouldn't you?"

"Admirable?" Mr. Parker shrugged his narrow shoulders. "For a woman your age, I suppose it is, but Lacey—"

Sadie turned her back on the storekeeper, dismissing him with a roll of her eyes that said she had heard it all before. Addressing Lacey directly, she said, "I couldn't help hearing your conversation, and I'm thinking it might be lucky for both of us that I happened to come in here to get some things I ran out of in the restaurant this morning. The fact is, I'm going to be shorthanded at the restaurant soon. Millie—you know, the redhead with all the freckles—she's leaving to get married at the end of the week. I'm going to be needing somebody who's looking for good, honest work."

Lacey's heart jumped a beat.

Sadie searched her expression. "It's not easy work, mind you. There's a lot of running involved when things get busy."

"I'm not afraid of hard work."

Appearing pleased at her response, Sadie replied, "Well then, as far as I'm concerned, you're hired. The restaurant is busiest in the early morning and during the supper hours. I have a woman who helps at night, so I'll try you out in the morning. If you're agreeable, you can start at the end of the week when Millie leaves. I'll pay you what I was paying her."

Sadie winked. "I'll be expecting to get more work out of you, though, because Millie's mind hasn't been on her job lately."

"That's fine with me." Lacey added, "And…thank you."

Lacey watched as Sadie walked to the back of the store to scout out her purchases. Her heart was pounding. She had a position and she'd start at the end of the week! She'd have money to pay for her board at the boarding house and she—

Lacey's high spirits plummeted as she bid the disapproving storekeeper goodbye and started back toward the Gold Nugget with the prospect of moving from the Gold Nugget suddenly looming closer. Also plaguing her was the prospect of informing Scully that she had agreed to take a job. He'd be angry, but she'd remind him that she'd be able to take the room at Mrs. McInnes's sooner than she thought. That would please him. Lacey pondered that thought. But how would *she* feel about moving to the boarding house? Mature…responsible…finally self-supporting?

Lonely.

She'd had enough of loneliness. She had thought her loneliness had come to an end when she came home and Scully had welcomed her with open arms.

It looked as if she was wrong.

Scully looked up at a knock on his office door. The knock was tentative…uncertain. It could be no one else.

"Come in, Lacey."

"How did you know it was me?"

Lacey stood framed in the doorway, platinum hair piled casually atop her head, intense blue eyes putting to shame the pale blue of her dress, delicate features composed in a half smile. A lovelier picture than Scully had ever expected would be his, even temporarily. The thought was disconcerting. He refrained from answering her question. Instead, he stood up, reached for his hat and said, "Come on with me. I have something to show you."

Around the desk in a moment, Scully took Lacey's arm. She hesitated momentarily, then said, "I suppose we can talk later."

Talk. Talk meant continuing the same argument they'd had earlier that morning. He'd had enough of it for the day.

He drew her out of the office with him toward the saloon's rear door.

"Where're we going, Scully?"

Again ignoring her inquiry, Scully ushered Lacey along with him, then pushed open the door of the back entrance and urged her out ahead of him into the narrow yard.

He felt the shock that rippled through her.

Lacey gulped. She took a deep breath. Tears brimmed in her eyes as she started toward the hitching post where the small burro was tethered.

It couldn't be…but it was!

"It's…*Careful!*"

The burro's name emerged from her lips with a sob as Lacey reached the animal in a few running steps. Careful turned his head toward her with a welcoming bray and tears streamed down her cheeks. She slid her arms around Careful's neck and hugged him tight….

She was a child again. The days were long and sun-filled, and Careful was her loyal playmate, helpmate and friend.

The choking stench of the fire hung on the air. Her grandfather lay dead in front of her and the charred remains of her home behind her. She was terrified and alone, but Careful stood steadfast nearby.

The road was long, the sun hot. Her head throbbed, her legs ached and her throat was parched. She was afraid. She couldn't walk any farther, but Careful trudged on beside her, limping every step of the way.

The Gold Nugget came into view at last. She couldn't make it. She couldn't walk another step, but Careful wouldn't give up, and neither could she.

She was sick. She didn't want to get better. She didn't want to remember...but Careful was alone, and he needed her.

She was fully recovered. She was leaving for boarding school to be educated as her grandpa always wanted. She was leaving Careful behind, and the emptiness inside her ached....

So many years in between. So many clouded memories and uncertainties, but she was home again at last. She knew that now, because Careful was with her again.

Uncertain how long it took to compose herself, Lacey turned back toward the big man who stood silently watchful behind her. Aware that words could not adequately express the full scope of her emotion, she said simply, "Thank you," then walked into Scully's embrace.

Enveloped in joyful tears as Scully held her comfortingly close, Lacey was not aware of the well-dressed man lurking in the shadows nearby. She had not seen him lingering in the mercantile, listening intently to her conversation at the counter. Nor had she noticed him following her at a safe distance when she left the store and started across the street.

Standing still unseen, Barret Gould paused to coldly assess the emotional scene unfolding. He had overheard the statement Lacey Stewart made in the store minutes earlier. She said she had returned to Weaver with plans for the future that had nothing to do with Jake Scully. She'd added that her plans didn't include waiting around for *the right man to come along*. Both were commendable statements that appeared innocent enough to the average person.

Yet the average person did not know Lacey's secret—a secret she did not know he shared.

A slow elation expanded inside Barret. He was being given a second chance for success in a plan that had met with devastating failure ten years earlier.

He would succeed this time, and the distinguished future that had escaped him—for which he was destined—would finally be his.

Lacey Stewart didn't stand a chance.

Chapter Three

"The answer is no!"

Lacey stood opposite Scully in the morning shadows of her room. The events of the previous day, when Careful was returned to her, had left her shaken. She hadn't had the heart for the argument she knew was certain to ensue when Scully learned she had accepted a job in Sadie's restaurant, but he had appeared at her door that morning for breakfast, and she had known it was now or never.

Never was not an option.

Lacey took a deep breath, then said, "Try to understand, Scully. I—"

"I said, the answer is no. You aren't going to do that kind of work."

Her reply was spontaneous. "I don't recall asking your permission."

Scully's gray eyes pinned her. Somehow, he had never looked bigger or more intimidating than he did at that moment as he towered over her in his anger, but Lacey did not back down when he replied, "No, you didn't ask my permission, but you should have."

"You forget. I'm eighteen years old—an adult. You're not my guardian anymore."

"I'm not, huh?"

Regretting her harsh statement, Lacey took a conciliatory step toward him and said, "Please…I don't want to argue with you, especially after yesterday. You've done so much for me, and taking care of Careful all those years while I was gone… I appreciate every bit of it, but I can't let it go on, don't you see? I have to start out on my own sometime."

"Sometime…but not now."

"When, Scully? Am I supposed to let you support me until I wither on the vine waiting for 'the right fella'?"

"You don't stand a chance of 'withering on the vine,' and you know it."

"No, I don't know it. And neither do I care. It's time for me to take responsibility for my own life."

"That's good thinking. It's premature, that's all. You need time to settle down here for a while so you can get reacquainted with the real world."

"The real world…" Lacey took a stabilizing breath. "You're right. The world I lived in these past ten years is far removed from Weaver. It wasn't a real world—not for me. I knew it then, and I know it now. Many of the memories of my life with my grandfather are unclear, but they aren't so dim that I wasn't able to see the differences. I belong *here.* This is my home, and the sooner I make myself fit back in, the better it will be."

"You're rushing things. You're not giving yourself a chance."

"I'm ready now to step back into my life, Scully. I need to, for so many reasons."

"None of those reasons are good enough. You need time. You deserve better than you're asking for yourself."

"Do I, really?" Lacey took another step closer. "Do I deserve better than working in a place where hardworking men like my grandpa felt privileged to have a good, hot meal set down in front of them at the beginning of the day? Do I deserve better than getting to know them so I can share a part of their sometimes lonely lives?"

Lacey paused, forcing back a gradual thickening in her throat as she continued, "I miss Grandpa, you know? He loved me. With his dying breath, he gave me the best advice he knew when he placed his Bible in my hands and told me to depend on it and the Lord to guide my way, and then when he sent me to you. He taught me so many things that'll stay with me the rest of my life. But somehow, so many of my memories of him have become vague and cloudy in my mind. I was robbed of those memories that last day, and I want them back. I don't know any other way to get them except to make a place for myself here so they'll eventually become clear."

Lacey looked up at Scully's still, unemotional expression. She said, "Those memories are all I have left of the only family I knew. The blank spots nag at me. They give me no rest. I need to fill them in so I can be whole again, and I'm doing that the only way I know how."

Lacey saw the brief flicker of change in the gray eyes regarding her so closely, yet she was unprepared when Scully said, "Are you ready for breakfast?"

Taking a moment to recover, she responded, "Y-yes, I guess I am."

"Let's go, then."

Lacey halted abruptly when they stepped out into the

hallway. When he looked down at her, she said, "You did hear what I said, didn't you, Scully?"

"I heard you."

"Then you understand."

Silence his only response, Scully ushered her toward the staircase.

The noisy hustle and bustle of Sadie's restaurant continued around him as Scully sat at the corner table he shared with Lacey. His empty plate in front of him, he sat silently as he had through the entire breakfast meal. Frowning, he glanced across the table at Lacey, who was picking at her food, then scanned the occupants of the crowded restaurant. They were a varied lot: transient wranglers obviously eager to be on their way, businessmen engaged in conversation, a few ranchers, some locals who looked to have spent a night on the town and a grizzly prospector or two in for their first good meal in months. He saw Doc Mayberry in deep conversation with Reverend Sykes at a table in the far corner. His frown darkened when he looked at the table occupied by three women from the Gold Nugget who looked to have remained active long after the Gold Nugget doors had closed for the night. Millie White, her plump, freckled face flushed and her hair in disarray, moved almost breathlessly between the tables.

Strangely, he hadn't given Millie much thought before this, except to wish her luck when he learned she had finally set the date for her wedding with her seemingly recalcitrant boyfriend. The thought that Lacey would assume her frantic pace between these same tables at the end of the week held little appeal.

Scully compared the two women. The result was no surprise. Lacey was slender, almost fragile in appearance. Her delicate features were faultless, almost mesmerizing. With her pale hair and vividly blue eyes, she drew speculation wherever she went. Conversely, Millie's only outstanding feature was her freckles. Although a pleasant enough girl, Millie could be easily lost in a crowd with her common appearance.

That could never be the case with Lacey. He had known the moment he saw Lacey that first time when she was a frightened, injured child that she was special in so many ways. The years had only served to confirm his opinion of her. She was lovely and sweet…and innocent. He needed to protect that innocence, to hold her safe. She was too friendly, too nice. The world held too many unnamed dangers for someone like her, and the mix of people she would meet in this place only increased the threat involved.

"Scully…" He hadn't realized he was staring at Lacey until she continued, "It's obvious that whatever you're thinking, it isn't good." She smiled…a glorious, apologetic smile as she added, "Don't worry so much. I'll be fine. Sadie's right behind the counter if I need her for anything, and you're across the street. What more could I ask?"

Scully was saved from a response to Lacey's question when Doc Mayberry appeared unexpectedly beside their table with an all-too-familiar man in a dark suit. He said, "Scully… nice to see you again."

Scully shook the hands extended to him and replied with limited courtesy, "Doc Mayberry…Reverend Sykes."

"And this must be the Lacey Stewart I've been hearing about all around town."

Doc's smile was too gracious. The old fellow had an agenda that went beyond a simple introduction. That thought was confirmed the moment he added, "Reverend Sykes and I haven't had the pleasure of meeting Lacey."

Enforced courtesy never his greatest strength, Scully said, "Lacey, it looks like these two fellas are determined to meet you."

Flushing slightly at Scully's brusque manner, Lacey replied, "I'm pleased to meet you both, gentlemen." She added without a moment's hesitation, "The girls at the Gold Nugget speak very highly of you, Doctor."

Scully's head jerked toward Lacey at the thought of what those conversations between Lacey and "the girls" had included.

Lacey continued, "And your name was one of the first I heard on my arrival in Weaver, Reverend Sykes—with an extremely favorable comment, of course."

"You're referring to Pete Loughlin, I'm sure." Reverend Sykes's smile broadened. "Pete told me you and he were passengers in the same stagecoach. He was very impressed with you, which is one of the reasons I wanted to meet you. Like you, my wife and I are recent arrivals in Weaver. Our church and the size of our congregation aren't very impressive yet, but we have great hopes for a change in the right direction. I'd like to extend an invitation for you to join us for worship." He added, "We'd appreciate any extra time you could spare for us, too. We need all the help we can get."

Appearing delighted at the invitation, Lacey replied, "Thank you. We'll both come, won't we, Scully?"

The brief silence that followed spoke volumes.

Scully stood up unexpectedly and said, "Lacey and I have some important business to tend to this morning. If you'll excuse us…"

Ignoring Lacey's shocked expression as he drew her to her feet, Scully dropped his coin on the table and turned her toward the door.

* * *

"I don't like seeing you taken advantage of."

"No one was taking *advantage* of me—except for you, that is."

Lacey was livid. Common courtesy had been thoroughly ingrained in her since childhood—common courtesy that had been severely abused when Scully dismissed both Reverend Sykes and Doc Mayberry so abruptly. Scully and she had arrived back in her room minutes earlier after their exit from the restaurant and a rush that had left her breathless. She continued with astonishment, "How could you be so *rude?*"

Scully did not smile. Without realizing it, Lacey proved his point. Of the many things he had been accused of in his lifetime, being rude ranked very low on the list—yet Lacey spoke as if he had committed one of the cardinal sins.

He hadn't, and he knew the difference.

"It should've been obvious to you what was happening, but it apparently wasn't, so I decided to save you from yourself."

"What are you talking about?"

"It was a ploy."

Lacey did not speak.

"Come on, Lacey, it's obvious what happened. Your *friend,* Pete Loughlin, went to see Reverend Sykes because he didn't like the idea that I was the man who was meeting you here—because he thought I'd be a bad influence on you."

"That's ridiculous! Why would he think that?"

"Because I threw Pete Loughlin out of the Gold Nugget a while back, and he obviously hasn't forgotten it."

"Why did you throw him out?"

"He claimed he had been cheated at one of the tables. He started a fight, and I stopped it."

"Anybody could make a mistake."

"Pete didn't make a mistake. He probably *was* cheated. I fired that dealer a week later when I found out he was dealing from the bottom of the deck so he could skim a profit off the top for himself."

"Oh…how terrible! You did make sure Pete got his money back, didn't you?"

"This is the West, Lacey. It's sometimes wild and sometimes unfair. I do the best I can."

"But, poor Pete—"

"I told you, I do the best I can, but that doesn't excuse Pete for going behind my back."

"Behind your back…"

"I told you, he doesn't approve of your association with me. He thinks Reverend Sykes can put an end to it."

"No!"

"Yes."

"I mean…I'd never let that happen! You believe that, don't you, Scully?"

Scully looked at Lacey. She was shocked and righteous. She didn't consider for a moment that Pete might be right, that maybe he *was* a bad influence on her.

Something inside Scully clenched tight. Doing his best to ignore it, Scully said, "I meant what I told them, you know."

Confused, Lacey shook her head. "What are you talking about?"

"We have some important business to tend to this morning—before it gets too late."

"What business?"

His expression sober, Scully said, "Wait here. I'll be right back."

"But—"

Lacey's reply went unfinished as Scully pulled the hallway door closed behind him.

Lacey looked down at the package Scully had tossed onto her bed. He had returned within the half hour, true to his word, but it was obvious she wasn't that easily mollified. She asked, "What's that?"

"Open it up and see."

"I asked you—"

"It's riding clothes. They should fit. Mrs. Parker said she's had a lot of experience fitting women with ready-made outfits."

"I'm sure they will, but I still want to know what all this is about."

Scully's irritation at the conversation with Doc Mayberry and Reverend Sykes still smarted. He resented the implication that he wasn't fit to properly oversee Lacey's future. Didn't they realize that he recognized Lacey's special qualities as well as they did? Didn't they realize he'd always done his best to protect her, and he was committed to that course?

Obviously not, and that thought rankled.

But it wouldn't change anything. He had always done the most he could for Lacey. His caretaking of old Careful was only a small part of it. He had known how much Lacey loved the animal, and how important a part the small burro had played in her survival on that last, desperate day. He had wanted to spare that beautiful, dear little girl as much grief as he could. He had instinctively sought to maintain her connection to Weaver any way he could.

He had made arrangements to have the burro stabled with his own horse over the years. He had taken Careful out with him on frequent overnight trips; and the truth was, he had grown as fond of the feisty little critter as he was of his own mount. Yet, the moment when Lacey and the burro were reunited had been more than he had ever hoped for.

He would never forget it, the way that reunion had made him feel.

Yes, he was committed to Lacey, with all that word entailed.

Aware that Lacey awaited a response to her question, he said, "What do I have in mind? Just put the riding clothes on. You'll see."

"I don't like mysteries."

Scully dismissed her reply with a glance. "Just put the clothes on. I'll be outside waiting."

The sun was hot and steady as the morning hours advanced. The terrain was flat as they traveled toward the distant mountains, and an inexplicable tension began assuming control of Lacey's senses.

Traces of her vexation still remaining, Lacey looked at Scully, who rode at her right. She had been upset at his attitude in the restaurant when Doc Mayberry and Reverend Sykes introduced themselves earlier, but she had gotten truly angry when he explained the reasoning behind his behavior. The thought that he might've believed for a moment that anyone could influence her against him had stunned her. He was her lifeline to a past she hoped to reclaim, her stability in the present and a stalwart presence as she looked toward an uncertain future. She considered the bond between them to be impervious to assault of any kind. The thought that Scully possibly did not feel the same had shaken her.

Those thoughts had deluged her as she had dressed in the

riding clothes he had brought. When she opened the door, she had found him waiting, his dark suit exchanged for more common western wear. It had not escaped her notice that the ordinary shirt and trousers he wore somehow emphasized his superior height and breadth of shoulder, which set him apart from the average fellow on the street, or that the brim of the weathered hat he wore pulled down low on his forehead added a new element of determination to the strength of his compelling features. She had frowned at her certainty that the gun belt he wore strapped around his hips was not for adornment.

Scully did not smile when they reached the street and approached the two mounts waiting for them at the rail. He said, "You do remember how to ride astride, don't you? We don't have sidesaddles in Weaver, and the trails are a bit rough for a buggy."

She had responded by mounting up in a fluid movement that had surprised even herself—a prideful display for which she now silently suffered stiff, aching muscles.

Her eyes straight forward, Lacey heard Scully say, "It's getting hot. You have water in your canteen if you're thirsty."

Lacey turned toward him, a tart response on her lips, only to have it fade at first contact with Scully's concerned gaze. In a flash of insight, it was suddenly clear to her that both she and Scully had gotten angry for the same reason—because, in one way or another, the bond between them had been questioned. She wondered why she hadn't realized that before, then silently thanked the Lord for relieving her distress by imparting a bit of wisdom that had escaped her.

Lacey responded, "I'm not thirsty, but I would like to know where we're going, Scully."

The shadows in Scully's eyes darkened with uncertainty as he replied, "Surely you realize where we're going by now."

A cold chill raced down Lacey's spine at his response. Her mounting tension exploded into breathlessness as she turned to scrutinize the terrain more closely.

Endless wilderness…a sunbaked trail…the mountains in the distance drawing ever closer…

Lacey gasped, "I-I'm not ready to go there yet!"

"Your grandfather's buried there."

"No, I don't want to go."

Suddenly trembling, Lacey shook her head. She couldn't go back to the site of her nightmares, not even to see her grandpa's final resting place. Not yet.

"Lacey, are you all right?"

The terrifying shadows began shifting in Lacey's mind.

The fire was all around her. Her skin was burning. She couldn't breathe. She tried to call for help.

She was afraid…afraid…

Lacey did not feel the strong arm that encircled her waist the moment before Scully swept her from her saddle and settled her on his horse in front of him. She was not aware of the sob that escaped her throat when his embrace closed around her. She felt his breath against her hair and heard Scully whisper, "It's all right, Lacey. It's over…in the past. You don't have to be frightened anymore. I'll take care of you."

Shuddering, Lacey burrowed closer against him. She knew it was true. She was safe with Scully. She'd always be safe with him.

Scully filled his canteen at the stream, then looked back at Lacey. She was sitting in the patch of shade where he had left her. Her skin was ashen, her eyes red-rimmed. Strands of pale hair hung loose at her hairline and trailed down the back of her neck, but she was unaware of her dishevelment as she leaned back and closed her eyes.

Crouched beside Lacey moments later, Scully untied the bandanna from around his neck and wetted it, then ran the damp cloth across Lacey's forehead.

Lacey opened her eyes, then looked away as she said, "I'm sorry, Scully. I don't know what happened to me. It was really thoughtful of you to think of taking me to see my grandfather's grave. I should want to see it, but somehow…"

"It was my fault." Scully's sober gaze met hers. "I did a lot of talking about it being too soon for you to do things, then I pushed you into something you weren't ready to face."

"It wasn't your fault."

"I should've realized how you'd feel."

"Scully, please…" Lacey gripped Scully's hand and held it tight. It was big and surprisingly callused, but she felt only its warmth as she rasped, "How could you realize how I'd feel if I didn't realize it myself? Besides, I haven't been completely honest with you. I wanted you to think of me as an adult ready to assume charge of her life, not as a frightened child still plagued by nightmares."

"Nightmares? What kind of nightmares?"

"Of that day…only they're all mixed up and unclear. They've been more frequent lately." A chill shook Lacey as she continued, "The heat and the fire are so vivid, but shadows surround everything else. The shadows move, Scully. They twist and turn. They advance toward Grandpa while we're outside the burning cabin, then they run away. And all the while, Grandpa is dying. He's trying to talk to me, but his voice is fading. I strain to hear him, but he can't talk any louder. He puts the Bible in my hand, and I hold it tight. It burns my skin, but I clutch it tighter and tighter, refusing to let it go, even when the shadows return and try to take it away from me. The shadows are suddenly chasing me. I run faster and faster, but they keep getting closer and closer. Suddenly I'm back at the fire again, and there's nowhere else to run but back into the flames."

"That's enough." Scully's voice was sharp. He clutched her close to halt her shuddering. "You don't have to tell me any more."

"There's no more to tell. I don't know how it all ends. It's all…shadows."

Scully stroked Lacey's fair hair as he held her in his comforting embrace. When he moved her away from him at last, he whispered, "You don't have to be afraid of the shadows anymore, Lacey. That's what I'm here for…to chase the shadows away." He smiled and wiped the dampness from her cheeks with his palms, "That's why your grandpa sent you to me, and there's no way I'd let that old man down."

"We share that, don't we, Scully?" Lacey's small smile was shaky. "We both loved him."

"Yeah…we share that."

"And he loved us both."

Scully appeared to consider Lacey's statement for a moment before he responded, "Yes, I suppose he did."

"He would never think you aren't *respectable* enough."

"Lacey…"

"I'm not moving from the Gold Nugget."

"Lacey…"

"Not yet."

Scully looked down into Lacey's resolute expression. He would pursue that argument another time.

* * *

It was happening again.

Barret Gould stood behind the carved mahogany desk in his impressive office, his expression tight as he faced his two hirelings. Blackie Oaks had been an itinerant wrangler who couldn't hold a job and Larry Hayes had been a waster too lazy to labor honestly to support himself when he'd run across them shortly after arriving in Weaver years earlier. He had used their services openly whenever their meager talents served his purposes as Weaver's best and only attorney, and as one of its best-respected citizens. His "generosity" in giving the two "good, honest work to do" had been commended by many. What Weaver's residents didn't know, however, was that he had also used Larry and Blackie's services covertly when opportunities to advance himself financially beyond the confines of the law were presented.

In both situations, however, his contempt for the limited mentalities of the two men was boundless.

Barret struggled to control his ire. He had been raised in San Francisco, the only child of wealthy parents. He had made good use of his pleasing appearance—thick brown hair, deceivingly warm brown eyes and even, patrician features—from an early age, and had employed it to great advantage when attending the best schools. Scholastically and socially successful, he had graduated as a lawyer with a great future in store while enjoying a clandestine lifestyle that went unsuspected.

But that was before his father was found to have participated in illegal activities and the family wealth was confiscated. That was also before his father was sent to prison a broken man and his mother took whatever family funds could be salvaged and ran off with her lover.

When he'd discovered he was also being investigated for participation in his father's illegal affairs and the same fate might follow for him, he made a fast escape. He had chosen the vast, wild interior of the country as the best place for him to hide, yet Weaver, Arizona, had been as far as he had been willing to run.

Barret would never forget his disgust when he arrived in the small, unimpressive town wearing hand-tailored clothes and a deceptive smile. He had since used his practiced facade to become a valued member of the community while silently despising Weaver for its ignorance, for its location in the middle of nowhere and for its lack of proximity to any city of reasonable refinement. He had sworn that he'd find a way to restore himself to the civilized world before his youth was spent.

Eleven years had passed since then, eleven years of silent frustration made bearable only by the sum accumulating too slowly in his name to have made the lost time worthwhile.

Barret struggled to suppress his disdain at Blackie's undiscerning observances as he said, "You're telling me Scully and Lacey Stewart rode out into the wilderness with no apparent destination in mind, then turned around and came right back to Weaver. That doesn't make any sense. Lacey has waited more than half her lifetime to claim her grandfather's strike. There's only one place she'd want to go if she went out riding."

Larry, the smaller of the two men, interjected, "Scully and the lady didn't come right back. They stopped at a stream for a while to cool off."

Barret glared with impatience. "'The lady…?' That 'lady' you're talking about is Lacey Stewart, you know… the same Lacey Stewart who was a child at her grandfather's cabin ten years ago. The same Lacey Stewart who could've identified you and Blackie as the men who shot her grandfather."

"Yeah, but she's all growed up and she's a lady now. And she didn't blink an eye when she saw me and Blackie on the street a few days ago."

"She saw you?"

"Yeah, and she didn't give us a second look."

Barret took a firm hold on his forbearance. "So you're telling me, that's it…they just stopped at a stream to cool off? They didn't get as much as halfway toward the old man's cabin?"

"Right."

Silence.

"They did a little cuddling while they were at the stream, is all."

"Cuddling…"

"Yeah, it looked to me like the lady was crying for some reason, and Scully was trying to comfort her."

"They didn't…you know…?"

"No, they didn't even come close. They just stayed for a while until the lady got herself back together, and then they headed back."

"Was it Scully's idea to turn back, or was it the woman's?"

The two men exchanged glances before Blackie replied, "I'd say it was the lady's. She didn't want to go on."

Barret nodded. She didn't want to look anxious. The girl was smarter than he thought.

He said, "All right, that's all I need to know for now. Get out, and remember what I said. Don't let that 'lady' out of your sight."

Waiting until both men had left his office and closed the door behind them, Barret sat down at his desk and reached into his drawer for the small sack that was never far from his reach. He withdrew the gold nugget from inside the sack and held it tight in his hand as he had many times before. He recalled the moment when Charlie Pratt had walked into his office late that first day. Short, wiry, unkempt, Charlie had been indistinguishable from any other prospector he had ever seen, but when the old man smiled and put the nugget down on the desk in front of him, Barret knew his moment had come.

A man of few words, Charlie told him he'd struck it rich, that he wanted to register his claim in his own name and that of his granddaughter, and he wanted to do it "real legal like, so there'd be no problem afterward." Charlie left the nugget behind for a "retainer" without disclosing the location of the claim, and said he'd return to sign whatever papers were necessary in a couple of days.

Barret's heart pounded in vivid recall. He had immediately set Blackie and Larry on the old man's trail. His plan had been simple. Charlie had kept his strike a secret. He had been cautious enough not to tell anyone but Barret about it. Blackie and Larry would follow the old man, find his claim and report the location back to him so he could record it in his own name before the old man returned—"real legal like, so there'd be no problem afterward."

A familiar knot of frustration twisted tight inside Barret as memory returned the details of the debacle that followed.

Charlie also had been smarter than he thought. Charlie had evidently spotted Blackie and Larry following him and had led them on a circuitous trail obviously meant to confuse them before reaching his cabin in darkness. He had then tricked them into thinking he had gone to his bed, only to appear unexpectedly behind them with a gun, demanding to know what they were after.

According to Blackie, the situation deteriorated into chaos from that point, ending up with Charlie being shot and with Blackie and Larry determined to hide their crime by throwing Charlie's body into the cabin and setting the structure afire.

Furious when they returned with their story, Barret had still considered the situation salvageable. It had seemed a matter of simply scouting the area Charlie had been working to find the source of the gold.

Barret remembered his panic at the news that Charlie's eight-year-old granddaughter, Lacey Stewart, had arrived in town injured and bleeding, fresh from the scene of the burned-out cabin. He'd been sure she would tell someone about her grandfather's strike, that she might even know its exact location. He had been furious with both his men for having allowed her to survive.

Fearing Lacey would be able to identify his men and the identification would eventually lead back to him, he had paid them off and told them to leave town. They had obediently stayed away until Lacey was sent to a school back east and it was safe for them to return. The girl never spoke of her grandfather's strike. He had been overjoyed at that, but his dream of a return to the wealth and prosperity of his youth had died when all manner of prospecting and excavation in the area of Charlie's cabin had failed to locate Charlie's gold.

Now Charlie's granddaughter had returned to Weaver, and with her return, his dream had been revived.

Barret clutched the nugget tighter. Lacey Stewart may have fooled everyone else, but she didn't fool him. She wouldn't have traveled back from the big city to a town in the middle of nowhere if she didn't think it would be worth her while—if she didn't have some idea where to look for the strike her grandfather had made.

It appeared, however, that she wasn't about to share the strike with Jake Scully.

It also appeared that Jake Scully was totally taken in by her.

But Lacey Stewart didn't fool him. He would get that claim—one way or another.

Chapter Four

The sun had barely risen and Weaver had not yet fully awakened when Lacey crossed the empty main street and headed toward Sadie Wilson's restaurant. Against Scully's adamant protests, she had started working there a few days ago. She had made certain to rise at dawn so she would be at the restaurant before the first customer even thought of appearing at the door, and she now knew she would find Sadie already at work in the kitchen when she arrived.

Lacey smoothed the apron tied around her narrow waist. Sadie had provided it the first day of her employment and she wore it proudly. It was important to her that she do well in her new position. Scully had not mentioned again her near hysteria on the trail when he'd attempted to take her to her grandfather's gravesite, and she was grateful. His solicitude during those frightening moments, however, made her more determined than ever to become independent. Scully was too good, too caring of her welfare. She could not bear the thought of telling him that her nightmares had grown more vivid since that day, nor of becoming a burden to him that he did not deserve.

A smile touched Lacey's lips as she neared the restaurant. She had prayed, asking the Lord to help her do well so Sadie would be satisfied with her work, and her prayers had been answered. She hadn't made any major mistakes so far in serving the customers, she was adapting well to the restaurant routine and Sadie had complimented her on the job she was doing.

Her thoughts were interrupted at the sight of the person waiting outside the restaurant door. Lacey hastened her step. She tapped Rosie on the arm when she reached her side. She liked Rosie and her friend, Jewel. Unlike some of the other Gold Nugget women, they had been friendly to her, and she appreciated their openness.

Rosie turned hesitantly toward her, and Lacey gasped with surprise. Wearing a plain cotton dress that bore no resemblance to the gaudy satin she normally wore, and without the heavy makeup of her trade, Rosie looked so young—certainly no older than Lacey, herself—but it was not that thought that stunned her.

A large bruise marked Rosie's pale cheek.

Lacey asked spontaneously, "What happened to your face, Rosie? Did you fall?"

Rosie flashed a weak smile. "Yes…that's what I did. I fell. I'm just clumsy, I guess." She hastened to add, "But I'm all right. The mark won't show under my makeup tonight, so Scully won't have to worry about it when I work."

"I'm sure Scully will just be glad as I am that you're all right."

Rosie changed the subject, saying, "Sadie hasn't opened the door yet. I guess I'm early, but I didn't get a chance to eat supper last night, and breakfast at the boarding house won't be ready for hours yet. I couldn't sleep for the loud complaints my stomach was making, so here I am."

Somehow hesitant, Lacey replied, "I don't think Sadie has everything ready, but you can come inside with me and wait, if you like."

"No, I'll wait outside." Rosie took a backward step. "Some of the ladies in town don't approve of Gold Nugget women, and I don't want to cause any trouble."

"Sadie's not like that." Lacey took Rosie's arm. "Besides, you're hungry, and that's what the restaurant's here for."

"That's all right. I'll wait here."

"Rosie, please." Lacey smiled encouragingly and said, "It's no trouble if you come inside now...really."

Lacey drew Rosie reluctantly behind her as she entered. She called out to Sadie as the older woman worked at the stove, "Good morning, Sadie. I told Rosie it would be all right to wait at a table until you're ready to open up."

Sadie glanced over her shoulder. "That's fine. I'll be ready in a few minutes."

Standing beside Sadie moments later, Lacey whispered, "I hope you don't mind, Sadie. I didn't want Rosie to wait outside. She fell and hurt herself. She's kind of pale, and her face is bruised. I don't think she feels too well."

"Fell and hurt herself, huh? Is that what she told you?" Sadie looked back at Rosie, then shook her head. "It's that boyfriend of hers. That Riley fella uses his hands on her when he has too much to drink. Everybody knows it."

"You mean he *hits* her?" Lacey was stunned. "Why does she let him do that to her?"

"Life is sometimes hard for a woman out here, Lacey, especially somebody like Rosie who doesn't have much to fall back on. I guess she figures she's better off with Riley than without him."

"But—"

"I know. It's not right or fair."

"But—"

"But that's the way things are."

Voices at the door turned Sadie's attention to the four cowpokes who entered and sat down at a table. She said, "It looks like the restaurant's open whether I'm ready or not. You'd better get started with the customers, Lacey. We're going to fill up in here in a hurry."

Lacey looked at Rosie.

"But take care of Rosie first. Like you said, she looks like she doesn't feel too good."

Lacey nodded. She swallowed the thickness in her throat as she turned in Rosie's direction.

"You're looking very fine today, Lacey."

"Thank you, Mr. Gould. What can I get for you this morning?"

Barret smiled his practiced smile as Lacey awaited his reply. He had entered the busy restaurant for breakfast a few minutes earlier, as he had for the past few days since Lacey started working there. He knew he made a good appearance. He knew his clothes were impressive, and that the deference the customers of the restaurant showed him made him stand out favorably in Lacey's mind. He also knew gaining Lacey's confidence could be useful in so many ways.

He looked at Lacey as she smiled at him, showing even, white teeth with a candid, guileless expression.

He said softly, "You forgot to call me Barret, Lacey."

To her credit, Lacey managed a demure flush. "Of course. I'm sorry."

"No need to apologize. I'd like us to be friends." Responding to her initial inquiry, he said, "I'll have some of Sadie's fine hotcakes and eggs this morning, but I know they couldn't be any finer than the service."

Barret complimented himself on the inroads he was certain he had made into Lacey's esteem as she returned to work and he nodded at the familiar faces quickly filling the restaurant. Amused, he watched the cowhands at a nearby table scramble to retrieve a fork Lacey had dropped. He almost laughed. She had everyone fooled with her innocent appearance—everyone but him. He wondered what they would think if they knew how carefully she was guarding her real reason for returning to Weaver.

Those thoughts were still prominent in Barret's mind when Lacey returned with his breakfast in hand. He patted her slender, ladylike hand as she placed his plate on the table and he commented, "Reverend Sykes and I look forward to seeing you at Sunday services this weekend."

Withdrawing her hand, Lacey responded, "Yes, I'm looking forward to attending services, too."

She walked quickly back to the counter to retrieve another customer's breakfast. Barret turned under the weight of someone's stare to see Jake Scully looking at him from the doorway. Scully did not return his smile of acknowledgment and Barret turned his attention to his breakfast in an effort to conceal his anger at the slight.

Barret inwardly smarted. He had never liked Jake Scully. Scully had never shown him the same respect that other residents of Weaver displayed toward him. As unbelievable as it seemed, he had the feeling Jake Scully looked down on him.

On him!

Actually, he was astounded that a man of the world like Scully could possibly have deceived himself into believing Lacey had left the refinement of city life behind and returned to Weaver without having greater prospects in mind. Could he possibly believe Lacey had come "home" because of a sense of obligation to him?

If so, he was a fool.

Barret watched covertly as Scully settled himself at a corner table. Scully's gaze was fixed on Lacey with an intensity that appeared almost proprietary, and Barret's questions were answered.

Jake Scully—a man who had seen it all, taken in by the wiles of a cunning woman!

The thought was delicious.

He didn't like it…not one little bit.

Scully scrutinized the patrons who had filled Sadie's restaurant to capacity although the day had hardly begun. His breakfast lay untouched in front of him as Lacey moved between the tables serving customers.

He seethed.

He watched as Barret Gould again called Lacey to his table, as Barret looked up at her with his suave, cultivated smile. His stomach churned as Barret stood up and whispered into Lacey's ear before paying his bill, his hand lingering on hers a second too long.

He hadn't needed that display to realize Lacey was out of her depth here. Lacey was too naive, too sincere. She wasn't experienced with the divergent personalities frequenting Sadie's establishment—just as Sadie's customers weren't accustomed to a person like Lacey.

Nor was Lacey accustomed to or deserving of the type of treatment she was subjected to by them. He had heard the occasional complaints if the food took too long in reaching the table, the demands that kept Lacey running. He had noted the assumptions about her instinctively friendly manner. One misguided cowhand had actually whistled to get her attention! True, Lacey seemed to handle it all gracefully, but it galled him.

As Scully watched, a young cowpoke summoned Lacey back to his table for the fourth time, smiling broadly. Obviously intent on impressing her, he joked and teased until Sadie called her away with a flimsy excuse. He saw the table of cowboys seated nearby whisper as Lacey passed, then laugh aloud. He noted the glances two matrons seated nearby exchanged when their husbands followed Lacey's progress across the room with more than common interest, and he observed with growing heat the drummer who called Lacey to his table, then pressed a coin into her hand with a wink. If that man thought he could buy his way into Lacey's affections—

"Say now, what does a fella have to do in here to get some service?" Scully's rioting thoughts were interrupted by the loud complaint of an unshaven cowpoke who stood up unsteadily at his table and slurred, "I've been waiting an hour in here, Sadie. Ain't your new girl going to wait on me? I'm a good customer!"

Scully tensed. Everyone in the restaurant knew Jud Hall had walked through the doorway only a few minutes previously, just as everyone knew Jud was trouble. He knew, because he had tossed the drunken cowpoke out of his saloon on too many occasions to count.

Tensing, Scully watched as Lacey approached Jud, her face hot. He saw Jud's face change as she drew closer. He didn't like what Jud was obviously thinking when Lacey said, "What would you like Sadie to make for you this morning?"

A leering Jud answered, "Maybe I don't want Sadie to make nothin' for me this morning, darlin'. Maybe I want *you* to cook me my breakfast."

Interrupting from her place beside the stove, Sadie called out, "I'm the cook in this restaurant, Jud. If you don't like it, you can leave."

"Maybe I don't want to leave." His leer turning aggressive, Jud continued, "Maybe I want this girlie here to—"

Scully was on his feet in a flash. Gripping Jud by the back of the neck, he paid no attention to the chairs that scraped out of his way and the customers who dodged Jud's flailing arms and legs as he propelled him toward the door. He waited deliberately until Jud hit the street with a thud before walking back into the restaurant and closing the door behind him. He did not look at Lacey as he slapped his coin down beside his uneaten breakfast, then walked over to her and said in a voice meant for her ears alone, "When you finish up work here today, tell Sadie you're not coming back."

Lacey looked up at him, her face red.

"Tell her."

He did not wait for Lacey's response as he walked out the door.

Barret observed the scene from the street.

A saloonkeeper protecting the virtue of a prospector's granddaughter.

How quaint.

How noble.

How *stupid*.

But it told him something. He had been right in everything he had been thinking. Scully was totally taken in by Lacey's pretended innocence.

Barret watched as Scully exited the restaurant. Scully's involvement with Lacey complicated an already difficult situation. He need tread lightly in dealing with Lacey because of Scully, and Lacey would need to tread just as lightly if she expected to claim her grandfather's strike without her unwanted protector following at her heels.

Barret considered that thought. It appeared he could be in for a long siege.

Unless...

Barret frowned.

Unless he could find a better way.

Lacey walked across the saloon floor toward the staircase to the second floor where her room awaited her. It had been a difficult morning at the restaurant—the most trying so far because of the incident with Jud Hall and Scully. She recalled the silence that had followed Scully's departure from the restaurant, then the gradual hum of speculative conversation that had ensued. She was glad it was over. She was anxious to reach the silence of her room, but she knew she would first meet another brief, revealing silence—the one her appearance always elicited when she walked through the saloon doors.

Lacey knew that silence was one of the reasons Scully was so adamant about her taking a room at Mary McInnes's boarding house. She also knew it was the reason he had arranged for the dilapidated outside entrance to the saloon's second floor, previously unusable, to be repaired.

Lacey nodded at a few familiar faces in passing, then

climbed the staircase, head high. She would be glad when the outer staircase was finished, actually more for Scully's sake than her own. It would relieve some of his stress. Yet she knew Scully would not be truly satisfied until she had severed all connection with the saloon and its patrons.

Lacey considered that possibility seriously for the first time. Her room above the Gold Nugget was the only home that remained for her. It was her haven. It was the place where she had recuperated from the most traumatic experience of her life. In it, she had known she was safe because Scully was nearby. She felt the same way now, but she was becoming acutely aware of the disservice she did to Scully in insisting that she stay.

Gasping with surprise when Scully stepped unexpectedly into sight at the top of the stairs, Lacey did not protest when he took her arm and said with an expression that suffered no protest, "I need to talk to you."

Lacey turned toward Scully when he ushered her into her room, leaving the door ajar as he turned toward her to ask, "Did you tell Sadie you won't be back to work at the restaurant again?"

"No."

Scully did not look pleased.

"I'm not going to quit, Scully."

"Yes, you are."

"No, I'm not."

Scully's chest began an angry heaving. He said tightly, "You tried and did your best, but working at the restaurant was a bad idea in the first place."

"It isn't."

"You saw what happened this morning."

"I could've handled it, Scully."

"Really."

"I could have! Sadie warned me about Jud. He causes trouble every now and then, but he's always been manageable in the past."

"In the past...before you started working there."

"What's that supposed to mean?"

"You have a mirror, Lacey."

"I don't understand."

Scully paused a moment, then grasped Lacey by the shoulders and turned her toward the washstand mirror. He held her facing her reflection as he demanded, "What do you see when you look at yourself, Lacey?"

"Scully..."

"Tell me."

Lacey frowned as she studied her image, then said, "I see a young woman with blond hair and blue eyes whose hairdo needs repairing and who looks confused."

Standing behind her, Scully stared at her reflection as he said, "I'll tell you what I see...what every man in that restaurant saw this morning. I see a young woman whose fair hair and womanly figure catches a man's attention even before he gets a closer look that stops him in his tracks."

"Scully..." Lacey gave a short, embarrassed laugh. "That's ridiculous."

"Is it? Look at yourself more closely. Is there another woman in this town who looks as good as you do?"

"Of course there is!"

"Who?"

Momentarily taken aback, Lacey stuttered, "There's... ah-ah...Noelle Leach, the blacksmith's daughter. She's a natural beauty."

"Right, and she smells like horses."

"Scully!"

"Go ahead, name another."

"There's Rita Johnson, the apothecary's niece. I haven't met her personally, but I've seen her, and she's lovely."

"Lovely? She's also so snobbish and impressed with herself that she repulses any man who might think of looking her way."

"You're not being fair." Lacey shook off Scully's grip and turned back toward him with a touch of irritation. "What difference does that all make, anyway?"

"What I'm trying to tell you, Lacey, is that you're different from the women in this town. You're kind and innocent, and too friendly for your own good. You trust people too much. You don't seem to realize that some of the men who look at you in that restaurant don't have the best of intentions."

"Oh, pooh!"

Scully's expression darkened. "Take Gould, for instance."

"Barret?"

"He can't be trusted."

"How can you say that? He's a lawyer."

"Is that supposed to prove something?"

"He's educated, and dedicated to serving the law."

"Is he?"

"He's also a member in good standing of Reverend Sykes's church."

"Oh, so that's supposed to mean something?"

"Of course it does!"

"Lacey, Reverend Sykes arrived in town only a few weeks before you. He doesn't know the townsfolk any better than you do."

"Scully…"

"But even Reverend Sykes accepts that people aren't always what they represent themselves to be. And as far as our town lawyer is concerned, I've seen too many peculiar things happen over the years after some poor fellows wandered into town and went to Barret Gould for advice. He isn't to be trusted, Lacey."

"No one else in Weaver seems to feel that way."

"I'm in a unique position in Weaver, Lacey. I see people come and go that the respectable members of the community don't give a second glance."

"I can't believe that."

"You should, and the fact that you don't is just my point. You're too gullible to be exposed to the element that frequents the restaurant."

"You and I have eaten there every morning since I arrived!"

"That's right, but you weren't working there, where everybody feels you're at their beck and call."

"Everyone respects me there."

"Oh? What about Jud?"

"That was different. He got out of hand. One of the customers in the restaurant would've stepped in to take care of him if you hadn't."

"Is that what you want…to be exposed to that kind of treatment, hoping somebody will step in to stop it?"

"It's not what I *want,* Scully."

"It's not what I want, either."

"But it's not the norm at the restaurant—and I don't want to discuss this with you anymore. Please understand. I won't quit my job there. Sadie needs me…and I need this job."

"Why, Lacey?"

"Why?" Lacey took a deep breath. She swallowed against the emotion that abruptly choked her throat as she attempted to continue. "You…you had a very pleasant life here before I came back, but since I arrived, you've done nothing but worry about me."

"That isn't the point I'm trying to make, Lacey."

"But it's the point *I'm* making. Please listen, and try to understand. You've been so good to me, Scully—and I've rewarded you with one problem after another." Lacey hesitated, dreading the words she was about to say before saying, "I've been wrong. I need to admit that to you. I need to move away from this room and give you some space so you won't feel so responsible for me."

"Lacey…"

"I'll go to see Mrs. McInnes today. If she still has that room, I'll take it and tell her I'll pay for my board at the end of the week, when Sadie pays me."

Scully's hands dropped back to his sides.

"That is what you wanted, isn't it?"

"Maybe."

"Maybe?"

"What I want is for you to be safe."

"I'll be safe there. You said so yourself."

"What about the nightmares?"

Lacey took a short breath. "I have to grow up sometime."

Scully looked at her for silent moments, then nodded. "All right. Mary is saving the empty room at the boarding house for you."

"How—"

"I told her you'd be taking it soon."

"So she held it for me…no charge?"

Scully did not reply.

"Thank you, Scully."

Expressionless, Scully said, "Let me know when you're ready to move."

Lacey stared at the door that closed behind Scully as she heard his footsteps retreat down the hallway. When she could hear him no longer, she frowned, suddenly at a loss.

She had done it...broken a tie that she had not truly wanted to sever.

What had she done?

What had he done?

Scully walked down the hallway, entered his room, closed the door behind him, then stood still. He had wanted Lacey out of the Gold Nugget environment, hadn't he? He had insisted that she move into the boarding house...had even paid the rent on the vacant room while Mary McInnes held it for Lacey. He had reasoned it was best for Lacey that way.

What he had not considered, however, was if it was best for him. He was, in effect, thrusting Lacey out on her own even more surely than she was with her job in the restaurant.

Scully shook his head. Her job in the restaurant...that was the problem. His respect for Sadie aside, Sadie was not prepared to handle the complications that having a beautiful, sincere young woman like Lacey working for her would entail.

Lacey needed to find a place that was more secure...more protected. The problem was, that place did not exist in Weaver, except in her room near his.

Yes, what had he done?

Chapter Five

"Are you sure you can't stop for breakfast, dear?" Mary McInnes's lined face moved into a frown of concern as Lacey passed through the boarding house kitchen on her way to the street. "You haven't been taking any of your meals here. I worry that you aren't eating right."

"I'm fine, Mary." Breathless with haste, Lacey continued, "Sadie will be waiting for me at the restaurant. I can eat there if I get hungry."

"But the restaurant is so busy…"

"I'm fine, thank you."

Outside moments later, Lacey walked quickly toward the main street. Mary was a dear woman. A widow with grown children who had made their homes away from Weaver, she looked after the residents of her boarding house with a surfeit of motherly love, which Lacey appreciated, and which she was certain Scully had taken into consideration when arranging for her room there.

Scully…

Lacey took a deep breath as she approached the corner of

the street. Scully had helped her move her things when she had said goodbye to Helen and taken her room at the boarding house a few days earlier. Mary had had no problem with allowing Scully into her room to help her—a privilege that Lacey had learned Mary granted to few male visitors to her respectable establishment. She had been comforted by the warmth Mary displayed toward Scully and had been pleased to see Mary show insight into Scully's character.

As for herself...

Lacey's step faltered.

She missed Scully. Not that he had distanced himself from her since she had moved. He hadn't, but the physical distance between them had been as difficult for her as she had expected. She was lonely in her room with strangers on all sides—residents of the boarding house who were friendly, who said all the right things intended to make her feel at home, but with whom she had no connection that even approached the bond Scully and she shared.

She had been so cautious in staying out of Scully's way during the nighttime hours at the Gold Nugget. She had remained in her room and busied herself with countless necessary tasks. When they were completed, she had sat down with her Bible to reread the familiar words she had virtually committed to memory, while images of nights spent in that same way with her grandfather grew gradually clearer in her mind. She suspected that the sense of security she had felt knowing Scully was nearby had somehow facilitated the clarification of those memories. She had come to anticipate with true warmth Scully's knock on the door before she retired for the night, when they would spend unhurried time talking in the doorway, no matter how heavy the traffic in the saloon below had become.

Those moments with Scully had meant so much to her. Losing them had cost her dearly.

Even her nightmares…

A chill raced down Lacey's spine. The intensity of her nightmares continued to increase. When she awoke in her silent room after those nighttime terrors, the shadows seemed somehow darker still.

Lacey murmured a prayer for the strength she needed to combat her fears. She was an adult now. She had come home to Weaver to repay Scully for his generosity and his caring over the years, and to regain memories of her grandfather that eluded her. She couldn't accomplish either of those purposes if she allowed her fears to gain control.

In the meantime, she was anxious for Scully's morning visit to Sadie's restaurant, anxious to see in Scully's sober gray eyes a warmth that was meant for her alone. She—

Lacey stopped still as the sound of a slap turned her toward the less respectable boarding house on the opposite end of the side street, where most of the Gold Nugget women lived. Rosie was standing outside the door, holding her cheek and sobbing while an unfamiliar fellow turned and walked angrily away from her. He was gone in an instant, the same instant it took for Lacey to start in Rosie's direction.

Rosie had already slipped through her boarding house doorway when Lacey reached it. Determined, Lacey was about to follow when she heard a female voice say, "Don't do that. It won't help."

Lacey turned to see Jewel behind her. A tall cowboy stood silently at her side. Not bothering with an introduction, Jewel turned toward him and said, "Go back to the ranch, Buddy. I'm all right. I can take care of Rosie."

Lacey noted the fellow's reluctance before he nodded. With a tip of his hat in her direction, he was on his way.

Jewel turned back toward Lacey. She still wore the satin dress and heavy makeup of her dancehall trade, but her expression was sober and concerned when she pushed back a straying strand of dark hair and said, "Rosie wouldn't like it if you saw her right now. She'd be embarrassed. She always is when Riley treats her like that, but she'd be especially embarrassed if she knew you saw him hit her."

"But she might be hurt. I only want to help."

"If you want to help her, don't let her know you know what happened. Rosie likes you. She likes to think you like her, too."

"I do like her."

"Then let her believe you don't know about the way Riley treats her. She thinks you'd lose respect for her. She doesn't have much, and that's important to her."

"But—"

Jewel's dark eyes grew suddenly moist and her voice hoarse. "Rosie's a good girl who's had a hard life, Lacey. Riley treats her pretty good for the most part. He just gets out of hand sometimes."

"But he hit her."

"And he'll come back tomorrow and tell her he loves her. To Rosie, that means a lot. Not too many people have told Rosie they love her in her life."

"That Riley fellow couldn't love her if he'd do that to her."

Jewel shook her head.

"What does that mean?"

"I know Riley doesn't really love Rosie. He just enjoys his power over her. You know it…and in my heart, I think Rosie knows it, too. But she's alone, and right now she figures he's the best she can do. I know how she feels because I've been there, too."

Lacey glanced spontaneously in the direction into which Jewel's quiet cowboy had ridden off, and Jewel responded, "No, not Buddy. He's all right." Her voice softened with suppressed emotion as she said, "Buddy's a fine fella, but he's not the first man in my life. I don't expect he'll be the last."

Sadness and frustration combined to tighten Lacey's throat as she whispered, "What can I do for you both, Jewel?"

"I'm all right. Rosie's the one who has trouble right now. If you want to help her, just be her friend. You're not like the other people in this town. You don't treat Rosie any different than anybody else just because she works at the Gold Nugget. She appreciates that." Jewel hesitated, then said, "I do, too."

Lacey still had not found the words to respond when Jewel turned away and slipped through the boarding house doorway.

"Can I have some more coffee here, Lacey?"

Lacey turned toward the young, curly-haired wrangler who had made the request. The restaurant had been filled since the door opened that morning. She had responded to the rush with instinctive haste, but her mind had not yet left the moments she had spent with Jewel in the doorway of her boarding house.

Lacey refilled Todd Fulton's cup, then felt his callused hand touch her forearm to stay her as he said, "Is something wrong, Lacey?"

The thought that if not for her grandfather's Christian teachings, his dying guidance and Scully's boundless generosity, she might now be standing in Rosie's or Jewel's shoes had lodged deep inside Lacey.

"Lacey…?"

Todd's hand tightened on her arm, bringing her back to the present, and Lacey replied, "I'm fine, Todd, just a little distracted this morning, I guess."

Todd's brown eyes searched hers before he said, "I was beginning to worry. I haven't seen you smile since I got here."

"Well…" Lacey forced her expression brighter. "I'm smiling now."

"You are all right, aren't you? You'd tell me if you weren't…."

Lacey replied sincerely, "It's nice of you to be concerned, but I'm fine."

"Good." Todd scrutinized her a moment longer, then said, "Because I came here this morning with a purpose in mind."

"A purpose?"

Lacey saw warm color creep up Todd's neck as he said, "Talk was that Jake Scully was looking after you, then somebody said you moved out into the boarding house to be on your own."

"You aren't another fellow who's going to say you're glad because Scully wasn't a good influence on me, or that my job here isn't right for me, either, are you?"

"No, ma'am. I'd never say that."

"Well, in that case, my response to you is, it's about time I started out on my own, don't you think? Scully is family— all the family I've got, anyway. He'll always be my closest friend, even if I am living at the boarding house."

"Then he wouldn't mind if another friend asked you to have supper with him on Saturday."

"Another friend? Who?"

"Me."

"Oh…" Somehow startled, Lacey responded, "Why would you do that?"

Todd grinned. "Let me see…so we could get to know each other better, maybe?"

"That's so kind of you, Todd," Lacey responded, "but I've been eating my meals with Scully."

Lacey frowned at her own response, suddenly realizing how presumptuous she had been in taking for granted that Scully would always give her needs precedence. Determined to correct that mistake but somehow reluctant to commit to Todd, she continued, "I can't have dinner with you on Saturday, but if you'll ask me again sometime, it'll be my pleasure."

"Fine. That's fine. I'll do that…soon."

Gratified to see that Todd's response and his smile were genuine, Lacey hurried to answer Sadie's call. She was returning with another breakfast in hand when she saw Scully sitting in the corner and realized she had been so preoccupied that she hadn't seen him enter. Uncertain how long he had been sitting there, she met his gaze with a sense of relief inexplicably so great that it brought a rush of tears to her eyes.

At his table moments later, Lacey saw Scully's fists slowly clench as he asked, "What did Todd say to upset you?"

"He didn't upset me."

"No?"

"No. I just…before I came here this morning…" Lacey halted. Scully was Rosie's boss, and Jewel had asked her not to embarrass Rosie. She couldn't relieve her own distress by talking the situation out with Scully and asking his advice. Rosie would be mortified.

Scully was waiting for her to finish her statement.

Lacey said sincerely, "I was feeling a little lost this morning until you came. I feel better now."

Lacey had spoken those words automatically, and she

suddenly realized how true they were. Just to know Scully was nearby made her feel better. What would she do without him?

Lacey was looking at him with her great blue eyes so open and earnest that Scully could barely restrain the impulse to hug her protectively close. If he were honest, he would say the same—that he'd been feeling a little lost until he saw her, and he felt better now.

Well, almost better.

Scully scrutinized Lacey's pale face more closely. She had been frowning as she worked, something she rarely did, and there were light shadows under her eyes, indicating a lack of sleep. Something was bothering her...and whatever bothered her, bothered him. He asked softly, "Are you all right, Lacey?"

"Yes, I suppose I will be when I learn to use the resources the Lord gave me to depend on myself a little more. You don't seem to have that problem, but I do."

Scully said flatly, "I wouldn't exactly say the Lord has much to do with my line of work."

With unexpected sobriety, Lacey replied, "It's more clear to me today than ever before that whether you realize it or not, you've been doing the Lord's work in caring for my needs over the years. And if that's clear to me, I know it's clear to Him."

Scully pondered Lacey's response. He had been doing the Lord's work? He was suddenly aware that, before Lacey's return to Weaver, he would not have given a thought to the gulf that lay between the Lord's work and his.

He pondered that reality, then dismissed it.

Lacey seemed to have dismissed it as well when she said, "You do want breakfast, don't you?"

He nodded. "The usual."

"Hotcakes and eggs." Lacey smiled into his eyes and all was momentarily well. She was back with his breakfast within a few minutes, and he mentioned casually, "Careful's due for some exercise. I take him with me occasionally when I go riding. The little critter seems to enjoy it. I'm going to take him out this afternoon after I finish some work at the Gold Nugget." He paused, then asked, "Do you want to come?"

Before she could respond, Scully stressed, "You don't have to worry. I don't have any particular destination in mind."

"Oh, I'd like that, but I have to do something first. It'll only take a few minutes. I could meet you at the livery stable afterward." She hesitated. "Unless that'll interfere with your plans."

Unless that'll interfere with your plans...

Didn't Lacey realize he wouldn't *let* it interfere with his plans?

It occurred to him that she did not.

Scully nodded his assent and saw her relief. He watched her walk away, wondering what was so important to Lacey that she'd chance missing a ride with Careful.

"How are you, Reverend Sykes?"

Lacey neared the small, dilapidated church situated in a less frequented area of town. She was uncertain exactly when that morning she had decided the visit was a necessity. She only knew it was.

Paintbrush in hand, Reverend Sykes turned at the sound of her voice. He had abandoned his customary dark suit for work clothes, and he seemed to be wearing more of the paint than he was successfully applying to the outside of the building. Yet the front portion of the church was already done, and he appeared determined to continue.

Reverend Sykes responded, "Well, I've been better. Painting isn't my specialty, but Leticia said we needed to do something to freshen up the church, and I've learned that she knows more about these things than I do. So, she's working on the inside, and I'm working on the outside."

"You're doing a fine job."

"You're a true diplomat, Lacey." Reverend Sykes's lean face moved into a smile. He searched her expression, then glanced at her riding apparel and said, "You're on your way somewhere, it seems. What can I do for you?"

"I wanted to stop by and tell you how much I enjoyed your sermon last Sunday." She had slipped into a back pew alone. She had wished Scully would offer to accompany her, but when he did not, she had left for Sunday services with a smile on her face and a strong hope for the future. She added, "I'll be there next Sunday, of course."

"I'm pleased to hear you enjoyed my sermon and we certainly look forward to seeing you again, but you needn't have made a special trip to tell me that."

Lacey hesitated. "I came for another reason, too, Reverend, but I can see this isn't a good time."

"Anytime is a good time, Lacey."

"I just…need some advice."

Reverend Sykes's expression sobered.

"About how to help someone who's in trouble without embarrassing that person with my concern."

Reverend Sykes responded bluntly, "Is this person in desperate need of help?"

"I think she is."

"She?"

"Yes."

Reverend Sykes nodded. "You might send her to me. I'm experienced in helping people, both socially and spiritually, and Leticia is especially good in dealing with women."

"No, Reverend, I can't do that. I don't want to embarrass her. It would damage our friendship."

"And if the friendship was damaged, you wouldn't be able to help her at all…is that it?"

Lacey's brief nod was her only reply, and Reverend Sykes's expression grew thoughtful. "You've caught me off guard here, Lacey. I don't know this person, so advice is difficult to give." He hesitated at her frown. "You want to hear my thoughts right now, is that it?"

Lacey nodded again.

"Well, I could tell you to pray for this woman. Prayer is powerful, but it's apparent you don't need me to tell you that. You obviously want to use the gifts God gave you to do more."

Reverend Sykes paused again to scrutinize Lacey's expression, then continued. "So, my advice is to do just that. You know this woman better than I. Use the gifts the Lord gave you, and use them well. I can see you have many. You're honest and concerned about someone who needs your help, yet with all your good intentions and determination, you are also conscientious enough to recognize this person's need to retain a sense of dignity, however limited it might be. From my observation, the particular gift you bring to this situation is your realization that God's work is sometimes a very delicate task, that we occasionally need to tread lightly in order to bring Christ into the lives of someone we wish to help. Pete mentioned to me that you spent a good portion of your journey toward Weaver reading the Bible. I would encourage you to use what you've learned there to guide you."

Searching Lacey's gaze a moment longer, Reverend Sykes quoted softly, "'Trust in the Lord with all your heart, and lean not unto your own understanding. In all your ways, acknowledge Him, and He will direct your path.'" He smiled. "I don't think I could give you better advice than that."

Of course. She should have known. The Lord would show her the way, just as He had shown her the need. She need only remain open to the opportunities he presented.

Intensely relieved, Lacey said sincerely, "Thank you so much, Reverend."

A few pleasantries then concluded the visit, and Lacey turned back toward Weaver's main street. She had come for advice and had received the best that could possibly be offered.

Lacey looked up at the position of the sun in the cloudless sky, then hastened her step. But for now, Scully was waiting.

Barret stood at his office window. He had walked away from his desk in exasperation a few minutes earlier. He was tired of the inane paperwork that seemed to comprise the sum total of his work as Weaver's only attorney. He looked out at the main thoroughfare, at the unfashionably dressed citizenry who trod the boardwalk, then at the traffic of bearded horsemen and broken-down wagons on the unpaved street. He remembered the gaiety and color of San Francisco…the excitement around every corner that awaited a man of imagination and means. His imagination had not faltered over the years. It was only the means that had made those wonders unavailable to him.

He had always known how to fix his situation with the law in San Francisco. All he had needed to erase any connection to his father's crimes was a sum sizable enough to convince a chosen few that he'd had no part in his father's illegal activities.

Had not suspicious deaths been included in that list of illegal activities, he knew his situation could have been resolved more easily, but that recourse still was not available to him. An adequate incentive was the only answer to his problem.

An adequate incentive…

It galled him that his life was being wasted because of his inability to accumulate a large enough sum of money to erase the charges against him—and he had little patience for delay.

Barret's thoughts came to an abrupt halt with Lacey's un-expected appearance on the walk a distance away. She was dressed in riding clothes, and if he didn't miss his guess, she was presently hurrying toward the livery stable.

Barret's heart began a slow pounding. In this desolate country, she could have only one destination in mind.

Barret searched the street for a sign of Blackie or Larry. Where were they? He had given them instructions not to let Lacey out of their sights.

Panicking, Barret stepped out onto the boardwalk as Lacey neared. He stood boldly in her path as she approached, search-ing his mind for a way to delay her. If his hirelings didn't show their faces soon…

Barret smiled as Lacey approached. He said, "Riding clothes. Are you intending an extended foray into Weaver's countryside?"

"Yes, I suppose I am." Lacey's smile was tight. "Scully's waiting for me."

"I expect Scully's not a man to tolerate being kept waiting, but I'm sure he'd make an exception for you. He does seem to be concerned about you, although his behavior isn't exactly in your best interest."

Barret saw the flicker of displeasure that crossed Lacey's

face at the casual negativity of his comment. He knew he had made a mistake even before she responded levelly, "I think you're mistaken in that observance, Barret. Scully's behavior *is* in my best interest, because he cares about me. He was responsible for my education and welfare. His concern for me has never lapsed, and he's now intent on helping me reestablish myself in Weaver."

"Of course, Lacey, dear. Scully's devotion to your well-being is obvious. It's just difficult sometimes when good intentions go astray."

"Astray?"

Barret took a conciliatory step toward her. "He means well, I know."

"He not only means well. He's *done* well."

"Yes, but, dear…" Barret made his handsome, patrician features sober. He glanced at the street behind Lacey and noted Larry's appearance in the doorway of the Gold Nugget. He saw Larry's momentary panic when he noticed Lacey on the street wearing riding attire.

Larry and Blackie stepped out onto the walk and began approaching as Barret continued casually, "Well, I don't expect we should be discussing these matters on the street when you're obviously pressed for time, Lacey. But I would like an opportunity to discuss your situation in Weaver with you in the near future. I knew your grandfather only casually, but I know he'd want the best for you."

"You're right. My grandfather wanted the best for me. That's why he sent me to Scully."

"But that was then, Lacey. This is now. Circumstances have changed since you've matured. Association with Scully could prove detrimental to your future."

"No."

Uncertain of the meaning of Lacey's response, Barret said, "What was that, dear?"

"I said, no. Association with Scully could never prove detrimental to me." Lacey paused, her gaze direct. "I hope I've made that point plainly enough."

"Of course you have, but inexperience sometimes guides one falsely." Barret offered his most concerned smile. "You're a lovely young woman. I wouldn't want you to find yourself in embarrassing circumstances because of a situation that's not of your making."

"I'm sorry. I'm in a rush."

"Now you're angry with me."

"Yes."

Marveling at her boldness, Barret said earnestly, "Now it's my turn to be sorry. It wasn't my intention to offend you. I hope you'll accept my apology."

"Perhaps I will when my anger fades, but right now it's impossible for me to accept your apology since I consider your observations ignorant and untrue, and your intentions questionable."

"My intentions questionable?"

"You obviously don't like Scully."

"I admit to that."

"Well, he doesn't like you, either. That said, I bid you good day."

"Lacey, please…" Forcing himself to stay her with a touch on her arm and a conciliatory expression, Barret offered, "Please accept my apology. It is sincerely meant."

"I'll consider it." Lacey shook off his touch. "Good day."

Barely concealing his silent ire at Lacey's abrupt dismissal, Barret stepped back into his office as she continued on down the street. She would *consider* accepting his apology, would she? Who did she think she was talking to?

Barret took a firm grip on his temper. He had intended his conversation with Lacey to be a casual flirtation that would delay her long enough for his insipid hirelings to appear. She should have been flattered. After all, he was good-looking and still in his prime. There wasn't a young woman in town wouldn't have been flattered to have a man of his stature show an interest in her. He had actually even briefly indulged the thought of a casual liaison with her.

That was a mistake.

Barret reviewed their conversation again in his mind. In retrospect, a simple, pernicious phrase had turned Lacey against him.

Although Scully's behavior isn't exactly in your best interest.

With those words, their conversation had taken a fast track toward disaster.

Barret waited until Blackie and Larry reached the walk outside his office. His anger erupted when they appeared intent on walking past. He opened the door and snapped, "Get in here!"

Waiting only until the door had closed behind them, he said, "Incompetent…that's what you both are!"

"You don't need to get upset, boss. Blackie and me was right behind her. She wasn't going nowhere without us."

"That isn't what it looked like to me."

"We was watching from the Gold Nugget window."

"You were, huh?"

Blackie chimed in, "You don't have nothing to worry about with me and Larry on the job. We aren't going to let nothing go wrong like it did last time."

"I suppose you know she's off to ride with Jake Scully."

"Sure…" Blackie attempted a smile. "That's what we figured when we saw her riding clothes."

"I don't want you to let them out of your sight…*out of your sight,* do you hear?"

"We hear you, boss. I told you—"

"I don't care what you told me. Mess this up, and you're on your own—both of you."

Barret watched as the frowning duo continued down the street, agitation twitching inside him. He had meant what he said to those two fools. What they didn't know, however, was that if they failed this time…if they lost him his opportunity to return to the life he had been born for, they wouldn't need to apologize—because they would not live to regret it.

Careful trotted briskly behind them as Scully and Lacey rode slowly along the narrow trail. Scully glanced around at the flat, broad valley spotted with cholla, prickly pear and barrel cactus, at the giant saguaros and the palo verde and mesquite trees outlined against rugged mountains in the distance. He was familiar with the trail. It would lead them to one of the occasional running streams where they would water their horses and where small trees would provide a measure of protection against the relentless sun as they spent a few leisurely moments.

Engrossed in her thoughts, however, Lacey seemed to be paying little attention to the passing terrain. She had apologized for keeping him waiting when she arrived at the livery stable for their ride, but the apology had been unnecessary. He knew whatever had been on her mind and had necessitated the delay was important to her, or she would not have kept him waiting. He wondered, however, if that important matter was the cause of her silence and preoccupation since the beginning of their ride.

"What's wrong, Lacey?"

Snapped from her reverie, Lacey turned toward him. Her expression still sober, she replied, "What makes you think something's wrong?"

"You're quiet. If there's one thing I've learned since you came home, silence is not one of your characteristics."

"Scully…are you saying I'm a chatterbox?"

"No, but you normally speak up when something's on your mind."

"Oh. Well, nothing's wrong."

Choosing not to reply, Scully turned his mount toward the distant stream. Careful made his way directly to the water when they dismounted beside it minutes later. The horses and the small burro were ankle deep in the refreshing stream when Scully joined Lacey in the limited shade. She was still frowning.

"You might as well tell me what's wrong, Lacey. You're not doing a very good job of hiding the fact that you're upset."

"I'm not upset."

"Really?"

She looked up at him, still sober. "I suppose I owe you an apology."

"Another one?"

His reply meant humorously, Scully was surprised when Lacey responded seriously, "Yes, another one. I guess I'm not as good a judge of people as I thought I was."

Scully felt a heat unrelated to the temperature rise inside him. He snapped, "If that Todd Fulton can't take no for an answer—"

"Oh, it isn't Todd. He's a nice fellow."

Scully went silent.

"You were right. Barret Gould doesn't like you."

"Barret Gould." Scully paused to rein back an angry response, then said, "What did he say?"

"I talked to him briefly on the way to meet you. I think he intended to give me what he believed was some well-needed advice, but his dislike of you took over somewhere. It shone through bright and clear."

"What did he say?"

Lacey scrutinized Scully's tense expression, then said, "I'm only telling you this because I had said you were mistaken in judging Barret harshly. I don't want you to get angry."

"Too late."

"Scully…"

"Tell me what he said."

"It wasn't really bad. He just said your behavior wasn't exactly in my best interest."

Scully hardly breathed.

"Scully…"

"I'll take care of it."

"No!"

"I said—"

"Scully, please…" Suddenly so close to him that he could feel her sweet breath against his cheek and see the silver specks of agitation in her eyes, Lacey rasped, "Promise me you won't confront Barret. It's important to me. I don't want to stir up any trouble for you."

"You didn't stir anything up. Barret did."

"I'm sure he meant it for my own good."

"I'm not."

Somehow unwilling to concede that point, Lacey responded, "Whether he did or not doesn't matter. I didn't come back to cause you problems."

"You came back because Weaver is your home."

"I want Weaver to be my home, but it's *your* home first, Scully. You've made a life for yourself here. I don't intend for my presence to complicate things for you."

Lacey was so close. Scully took an unsteady breath before responding, "You aren't the one complicating things for me here."

"Yes, I am, and I don't want to. I'd rather go back east and take a position at the school than cause trouble for you."

"Back east..." He shook his head. "Not a chance."

"Then promise me," Lacey begged. "Please."

"Lacey..." Scully stared into Lacey's disturbed expression.

"Please."

Scully slid his arms around her and drew her against his chest. He hugged her tight, a myriad of emotions assaulting him as he said, "All right. I won't confront Barret about what he said this time. I promise, but if there's a next time—"

"You don't have to worry, there won't be a next time." Drawing back from his embrace, Lacey smiled sheepishly. "I got a little angry when he admitted he didn't like you, so I told him that was all right, because you didn't like him, either."

Scully gave a hard laugh.

"He did apologize for what he said, you know, but I told him I couldn't accept his apology because his remarks were ignorant and untrue, and his intentions questionable."

Scully listened intently.

"He asked me to reconsider accepting his apology, and I said maybe I would, but I didn't want to talk about it anymore." Lacey paused, then added, "Truthfully, I may accept Barret's *need* to apologize, but I won't ever accept what he said about you."

Scully stared at Lacey a moment longer, then offered, "Even if it's partially true?"

"It isn't."

"You're so sure of that?"

"Yes."

Scully had no words to reply as he scrutinized Lacey's sincere expression. She believed in him without exception. The thought was sobering.

At the sound of a soft bray, Scully looked up to see Careful approaching them. Lacey laughed as Careful nudged her head with a look that could only be called a half smile, and then grasped a lock of her fair hair with his teeth and pulled.

Scully was about to chastise the brazen burro when Lacey said, "No, don't. Careful pulled my hair in order to get my full attention. He always did that when I was a child." She stroked the animal's muzzle and added with a touch of seriousness in her tone, "See that, Scully? Time and circumstances don't change real friendships. If friendships are true, they're impervious to all assaults."

Scully watched as Lacey stood up unexpectedly. She drew Careful back with her to the stream, took off her boots, then waded into the water and splashed the burro playfully. He realized that what she had said was true. Time and circumstances didn't change true affection.

Or did they?

Succumbing to impulse, Scully pulled off his boots and walked toward the stream.

* * *

"They didn't do nothin', boss."

Blackie stood opposite Barret in the cool confines of his office, but the unkempt boor hadn't yet stopped sweating. Barret attempted to ignore Blackie's offensive odor as he replied, "What do you mean? They certainly didn't ride out just to pass some time. It's hot out there, in the event you didn't realize it."

"Me and Larry realized it, all right." Blackie pulled off his hat and ran his hand through hair stuck slickly to his scalp with perspiration, then wiped his arm across his forehead before continuing. "Larry and me was stuck out there in the sun, watching, while them two took off their boots and walked around in the stream to cool off."

"You're telling me—" Barret took a firmer grip on his agitation "—that Jake Scully rode out into the afternoon heat just to splash around in a stream?"

"It sure looked that way."

"Well, maybe you weren't looking hard enough!"

"Look, boss…" His bearded face growing unexpectedly menacing, Blackie snapped, "Me and Larry spent a long afternoon trying to cool off in the shade of a few, miserable bushes while them two was kicking up some fun in the stream. We was looking hard enough, all right, and it wasn't easy."

Barret gauged Blackie's reaction critically. The man was irritated because he had been sent out on a wild-goose chase in the heat of the day, but that was too bad. He snapped back, "Where's Larry?"

"He went straight to the Gold Nugget to get a drink."

"And he left you to carry the 'good news' to me."

"Like you said, it was hot out there."

Barret nodded. He pressed, "They didn't travel in the direction of Charlie Pratt's burned-out cabin?"

"I told you, they didn't go nowheres near it."

Barret paused to consider the situation. Lacey Stewart had waited ten years and it appeared she was content to wait a few more weeks until she was again familiar enough with the territory to be able to locate her grandfather's strike without Scully. That could be the only explanation, because if she intended sharing the claim with Scully, they would have headed directly for it that afternoon.

So he need wait a little longer.

Barret felt a hot flush suffuse his skin. But *he* had waited ten years, too, and he wasn't as patient as Lacey Stewart obviously was. It occurred to him that the way the situation presently stood, Lacey would find it difficult to ride off alone when she was ready to search, without Scully trailing behind her. He'd need to figure out a way to separate the two of them. He hadn't been successful in ingratiating himself with Lacey earlier that day, but he was no longer concerned about that failure.

An uncouth, barbaric adage commonly used by Weaver residents sprang into Barret's mind. He despised it, but the truth of the saying was so appropriate.

Yes, *there was more than one way to skin a cat.*

Chapter Six

Lacey took a deep breath as she walked down the hallway toward her boarding house room. The afternoon spent with Scully in the wild Arizona terrain had been exceedingly pleasant, even though the day had started out poorly in so many ways.

Lacey's mind returned to the scene between Rosie and her beau earlier that morning. The image of Rosie sobbing as a result of Riley's blow shook Lacey even in retrospect. She had not quite recovered from witnessing that devastating encounter or her revealing conversation with Jewel when she was stopped by Barret Gould. Lacey recalled the unpleasantries of the exchange that had followed. Barret's audacity in criticizing Scully so boldly had been infuriating. She wondered how he could believe for a moment that she would prefer his advice to Scully's about any portion of her life.

She supposed she shouldn't have told Scully about that conversation, but she had needed to let him know he was correct in his assessment of the haughty lawyer, and that she had been wrong.

But the remainder of the afternoon, while they had stopped at the stream to cool off themselves and their mounts, had been one of the most pleasant times she could recall in recent years. Sitting so close to Scully and speaking to him so honestly from the heart, she had been even more conscious of the special intimacy they shared. Careful's affectionate bid for attention had interrupted their dialogue, but the display had warmed her heart and returned her briefly to a carefree period of her life that she cherished in memory.

She recalled her astonishment when Scully waded into the stream behind her, his feet as bare as hers. She remembered how they had both stomped around in the cool water. She recalled the moment when Scully laughed out loud in spontaneous enjoyment. Her heart had jumped a beat at the sheer beauty of the sound.

She truly was fond of Scully. There was no one whose affection was presently more dear to her. She whispered another brief prayer of gratitude, knowing she could never give enough thanks to the Lord for His having placed Scully in her life—although she wondered why she deserved such a precious gift.

Lacey closed the door behind her. Their visit to the stream had been invigorating, a relief from the intense heat of the day. Their damp clothing had cooled them for the greater portion of their ride home, but once their clothes had dried, the heat had become oppressive. She was presently looking forward to sponging herself with cool water from her washstand and refreshing herself with the delicate fragrance of the lilac-scented soap she favored.

Lacey looked at the clock on the mantle. She had a few hours until Scully and she would go to the restaurant for their evening meal. It occurred to her that Mary was right. She had yet to take advantage of the food the dear woman provided her guests—meals reputed to be consistently excellent. She knew, however, that even if she were given the choice, she would prefer Scully's company to a meal fit for royalty.

Lacey turned to the washstand. She was unbuttoning her shirtwaist when she looked at the soap dish and stopped cold. She had used up the last of her soap that morning.

Impatient with herself for having forgotten to stop at the mercantile to buy another bar, Lacey checked her small purse for change. Satisfied, she started for the door.

Lacey walked briskly toward the store. Her path lay past Barret Gould's office, but the possibility of a second encounter with him that day was more than she could presently face. Deciding to avoid it if she could, Lacey crossed the street and walked quickly along the crowded walk, hoping no one would notice her circuitous route when she crossed back again to the other side.

Lacey moved quickly between the last straggling shoppers of the day and the influx of wranglers just beginning to arrive for the weekend's entertainment. She approached a small boutique where it was rumored that many of the Gold Nugget women did their shopping. According to the whispers of two matrons standing behind her while she had waited for her order to be filled at the mercantile a few days earlier, the clothing at the boutique was fashionable, direct from Paris and well beyond the reach of the "decent" women in town.

He who guards his lips, guards his soul.

She had wondered if those two "decent" women were familiar with that passage. Less important than that, she had then wondered if the clothing in the store was really direct from Paris.

That thought lingered as Lacey spotted a familiar figure standing in front of the boutique. She recognized the distinctive shopping basket Rosie carried. Rosie's surprising talent for weaving was well-known at the Gold Nugget, and her baskets were easy to pick out.

Lacey's step slowed as she approached the thin dancehall girl and said, "I thought it was you standing here, Rosie."

Rosie turned toward her, then glanced away—but not before Lacey saw the fresh bruise at the corner of her eye.

Rosie replied, "Marcella told me that Madame Lilly had reduced her prices on some dresses because she expects new stock to arrive on the stage at the end of the week." Referring to the voluptuous brunette rumored to be so popular in the Gold Nugget, Rosie continued, "Marcella bought herself a beautiful dress. I thought I might be able to find something. My old gold satin got ripped somehow."

Lacey paused in her response. She knew how Rosie's dress had gotten ripped, all right.

Lacey said simply, "Maybe I can help you fix it. I've done a pretty good job of repairing my own dresses from time to time."

"No…I don't think so. It's ripped beyond repair."

Her heart aching for Rosie, Lacey looked at the sign in the window and said, "It seems there are a few more dresses left at reduced prices."

Rosie turned back hopefully toward her. "How do you know that?"

"It says so right there on the sign." Lacey read, "'Only six dresses remaining at greatly reduced prices.'"

"I won't get paid for another few days. Does it say how much longer Madame will keep the prices reduced?"

Lacey looked back at the sign. The sign was clearly written

in bold letters. Momentarily confused by the question, Lacey responded, "No, that's all it says."

Realization then struck her, and Lacey asked, "Don't you know how to read, Rosie?"

Rosie stiffened and took a backward step.

"Rosie?"

Rosie's lips wobbled. "No."

"Oh."

"My Ma and Pa died in an accident when I was six. My uncle didn't have any choice but to take me in." She shrugged. "That's what he said, anyway. He raised me until I was ten. I guess he figured a girl like me wouldn't have no use for book learning."

"A girl like you?"

Rosie ignored the question. "He ran off when I was ten."

"He left you alone?"

"He said I always had too much to say."

Lacey took a breath, then forced a smile. "Well, I suppose I wouldn't know how to read, either, if it wasn't for my grandpa. He took me in when my mother died, too, you know."

"I know."

Lacey's brows rose with surprise.

"Everybody at the Nugget knows that story. Your grandpa was killed, and before he died, he told you to go to town and ask for Scully, so Scully could take care of you. Then Scully sent you back east to school, so you could learn to be a lady."

A lady.

Rosie had used that word with profound admiration, and Lacey felt her own eyes moisten. She heard herself say, "Yes, Scully did all that for me, but I could already read by the time I met him. My grandpa taught me easily enough. I could teach you, too."

"No, it's too late for me."

"Oh, pooh! I never heard such nonsense!" Realizing she had startled Rosie with the sudden vehemence of her response, Lacey continued more softly, "I'd really enjoy teaching you to read, Rosie. It would be fun."

"Everybody would laugh at me. Besides, Scully wouldn't like it if you spent too much time with me."

"He wouldn't care."

"Yes, he would."

Rosie was adamant. Aware that she was losing the battle, Lacey said, "Then we don't have to tell anybody I'm teaching you to read."

"That won't work."

"Yes, it will."

A glimmer of hope shone in Rosie's eyes as she said, "You really think I could learn…it's not too late for me?"

"Of course it's not too late."

Rosie hesitated a moment longer, then said, "I could try— but only if I can pay you for teaching me."

"Pay me? Why?"

"Men get paid for the work they do. Women should, too."

The light of principle shone in Rosie's eyes—and a fragile fragment of a pride that was almost nil. Lacey could not infringe upon what little Rosie had left.

Lacey replied, "All right, I'll teach you to read if you'll—" Lacey continued smoothly after a moment's hesitation "—if you'll make me a basket just like yours. It's beautiful."

"That's not a fair exchange."

"We'll both be getting something we want. What's fairer than that?"

Rosie hesitated.

"Well, is it a deal?"

Rosie hesitated a moment longer, then nodded.

Elated, Lacey said, "We'll start tomorrow! You can come to my room at the boarding house when I'm done with work in the restaurant and we'll—"

"I couldn't do that. Mrs. McInnes wouldn't like it."

Lacey did not bother to argue the point. After a moment's thought, she said, "In that case, I know the perfect place."

Lacey walked out onto the boardwalk and waited as Scully closed the restaurant door behind them. She smiled up at him, then took his arm as they began walking. Yes, the day that had started out so badly had made a complete turnaround. She'd had a lovely afternoon with Scully and had taken the first step toward helping someone desperately in need. She had simply turned her perplexity over into His hands, and the Lord had provided the way to help Rosie. All she had needed to do was listen to His response.

Her heart rejoiced.

Lacey's smile briefly faded at the thought that night was approaching, and with it the possibility of the nightmares, which had increased in frequency. As pleased as she was that the situation with Rosie appeared to be headed in the right direction, she was forced to admit she had been unsuccessful in combating the shifting shadows of the terrors she faced in her dreams. Lacey glanced at Scully. Her inclination at that moment was to confide in Scully, to tell him about the nighttime anxieties she could not seem to overcome, but she was determined not to take a step backward in her independence, nor to allow fear to intrude even briefly into the beauty of the day they had shared.

Forcing those thoughts aside, Lacey watched as Scully observed the street with a practiced eye. Her gaze lingered. His skin had darkened to a golden hue while they had frolicked in the water. His eyes, always his most outstanding feature, appeared a lighter, softer gray in comparison, and his smile more brilliant.

She said candidly, "You're a very handsome man, do you know that, Scully?"

Scully looked back at her with a suddenly wary expression.

"Well, you are. I can't possibly be the first woman to tell you that."

Scully's gaze narrowed. "No, you're not…but, in my experience, that compliment is usually followed by a request for something extravagant."

"Scully…" Lacey replied sincerely without hesitation, "What could I possibly want from you that you haven't already given me?"

His expression unreadable, Scully did not respond, and Lacey continued with a hint of a smile, "I have something to confess, though. I didn't really remember what you looked like when I came home that first day. I saw that tall, grayhaired rancher who was in town when I stepped off the stage, and I thought he was you."

"Tall, gray-haired…" Scully frowned. "You mean Tom Belcher?" At Lacey's nod, he said, "He's more than fifty years old."

"I figured you had to be at least that old since you were already an adult when I first met you. I figured you'd be needing somebody to take care of you in your old age. I wanted to be that person."

"You wanted to spend your life taking care of an old man?"

"Not *any* old man. Just Jake Scully. But the joke was on me. You're young and handsome…and you're still taking care of me." Lacey sobered. "You're not only handsome, Jake Scully, but you're a good man."

Scully did not smile as he said, "Did you ever stop to think that I might not be the Good Samaritan you think I am?"

"Scully…you've read the Bible!"

"Does that surprise you? Do you really think I could've lived with your grandfather for a year without learning something?"

Lacey asked with a sober bluntness, "Is that why you left Grandpa? I know he didn't ask you to leave."

"No, that's not the reason." Scully's voice dropped a note softer. "I left because your grandpa set a criteria I needed to emulate. He was a man who had set his own goals and established his own way of life with standards he refused to compromise. As far as I was concerned, whether he ever struck it rich or not didn't really matter. I admired him. Although my own ambitions or standards weren't as clearly defined, I knew it was time for me to make my own way, too. Your grandpa understood that."

"My grandfather and grandmother were cut from the same cloth. I don't know if you knew that. Grandpa told me my grandmother could've stayed in a nice, comfortable home back in Illinois when he went west, but she chose to go with him. He said she accepted every day they had together as a blessing, no matter how difficult their circumstances, and he'd never forget that. It broke my grandpa's heart when she died in an epidemic. He raised my mother by himself, and when my mother died in an epidemic, just like my grandmother, he raised me, too."

"Your grandfather was a good man."

"You are, too."

"I'm not your grandfather, Lacey. Don't ever mistake me for him."

"I won't. I couldn't."

Appearing uncomfortable with their conversation, Scully turned his attention back to a cautious scrutiny of the street. He had behaved in the same way when the previous weekend was approaching. She supposed it was a reflex that had become instinctive over the years in a territory where civilization sometimes seemed to lapse when celebration took over, but she didn't yet feel the same way.

Twilight was a special time in Weaver. In that brief period before the darkness of night, Weaver came alive with lamplight, imparting a fairy tale quality to the primitive scene. The greatest transformation performed was on the Gold Nugget Saloon. The building glowed, boasting bright lights and gaiety that came to full blossom only after the sun had set. She knew the sometimes cruel light of dawn would dispel that metamorphosis, but she never failed to enjoy the deceiving sight.

Lacey's smile dimmed as Scully's step slowed. His gaze had halted on a couple locked in a passionate embrace in a dark alleyway beside the Gold Nugget. Scully drew Lacey determinedly forward.

Out of view of the embarrassing scene, Scully turned to her and said, "I'm sorry to have exposed you to this kind of thing, Lacey. As far as Lucy and the rest of the women who work in the Gold Nugget are concerned, the Gold Nugget is a dancehall. That's all I expect of them when they entertain my customers. I can't control what the girls do on their own time, but I don't stand for that type of behavior while they're working. I'll tell Lucy she's no longer employed at the Gold Nugget tomorrow."

Lacey turned to glance back at Lucy as the smiling dance-hall girl freed herself from the cowboy's embrace and they walked arm and arm back into the saloon. She said instinctively, "Don't do that, Scully."

He turned darkly toward her.

"I know Lucy's not behaving properly, and I really don't know her, but I do know if she leaves the Gold Nugget, she'll probably end up someplace where more might be expected of her than it is here. Warn her, first. At least here she has a chance to discover the error of her ways."

"I don't have time for warnings. She knew the rules when she took the job."

"If you warn her and tell her what'll happen if there's a next time, she'll understand you meant what you said."

"I don't operate that way at the Gold Nugget."

"Please."

Still frowning, Scully said, "Why do you care what happens to Lucy?"

Lacey replied, "Why should I not?"

Silent a moment longer, Scully replied, "I guess that's as good an answer as any. All right. I'll give Lucy fair warning tonight. The rest is up to her."

"Thank you, Scully." Greatly relieved, Lacey tucked her arm more tightly under his.

Scully regarded her intently. He said, "You look tired."

"Thanks. I was feeling pretty good until now." Lacey gave him a wry smile, then admitted, "But you're right. I am tired."

"I'll walk back with you to the boarding house."

Aware that Scully's night had only begun, Lacey withdrew

her arm from his and said, "You don't have to do that. I don't have far to walk, and you have a business to take care of. I'll go back by myself."

"I'm not leaving you alone on the street at this time of night."

"It's barely dark." Lacey glanced around them. "There are any number of women still on the street."

Scully motioned toward four cowboys riding briskly toward them and said, "I don't have to look around to know those fellas wouldn't look twice at any of those other women—but they would at you."

"Scully…" Lacey could not help but laugh. "I'm a big girl now."

"That's the problem."

Suddenly realizing he was deadly serious, Lacey said, "I surrender."

"It's not a case of winning or losing, Lacey. It's a matter of being safe."

And of not becoming a burden to a man overly concerned for her welfare.

Yes, she understood far better than Scully realized.

That thought in mind, Lacey responded, "All right, let's go back now. I have a feeling Mary may be waiting for me. She treats her boarders like her children, you know."

"Lacey…"

"I really am tired, Scully."

They had reached the boarding house door when Mary called from inside, "Is that you, Lacey?" In the doorway within seconds, the dear woman said, "I'm glad you brought Lacey home early, Scully. I managed to save her some of my special apple pie, but it won't last much longer if any of my other boarders see it."

Lacey walked up the boarding house steps as Mary chattered on. She looked back as Scully tipped his hat and walked back down the street.

Barret stood at his office window, watching the growing activity on the street. Friday night, and the influx of weekend revelers had just begun. Within the hour, all respectable residents would be in the safe refuge of their homes and the streets would be abandoned to pleasure seekers. Hayseeds…hicks…ignoramuses. The town was full of them, and not a single one of them had any idea of the level of enjoyment one could reach in more civilized environs. Yet he had no desire to go home yet. As deficient as his office was in the refinements to which he was accustomed, his home was worse. It was by far the largest house in Weaver's small residential area on the next street, but it was still a miserly abode when compared to the mansion that had been his family's San Francisco home.

His life in Weaver was a bore. The only thing that made it bearable was a dream now held in abeyance in the dainty hands of Lacey Stewart. He needed to shake her up somehow…force her to make a move—which would be difficult indeed with Scully dogging her every step.

Barret's eyes glazed over as he stared out onto the street. He needed to think…and plan.

Lacey looked up from the page she had been reading as a thought struck her in the silence of her room.

Strangely enough, she'd had no desire to sleep after Scully dropped her off at the boarding house door and she was safely secured in her room. Sitting alone in the advent of night, her

mind again deluged with uncertainties, she had reached for
her grandfather's Bible, which had given her so much comfort
through the years. She was uncertain how long she'd been
reading when it came to her in a flash that if Rosie could not
read, she could not write—and if she could not write, she
could not read. There was no way of separating the two. The
lessons needed to be taught concurrently. She had everything
she would need in order to teach Rosie to read. It was all con-
tained in the one book she held in her hand. Writing, however,
was another matter.

Paper and pencil—Rosie needed that much, at least, so she
could practice in private between lessons. Without those
simple supplies, Rosie would be at a disadvantage that might
even discourage her enough to make her abandon the effort.

Lacey shook her head. She couldn't let that happen to a
young woman with such low self-esteem that she believed no
one, including God, truly loved her.

Lacey looked out her window at the darkening shadows of
the street below. There was no way she'd be able to purchase
the necessary supplies in the morning or after she finished up
work in the restaurant, without Scully's notice. She would have
to get them now, before the mercantile closed for the night.

She didn't have much time.

The brisk business of the saloon constant behind him,
Scully nodded to familiar faces in passing as he pushed his
way out through the Nugget's swinging doors onto the boardwalk. He walked a few steps into the shadows of the overhang,
then leaned back against the false front of the building,
frowning as the boisterous music and heavy smoke from the
saloon filtered out onto the street.

What in Sam Hill was wrong with him? Admittedly, his lifestyle had been beginning to pale of late. He had supposed he was getting older. He had thought it might be time to broaden his horizons. He had even considered moving on, but, somehow, none of those solutions had seemed the answer.

Then Lacey returned to Weaver, and his scrutiny of Weaver and the lifestyle he had adopted became sharper...clearer. It was almost as if Lacey's confidence in his "goodness" made him even more aware of his deficiencies; as if her innocent trust made him aware of the tawdry side of things he had previously accepted; as if her faith in the Lord and her devotion to His teachings made him conscious of the many ways in which he fell short.

Yet he felt none of the resentment he would have considered an ordinary reaction to his new consciousness. And the reason was simple. Lacey had brought him to those conclusions with only honest praise for him.

Rose-colored glasses.

She was too innocent, and too beautiful. She didn't realize how a man could be intrigued by that combination, or what he could be thinking each time she smiled at him so guilelessly. He wished he could make her realize those things, but he didn't want to if it would change her. He liked her the way she was, honest—outspoken, earnest...feisty, anxious to fight the good fight. He'd never met a woman like her.

"Well, stranger."

Scully turned toward the sound of the familiar female voice. The dazzling color of Charlotte's red hair was distinctive even in the limited light, as was her teasing smile as she continued, "I haven't seen much of you lately. I reminded you of that once before. I also reminded you that you knew where to find me, but it looks like it's time for me to stir your memory." She walked an intimate step closer as she said, "So, here I am. And don't tell me you've been busy. I won't accept that excuse. I know a man always makes time for things that are important to him." She halted for effect, then said, "Which brings me to a very unflattering conclusion."

Scully could not help but smile. Charlotte…out in the open…never mincing words. He could do no less than return the favor in kind.

"You're right, Charlotte, honey. A man does make time for the things that're his top priorities."

Charlotte sobered. She responded bluntly, "You're making a big mistake, Scully."

Scully was suddenly as serious as she. "Lacey's my responsibility, Charlotte. She's out of her element here. She needs guidance, and I'm the only family she has."

"Are you sure you're the one who should be giving her guidance?"

"Yes."

"Oh…ho!" Charlotte was smiling again. "You didn't even hesitate!"

"And what does that tell you?"

"That tells me you haven't changed as much as I thought you had." Charlotte reached up to stroke Scully's cheek with her smooth hand as she whispered, "And it also tells me, if I just relax and have some fun while I'm waiting, you'll walk right back into my arms."

Charlotte stood up on tiptoe unexpectedly and pressed a fleeting kiss against Scully's lips. Contrary to the reaction she expected, Scully drew back and said, "You haven't changed a bit, either, Charlotte—but I think it's time for us both to get back to business."

Scully slid his arm casually around Charlotte's shoulders and turned her back into the saloon. Charlotte hadn't bothered to be subtle. Even if she had been, he knew all the signals. The truth was, he wasn't interested anymore. He'd been as truthful as he could be with her. Lacey was his responsibility, and that was all that counted.

Lacey stood still in the shadows of the boardwalk. The street teemed with activity around her, but she was somehow unable to move. She had watched the two figures standing intimately close under the Gold Nugget's overhang. The brightly dressed, redheaded woman was Charlotte, who had never been overly friendly to her while she resided at the Gold Nugget. The other person was Scully.

Lacey had caught her breath as Charlotte stood up on tiptoe and pressed her mouth to Scully's. She saw the whispered conversation that followed when he drew back, and she glimpsed the smile on Scully's face before he slipped his arm around Charlotte's shoulders and they walked back into the saloon.

Lacey took a shaken breath. Although the kiss had been fleeting, Scully and Charlotte were obviously more than friendly.

Hard questions tormented Lacey. Had she imposed herself upon Scully's life to the extent that he had no time for the woman he loved?

Had she been so self-absorbed and determined to regain her past since returning to Weaver that she hadn't given a thought to Scully's hopes for his future?

Uncommon distress shuddered through Lacey when the answer to those questions became painfully clear.

Lacey swallowed past the lump in her throat, then forced herself on toward the mercantile. She needed to change all that now. She needed to allow Scully time for his own life by immediately taking full charge of her own. It wasn't only fair, it was the right thing to do. And if that necessity had somehow formed an aching knot inside her, she need remember to be thankful for the blessings God had given her and not lament the loss of something she had never owned.

As for Scully, she would have to depend on the Lord to guide him.

In the meantime, the mission that had brought her out onto the street at that late hour had not changed.

Her smile fixed, Lacey walked into the well-lit mercantile.

Barret blinked. Still at his office window as he liberally imbibed in the solitude, he struggled to clear his vision, then laughed aloud as Lacey stepped out of the boardwalk shadows and walked to the mercantile store.

Lacey had seen Scully and Charlotte together. He had seen the prim Miss Lacey Stewart's shocked expression when the sultry redhead kissed Scully boldly. He knew it had not missed her notice that Scully and Charlotte had looked quite cozy when they walked back into the brightly lit saloon.

Barret snickered with true enjoyment. It appeared he had judged Lacey harshly. He now believed she had been sincere in her enjoyment of Scully's attentions. She might even have been considering taking him with her when she went to locate her grandfather's strike.

However, if Lacey had entertained that intention even for a moment, she had obviously abandoned it now. And since she now knew her hero's true worth, he might even have been provided with a way back into her good graces. All he needed was a careful word here, and an inference there. That was his forte, after all.

Yet a simple point nagged at him. Scully was a clever, experienced man. It didn't make sense that he was should be so completely taken in by Lacey's innocent pose.

Could it be…?

Barret went suddenly cold. Did Scully suspect Charlie had made a strike? Was it possible that the old man had hinted at it during their conversation that last day? If so, he probably believed the strike existed because there was no other reason anyone would go after the old man.

Barret followed that trend of thought: *If* Scully believed Charlie had made a strike and *if* he had waited ten years to find out, he probably figured the payoff should be his.

Barret was suddenly deadly sober.

But *if* Scully had come to that conclusion…he would soon discover he was wrong.

Chapter Seven

"Oh, I'm sorry, Scully. I should've told you sooner that I couldn't have lunch with you." Her regret was sincere even if her excuse was deliberately misleading. Lacey continued, "I promised to be at the church after I finish work at eleven. I've been wanting to do something positive since I arrived in Weaver, and this is my chance to do it."

The early morning hum of the restaurant continued on around them as Scully questioned, "Is that smart? Doesn't Reverend Sykes think that's asking too much of you."

"It isn't Reverend Sykes's decision."

"I know your intentions are good, Lacey, but the restaurant is so busy that you go without breakfast most of the time. Now you won't have time for lunch."

"I'll find time to eat. Don't worry."

"But I do worry about it." Seated alone at a corner table, his untouched breakfast in front of him, Scully scrutinized her intently.

Lacey squirmed mentally under his stare.

The semidarkness before dawn…the fire…her grandfather's gasping words. The fear…

It had all returned the previous night, in nightmares so vividly terrifying that they had left her shuddering. She knew she had awakened overly wan because of the sleeplessness that had followed.

As if reading her mind, Scully said, "You're pale this morning, Lacey. Are you all right?"

"I'm fine." She smiled. "I have to go back to my customers."

Scully asked abruptly, "Has somebody been giving you trouble here?"

"No."

"Is the work too heavy for you?"

"No."

Scully did not appear convinced.

Lacey responded sincerely, "I don't want you to worry about me. I wasn't able to attend services regularly while traveling back to Weaver. I sorely miss my connection to the Lord's word, and this is good for me."

"I don't think the Lord would want you working yourself into the ground because of a sense of duty."

"It's not duty. It's pleasure."

Scully considered her reply, then said, "I'll come to get you at the boarding house at suppertime."

Lacey was about to make an excuse, but Scully's scrutiny was so intense that she was certain he'd see right through her if she tried.

Deciding to put that off for another day, Lacey said, "I'll be waiting."

Lacey was about to leave Scully's table when his touch on her arm stayed her. She swallowed as Scully's sober gaze met hers and he said, "You'd tell me if something was wrong, wouldn't you, Lacey?"

"Scully…" Lacey sighed. "Of course, I would."

Of course, I would.

Lacey had said those words so sincerely. So, why didn't he believe her?

Scully watched as Lacey moved back and forth between the restaurant tables, smiling at the customers as she snatched up empty plates from some and returned with filled plates for others. She was becoming more adept at her job with every day that passed, and he needed no one to tell him that Sadie was pleased. Neither did he need anyone to tell him that Sadie's customers—the majority of whom were male—were pleased as well.

Scully picked up his fork, poked at the hotcakes on his plate, then looked back up to watch Lacey's progress across the room. Todd Fulton was there again. The youthful cowboy couldn't take his eyes off her. Hiram Watts, Jerry Livingston and Mitch Carter had obviously also taken to coming in as often as their schedules allowed.

Could one of them be the reason Lacey was effectively distancing herself from him?

No, she wanted to make time to work at the church.

He understood.

Yes…he did.

"I'll never be able to do it." Rosie shook her head. Tears brimming, she glanced up from the slate on the table in front of her. "It's too confusing."

"No, it isn't."

Lacey slid her hand over Rosie's. Rosie's hand was trembling, and Lacey's heart ached. They were seated in the small anteroom that Reverend Sykes had made available when she had confided in him about Rosie's lessons the previous day. She had known he wouldn't refuse her space to conduct Rosie's lessons, and she had been equally sure he would respect her confidence. True to their agreement, he had allowed them complete privacy, and Rosie had appeared pleased. A half hour into the first lesson, however, the situation had taken a drastic change in course.

"I told you, it's too late for me." Rosie wiped away a tear with an angry hand. "What do I need to learn to read and write for, anyway? I've done all right so far without it."

"You're a good person, Rosie. I can't imagine how difficult it was for you just managing to survive, being out on your own as young as you were."

Rosie did not reply.

"But you can do even better, and doing better starts with feeling better about yourself."

"Marjorie knows how to read and write, and she's working at the Gold Nugget."

"That's Marjorie's choice. You didn't have a chance to make a choice."

"Nothing will probably change, even if I do learn to read. I'm a Gold Nugget girl, and everybody in Weaver knows it. I'll probably always be a Gold Nugget girl, either here or somewhere else."

"That could be true, of course, but even if it was, that doesn't mean you wouldn't profit from reading—even if it's only in the way you feel about yourself." When Rosie did not respond, Lacey picked up her Bible. She opened it to a familiar page and smiled. "Do you see these small drawings in the margin, Rosie? My Grandpa drew them to illustrate some of the stories when he was teaching me to read. Some of the drawings are faded and almost illegible, and I don't remember when he drew some of the others, but they all represent his love to me—a love that was an extension of God's love. Being able to read these words is a treasure beyond value that my Grandpa shared with me. One of the reasons I came back to Weaver was because I wanted to remember even more—about things that the night my grandfather was killed somehow made me forget. I expect I'll be able to clear up those memories when I finally get the courage to ride out and face the ruins of the cabin my grandfather and I shared. But since returning to Weaver and learning how others in situations similar to mine have suffered difficult lives, I've begun wondering how I could show my appreciation for being blessed with Scully's care over the years. I've found the answer, Rosie. I can show my appreciation by sharing my blessings, just like Grandpa and Scully shared theirs with me."

Her voice suddenly husky with emotion, Lacey whispered, "I know learning to read and write will be hard at the beginning, but it'll get easier. I know you can do it."

"It's too late, I'm telling you." Rosie's pale eyes were red-rimmed. "I don't know much, but I know I've done a lot of things that go against what's in the Bible. Just like my uncle said, everybody gave up on me—including God."

"Look…right here, Rosie." Lacey pointed again to the drawings on the Bible's page. "Do you see these two birds my Grandpa drew in the margin? He drew them when he read this to me.

"'Are not two sparrows sold for a farthing? And one of

them shall not fall on the ground without your Father. But the very hairs of your head are all numbered. Fear ye not, therefore, ye are of more value than many sparrows.'"

Rosie remained silent as Lacey whispered, "You see? You'll always have value to the Lord. It'll never be too late for you to Him."

Rosie took a breath. "Is that what it says…truly?"

Lacey nodded. "I'll read more to you from the scriptures—every day if you want me to. But when we're done with these lessons, you'll be able to read it all for yourself."

Rosie swallowed.

"It all starts with the alphabet you're scratching on that slate, and ends up with reading a book."

Rosie's lips wobbled as she said, "If you won't give up, I won't, either."

"It's a deal." Lacey cleared the thickness from her throat, then took the chalk from Rosie's hand. "D…for dog, that's how you write it." And as Rosie struggled to form the letter, "That's good, Rosie…really good!"

"She's at church, boss. The way she went sneaking off, I figured she'd finally be leading us somewhere important, but that's where she went, all right."

Barret stared at Blackie and considered his statement. Lacey had sneaked off to church.

Sneaked.

Confused and frustrated, Barret returned, "She must've seen you following her."

"No, she didn't boss."

"Why else would she waste her time going to church in the middle of the afternoon?"

"Maybe it has something to do with that Rosie from the Gold Nugget. She went into the church a few minutes after Lacey got there."

"Rosie…" Barret shook his head. If Lacey was enlisting that girl's help for some reason, she was making a big mistake. Rosie couldn't even help herself get out from underneath her abusive boyfriend's thumb. Barret said abruptly, "That doesn't make sense."

"Well, she's been in that church with Rosie for the past hour."

"Where is she now?"

"Still there, I suppose."

"You *suppose?*"

"Don't worry, boss. Larry's watching her. She ain't going nowhere without one of us trailing behind."

"Where's Jake Scully?"

"He's at the Gold Nugget, I guess. He saw Lacey at break-fast. The two of them looked real cozy, too."

Cozy? He had seen Lacey's expression when she saw Scully and Charlotte together the previous evening. That didn't sound right, either.

"She's up to something. Keep your eye on her," Barret ordered. "She's not going to get away with anything. I've waited too long."

His agitation increasing, Barret followed Blackie's progress as his hireling exited his office and started back up toward the church. Blackie was useless when it came to the subtleties of situations, but both Larry and he had learned the value of maintaining his confidence. They were the best he could do right now.

Barret took a breath, then made a decision. He presently had only one recourse.

* * *

"I thought I saw you approaching, dear."

Lacey looked up to see Barret standing in her path as she walked back down the boardwalk from the church.

Lacey attempted to stifle the surge of annoyance his appearance elicited. She had just begun feeling things might take a turn for the better. The midafternoon sun was shining and the heat of the day was bearable. She had stopped off to see Careful on the way back, and the burro's enthusiastic, braying welcome, as well as his sympathetic silence when she shared her troubles with him as she had done as a child, had soothed her sagging spirits. Most comforting of all, however, her first session with Rosie had gone exceedingly well after its rough start.

Lacey recalled Rosie's flush at the end of the lesson when she presented Rosie with a pencil and paper tablet with which to practice her newly learned skills. It had occurred to her when she saw Rosie's reaction that it was probably the first time in her life that someone had even thought to place paper and pencil in Rosie's hand. The thought had momentarily thickened Lacey's throat, but she had forced aside her emotion, determined that this instance would not be Rosie's last.

She had read a chapter of Bible text to Rosie at her request when their lesson was completed. The realization that Rosie had never heard the first chapter of Genesis or any other Bible verse before that day had stunned her. The words had become even more precious to her knowing that Rosie was hearing them for the first time, and she had been hard-pressed to keep the tears from falling. She had been inspired by Rosie's eagerness to listen and learn, and the resulting glow within had warmed her soul.

Then she had spotted Barret Gould standing in her path.

Irritated by the fact that she had not had the presence of mind to walk on the other side of the street to avoid such an encounter, Lacey did not respond to Barret's greeting.

His smile paling as Lacey remained silent, Barret continued, "I've been thinking about my unfortunate comments during our previous conversation, Lacey. I meant well but spoke in a way that was detrimental to any friendship we might form. It occurred to me in retrospect that I accused Scully of similar behavior—meaning well, but not acting in your best interest. I realize that now, and I want to apologize. I hope you will accept my apology, because it is sincerely meant."

"I accept your need to apologize...." Her eyes never moving from Barret's remorseful expression, Lacey heard herself say, "But I strongly resent what you said about Scully. You aren't his friend, so neither can you be mine."

"I hope you're wrong there, Lacey." A revealing anger flitted across Barret's expression before he continued in an almost fatherly manner, "I'm older than you, and I'm far more experienced in dealing with life's dilemmas. I saw in you an inclination to glorify Scully because of the admirable care he provided for you, and I hoped to spare you the disappointment I saw in your future."

"You needn't worry. Scully makes no pretense about himself, so he will never disappoint me."

"Dear...I was hoping to spare you disappointment of a more intimate nature."

Lacey felt the flush that transfused her skin as she responded, "Meaning?"

"Meaning, I...we..." Barret paused briefly, as if seeking the right words. He continued, "You're a beautiful young woman. You'll make a good man an excellent wife someday, and the man who wins your hand will be fortunate, indeed. I'm sure Scully feels the same way. He'd like to see you safely married with children to care for but—"

Losing patience, Lacey interrupted, "Mary is expecting me and she worries if I'm late."

"But," Barret continued with an indulgent smile, "Scully's preference for redheaded women is well-known in Weaver. It will always be his first priority, whether you realize that now or not. And that, my dear, was the main reason for my ill-advised comments that first day."

Incensed, Lacey barely maintained her calm as she replied, "Scully's social preferences, if indeed he has any, are not my concern. Neither, Mr. Gould, are they yours."

"I hoped to spare you some grief, dear."

"I'm not your 'dear.'"

"Nor did I wish to make you angry with me again."

"You've failed in that respect, too. In fact, you've made me angrier than anyone else in Weaver has since my arrival."

"That was not my intention. I'm sorry."

"You should be."

"My intentions were good, but I see they've been miscon-strued."

"No, I don't think so."

Barret did not immediately respond.

Rigid with anger, Lacey said, "I don't accept your claim that your intentions were good. Neither do I believe I've mis-construed them. You stopped me today to apologize for your previous comments about Scully, then proceeded to restate them in more positive terms. Let me save you the trouble of apologizing again by telling you you'll be wasting your time. So, if you'll excuse me—"

"Lacey—"

Lacey looked down at Barret's hand on her arm as he again attempted to stay her. She objected from between tightly clenched teeth, "Take your hand off me."

"Lacey, I—"

"And don't ever bother me with your insincere apologies again."

Waiting only until Barret's hand had dropped back to his side, Lacey walked off, head high.

She was still walking resolutely, refusing to look back, when Barret's words returned to tighten the knot that had formed deep inside her the previous night.

Scully's preference for redheaded women is well-known in Weaver.

Lacey reached up toward her platinum locks with tears suddenly brimming.

Barret walked back into his office, then turned to the window to watch as Lacey continued down the street. He mumbled an epithet, abandoning any further attempt to gain Lacey's confidence. She did not respond to his guile like the average woman—but the reason was simple. She was *not* the average woman. Her facade was carefully calculated. Her defense of Scully was somehow useful to her at the moment and it would not change.

There was one area, however, where he knew his barbs had lodged deeply. His remark about Scully's preference for redheads had struck home because Lacey had seen the evidence of it with her own eyes.

Lacey slipped out of sight, and Barret turned back to his desk with a single thought consoling him. He need not worry that

Lacey would consider confiding the location of her grandfather's mine to Scully now—not with Charlotte on the scene.

Barret smiled to himself with his certainty that Lacey would turn against Scully sooner or later. That was a reality he could count on.

Because that was the way women were.

Rosie was breathless with excitement when she reached her boarding house door. A small smile on her lips and a paper tablet and pencil in hand, she walked up the staircase toward her room on the second floor. She had worked so hard during her first lesson, but she honestly believed Lacey had worked even harder. She had seen the concern in Lacey's eyes when she had been briefly overwhelmed, and she had felt Lacey's driving desire to help her learn. She was no longer puzzled why a lady like Lacey would care about someone like her, because she now knew the answer. She'd have the answer to all her other questions, too, when she was able to read the Bible for herself.

Rosie reached the top of the stairs and turned toward her door, then glanced down at the tablet she carried. Lacey had printed her name on the first page.

Rosie Burns.

She had copied the letters with Lacey's instructions, and she would practice again as soon as she could.

She would be reading soon.

Very soon.

Rosie tucked her tablet under her arm as she pushed open the door to her room. One step inside and she froze. She looked at the half-empty bottle of red-eye on the nightstand beside the bed where Riley was reclining. She was unable to move as Riley sat up and demanded, "Where were you? I've been waiting for you for an hour."

Rosie tossed her precious tablet and pencil casually onto a chair, leaving the door open behind her as she said, "I didn't expect to see you here until tonight."

"I asked you where you were."

"At the boutique. I need a new dress."

"You didn't get one, though, did you?"

"No. I didn't have enough money."

Riley stood up and started slowly toward her. He was slight, wiry, tightly muscled. Rosie remembered a time when the sight of him—his curly blond hair, warm brown eyes and little-boy looks—had started her heart pounding with anticipation.

Now her heart pounded only with fear when he halted close beside her and whispered, "I don't believe you."

"But—"

"I went past the store and looked inside for you, but you weren't there."

"Maybe I was at the mercantile."

"You weren't there, either."

"Or the apothecary. I needed something for…"

"Stop lying! Who were you with?"

Rosie took a shaken breath. Riley looked at the chair where she had dropped the tablet. She took a step toward it as he reached over and picked it up. She held her breath when he opened the tablet to the first page where her name was printed, where her own, primitive attempts at drawing the letters were clearly visible.

"Rosie Burns…your name." He laughed aloud. "Well, either a kid is learning how to scribble, or somebody's trying to teach you to write your name. Which is it?"

"Riley..."

"I asked you..." Riley grasped her arm painfully tight. The smell of liquor was heavy on his breath as he said hotly, "Which is it?"

Tears squeezed out the corners of her eyes as Rosie replied, "I bought the book in the mercantile, and I asked Mrs. Wilson to print my name in it...so I could try to copy it."

"Why?"

"Because."

"You're thinking after you learn to write your name, you'll be too good for me, huh?"

"No, I didn't think any such thing. I just wanted to know how to write my name, is all."

Riley released Rosie so abruptly that she staggered back a few steps. She watched as he picked up the pencil Lacey had so carefully sharpened. He turned toward her and broke it in half, then, laughing at her gasp, tore the sheet containing her name out of the tablet and tossed it onto the floor. He was tearing the other pages out one by one when Rosie charged toward him.

"That's mine! Give it to me!"

Riley raised his hand to strike her when Jewel appeared unexpectedly in the doorway and said, "Leave her alone!"

Rosie looked up to see the derringer in Jewel's hand was pointed directly at Riley.

When Riley turned to advance toward Jewel, Jewel warned, "Don't make that mistake, Riley. I'm not afraid to shoot."

Riley slurred, "You wouldn't do that, would you, Jewel? I thought we was friends."

"We're not friends, and we never will be. You're drunk. Get out of here."

Riley took a step. "I'm not going nowhere."

"You'd better."

"If you're thinking that boyfriend of yours can protect you when that gun's not in your hand, you're wrong."

"I can protect myself."

"You think so, huh?"

Jewel aimed the pistol pointedly. "Either you get out of here now, or I'm going to fix it so neither Rosie or any other woman will ever have to worry about you bothering them again."

Riley went still. "You wouldn't do that."

"Wouldn't I?"

Riley turned back to Rosie and demanded, "Tell her, Rosie, honey. Tell her I didn't mean nothing."

Rosie stood stiffly. She did not respond.

Jewel did not blink. "Get out."

"You'll be sorry about this."

"Yeah, I know. Get out."

"You will, too, Rosie."

Rosie remained silent.

Riley took a lurching step forward as Jewel stepped aside. He mumbled under his breath as he walked out through the doorway.

Following him at a safe distance, Jewel watched as he stumbled down the staircase and out the front entrance, slamming the door behind him.

Back in Rosie's room, Jewel closed the door behind her, then looked at Rosie where she stood against the wall with tears streaming. She said, "Come on over to the washstand and wash your face. You'll feel better."

Rosie swallowed. She moved abruptly to gather up the broken pieces of pencil and the sheets torn from the tablet. She was still clutching them close when she walked to the washstand.

* * *

Sunday morning. The sun beamed down from a cloudless sky. Weaver's main street was silent. The Gold Nugget Saloon was dark.

Lacey stepped out through the boarding house doorway and started toward the small church hidden from view around the curve of the main street. She had intended to wait for Mary, but the older woman had waved her on ahead when the last-minute details of cleaning up after breakfast had taken longer than expected.

Dressed in her Sunday best, a simple blue cotton with a matching hat and reticule, Lacey walked at a modest pace, somehow feeling more alone than she had ever felt in her life. She clutched her Bible tightly and smiled at Weaver's prominent citizens as they emerged from their doorways, but she made no attempt to join them. She searched the growing parade and saw Wilson and Janine Parker from the mercantile store walking with Doc Mayberry; Rita Johnson, the apothecary's niece, with her stiff-necked mother and father; Noelle Leach, the blacksmith's daughter and her father, Noah, just turning the corner of the street ahead. She nodded at Hiram Watts, Jerry Livingston and Mitch Carter as they lounged against a storefront on the opposite side of the street and tipped their hats in her direction.

The church bells began ringing as if on cue, and doorways opened along the street as additional churchgoers emerged to join the silent parade. Lacey scanned the street, her spirits sinking lower when the person she had hoped to see did not appear.

Lacey thought back to her conversation with Barret Gould, and her anger again simmered. It was not Christian and her thoughts were not worthy of the Sabbath, but she truly disliked that man. Even more, she despised what he had said.

Scully's preference for redheaded women is well-known in Weaver.

Those words haunted her. They seemed to confirm what she had witnessed the previous night between Scully and Charlotte. They had stolen the joy from her successful first lesson with Rosie. They had left her silent and uncommunicative with Scully at supper later that night. They had made her more vulnerable than ever before to the nightmares, which had assaulted her vividly every time she had dozed during the night.

She was angry with herself because she hadn't had the courage to release Scully completely from the bondage of sharing his daily meals with her. Her excuse had been that Scully didn't appear to resent that ritual, but she vacillated, still uncertain. She had prayed for direction only to have awakened that morning still suffering indecision.

Lacey's step momentarily stilled as Barret Gould walked onto the main street to join the stream of worshippers. Frowning, she wondered at his reason for going out of his way to take the Main Street route to church instead of the shorter route from his house on the next street.

Barret was dallying. Lacey realized abruptly that at the present rate she was walking, she would soon reach his side.

No, that would never do.

Silently imploring the Lord's forgiveness, Lacey crossed the street to avoid Barret completely. She could not be sure that his dallying was a deliberate effort to again place himself in her path, but she rationalized it was far better to avoid interaction with him than to chance her reaction if he attempted to start another conversation.

The irrational ache in the pit of her stomach remaining, Lacey cast another surreptitious glance around her, then chastised herself for entertaining the hope that Scully would appear somewhere on the street to accompany her. Without saying the words, Scully had made it clear the first day she had met Reverend Sykes that he had no intention of taking the reverend up on his invitation to attend Sunday worship. She did not choose to judge him for that decision. Scully had already gone out of his way to accommodate her—far more than she had realized until she had glimpsed him with Charlotte.

The unhappiness inside her expanded.

"Lacey...good morning."

Lacey turned at the sound of her name. Todd Fulton stepped out from the shadows and walked up to her side. She noted that the young wrangler's dark hair was neatly combed underneath his hat as he tipped it politely, that he was freshly shaven and was wearing clothes that were obviously newly purchased as he confessed, "I was waiting in the doorway for you to pass. I knew you'd be going to church this morning. I was hoping you wouldn't mind if I joined you."

"Mind? Of course not." Lacey forced her smile brighter as she looked into Todd's uncertain expression. "I'd enjoy your company."

"I was hoping you would. I was also hoping you'd have dinner with me tonight. It would pleasure me greatly."

"I...well..." Lacey took a breath. If this was a sign, she couldn't ignore it. Her decision made, she forced herself to say, "I'll be happy to have dinner with you."

Todd was conversing easily as they approached the church, but Lacey's thoughts wandered. She was no longer walking alone...yet she still felt strangely alone.

Lacey scanned the street one last time as she approached the church doorway. Resigned, she walked inside.

* * *

Scully watched from a position out of sight of the procession making its way to church. Lacey disappeared through the church doorway with Todd walking proudly beside her. Scully lingered only until the church doors closed and the singing began before walking back in the direction from which he had come.

Somehow, he couldn't put a name to the feelings inside him. Nor could he quite understand what had driven him to the street to see Lacey so early that morning after the especially active Saturday night he had had at the Gold Nugget. Was it because she had been so quiet at supper, because he had sensed a distance widening between them, or was it because, if Todd hadn't stepped up unexpectedly to accompany her, he might've been the man to walk beside her though the church doors for Sunday service?

No matter. Todd was with her now, and as long as the cowpoke behaved himself, he supposed Lacey was better off.

Yes, of course, she was.

He was sure of it.

Chapter Eight

The fire burned hotter. It singed her skin.

Her lungs were on fire.

There was no way out.

She cried out, "Help! Help me..." but her scorched lips refused to allow the sound passage.

She was outside the burning cabin—but the danger remained.

Grandpa was dead! They had killed him, and still they lingered.

They came closer...nearer.

Help! Help me!

Lacey awoke with a start, her heart pounding. She struggled against the terror remaining in the silent shadows of her boarding house room. She closed her eyes, then snapped them open again, telling herself it would soon be Monday morning, the beginning of another week. She had only had another nightmare, like the many others she had suffered through before. She would survive. Dawn would bring relief from her fears.

Lacey sat up slowly in bed. She was still trembling and a glance at the window revealed that dawn was hours away. Determined to take charge of her emotions, Lacey forced herself to lie back again. She firmly closed her eyes. She would not surrender to fear.

Grandpa's image appeared vividly in the darkness of her mind's eye, and Lacey smiled. Those sparkling eyes and that dear, bearded face... But, the image was changing. It was being replaced by a sober, handsome face and a serious, gray-eyed gaze that held hers intently. That gaze warmed her, held her safe and she abandoned herself to its comfort.

Scully.

Of course.

He would always keep her safe.

Lacey emerged from the boarding house doorway and glanced up at the lightening sky. It was Monday morning, and dawn had not fully consumed the night, but she was already dressed and on her way. Sadie would be surprised to see her at the restaurant so early and she—

Lacey gasped as a figure stepped out of the shadows.

"Lacey."

Her fear dissipated.

"Scully, what are you doing here so early?"

Scully walked to her side and Lacey felt his warmth pervade her. His handsome face, his sober gaze, the sheer size and masculine power of him—all was gentleness and under-standing in his dealings with her.

She had felt that gentleness and understanding when she had explained the previous day that she would be having Sunday supper with Todd. She had seen the flicker of an unnamed emotion in his gaze before Scully had nodded and accepted her decision without comment. She had reasoned that the strange sense of abandonment she had felt when Scully left her at her door was unrealistic, that she needed to become more independent for Scully's sake, as much as for her own. She had enjoyed Todd's company that evening and had even tentatively consented to see him again, while still scanning the street for a sign of Scully in the hope of seeing *him* again before the day ended.

It had occurred to Lacey that her most recent nightmare— a dream more vivid and more terrifying than its predecessors—might have been related to that sense of abandonment, but she had forced that thought away. Scully had a life of his own. She needed to remember that.

Yet she did not question her joy at Scully's unexpected appearance in the predawn shadows as she smiled up into his uncertain expression and he said, "If I didn't know better, I'd think you're happy to see me waiting here for you this morning."

"And you'd be right, even if I'm surprised to see you, since the Gold Nugget probably only closed a few hours ago."

Scully sobered as he scrutinized her surprising lack of color and the dark shadows under her eyes. He said, "You look like you didn't sleep well, Lacey. Was it the nightmares again?"

"You always seem to open our conversations by telling me how tired I look." Lacey continued her light rejoinder with a shake of her head. "Everybody else tells me how *good* I look...."

"You do look good—better than any woman in this town— but that doesn't mean I can't see that you had a fitful night's rest."

"You see right through me, don't you, Scully?"

"No. If I could, I wouldn't be here this morning, wondering what's going on."

"What do you mean?"

"I'm glad you and Todd have struck up a friendship, Lacey.

I'm glad to see you're settling in—but I have a feeling there's something else going on." Scully hesitated, then continued, "I want you to talk to me, Lacey. I have the feeling you're trying to shut me out, even though you say you're glad to see me this morning."

"I told you, I *am* glad to see you."

"So?"

"Oh, Scully..." Unable to avoid telling him the truth any longer, Lacey blinked back the sudden heat of tears and said, "I'm trying not to be selfish."

"Selfish!"

"I've been claiming all your time since I came back to Weaver—as if I have a special right to it."

"You do have a special right."

"No, I don't. You have a life of your own. It doesn't necessarily coincide with mine, and I shouldn't expect it to. I came back to Weaver for a few purposes. I explained the first—to take care of you in your old age—which was a misconception on my part. The second was to lift the shadows from the memories I have of my grandfather. The third—" Lacey shrugged, unable to express a thought not totally clear in her own mind. "Well, it looks like I haven't done so well on any of those fronts."

"So you figure to start by pushing me out of your life and pretending you're no longer my responsibility."

"I'm an adult now, Scully. I'm responsible for myself. That's something I've had to make myself face."

"Why?"

"You need to go on with your own life."

"What's all this concern about my life all of a sudden?"

"'All of a sudden...'" Lacey's spirits sagged. "I guess that says it all."

"No, it doesn't. You came back to Weaver expecting I'd help you settle the past and situate yourself in the present, and you had a right to that assumption. So…what happened? Why has everything suddenly changed?" And when Lacey averted her gaze, he asked, "Come on, Lacey, tell me."

Lacey looked back up at Scully. How could she explain? How could she make him understand?

Truth was the only answer.

Lacey responded bluntly, "I saw you with Charlotte outside the Gold Nugget the other night. I'm sorry, Scully."

"Sorry about what?" Scully's broad frame tensed noticeably. "Charlotte's a friendly acquaintance, but neither of us have made our friendship out to be more than that."

"I saw you kiss her, Scully."

"I've kissed a lot of women in my life."

"There was something special about that kiss."

"Not on my part."

"Scully…"

"Is that what this is all about—a simple kiss? Lacey, you've been sheltered all your life, but the truth is, a kiss doesn't signify commitment. That's all it is—just a kiss."

Scully flushed as a thought suddenly struck him. He asked, "Why? Did Todd try to kiss you last night?"

"Of course not!" Lacey's reply was spontaneous. She then added, "But why would it matter if 'a kiss is only a kiss'?"

"Because you seem to think it means more."

"A kiss is an expression of caring, Scully. I'm not so *naive* that I don't understand that. I've been tempted to kiss you myself a few times."

Silent a few moments, Scully replied unexpectedly, "So, why didn't you?"

"Because I thought it would be forward. I thought you might resent—"

"I wouldn't have resented it."

Lacey was uncertain of the reason for the sudden thickness in her throat as she replied, "All right, then."

Standing on tiptoe, Lacey pressed a lingering kiss against Scully's cheek. Somehow dissatisfied, she impulsively slid her arms around his neck and hugged him close. She whispered, "I do love you, Scully. I always will. You're the best friend I'll ever have…dearer than anyone I know…closer to me than if you were actually my family, but I don't want my feelings to become a burden to you. You have a life of your own that's separate and apart from me. I want to make sure you don't end up resenting me for keeping you from it."

Scully's strong arms closed around her, and the tightness in Lacey's throat thickened as she said, "Please understand…I'll always love you, Scully, no matter how many Charlottes there are in your life."

Thrust abruptly an arm's length from him, Lacey looked up into Scully's stern expression as he repeated, "Charlotte is an *acquaintance.* That's all."

"I'm just using Charlotte as an example." Lacey hastened to explain, "I know you prefer redheaded women and I—"

"Who told you that?"

Lacey went still.

"It's untrue, and I want to know who said it."

"Does it matter?"

"Yes."

"I've already set him straight about it. I told him your personal preferences are nobody's business but yours, and they certainly aren't *my* business."

"Tell me who it was."

"No."

"Was it Todd?"

"No!"

"Who—"

"Don't ask me again, Scully. It doesn't matter."

"Yes, it does."

"Scully, please! I made a mistake mentioning it. Don't make me regret it even more than I do now. It doesn't matter, really it doesn't. He won't repeat what he said to anyone else. If he was trying to warn me against you, I've made it clear I didn't feel I had any need to be warned. I also told him I'm not interested in anything else he has to say, whether it's about you or anyone else."

"Was it Reverend Sykes?"

"Scully, I told you...I won't answer you."

"All right." His chest heaving with the anger he suppressed, Scully continued, "You won't tell me, so I'll make this point clear right now. That kiss you witnessed between Charlotte and me meant nothing more than casual friendship. I've kissed a lot of women and held a lot of women in my arms."

Unexpectedly drawing her against him, Scully brushed a kiss against her cheek and said, "Now I've kissed you, too. I'm also holding you in my arms, and you can believe me when I tell you that brief kiss I just gave you means more to me than any of those others."

When Lacey did not reply, Scully drew back and whispered, "I kissed you, Lacey, and you aren't even a redhead."

Lacey's spontaneous laugh was the signal he appeared to have been waiting for. Scully slid Lacey's arm through his and said, "Enough said. Come on. Sadie will be wondering where you are. Besides, I'm hungry, and I haven't been to bed yet. I'm going to take care of both those necessities in that order, as soon as possible."

Lacey walked beside Scully. Her cheek burned from the touch of his lips. His warmth filled her when he looked back down at her and added, "Now that all that nonsense is settled, I'll be back at noon to take you to lunch."

"Oh, no." Lacey shook her head regretfully. "I have to be at the church."

Scully's gaze narrowed. "Supper, then?"

"Yes."

They turned onto the main street's boardwalk and Lacey clutched Scully's arm unconsciously closer. The day was brighter and her heart had lightened.

How had she come to be so blessed?

"I'm going with you."

Rosie looked at Jewel as the taller saloon girl stood illuminated by a shaft of afternoon sunlight in the doorway of her room. Jewel's color was more vibrant than her own and her demeanor was more assured, but Rosie knew only too well that underneath her outward composure, Jewel was like her— still the abandoned child she had once been, still struggling to find her way. Their common backgrounds had made them instant friends after meeting at the Gold Nugget two years earlier, and the common problems they had shared since that time had brought them even closer.

Yet there were basic differences between them that made Rosie question Jewel's motivation as she replied, "You don't have to come to my lesson with me, Jewel. Riley won't be back for a few days. It always takes him that long to come to terms with the way he acted. Besides, he doesn't know anything about my lessons. He thinks I bought the tablet."

Jewel responded unexpectedly, "Did it ever occur to you that I might want to go with you because I'm as eager to learn as you are?"

"No." Rosie replied honestly, "I didn't think it mattered much to you."

"It doesn't, but it won't hurt, either."

"Then you're not coming with me because you think Riley will be waiting for me somewhere?"

"No."

"Truth, Jewel…"

"That's not my only reason."

"But you want to take your derringer with you."

Confidence returned to Jewel's expression. "I'm never without it."

"Lacey wouldn't want you to take a gun into the church."

"Don't tell her, then."

"Jewel…"

"I'm coming with you—like it or not."

"Jewel, please, leave the gun here."

"I told you, I don't go anywhere without it."

"You can go to the church without it."

Jewel did not respond.

"Jewel…"

Rosie saw the myriad of emotions that raced across Jewel's expression. She was not aware she was holding her breath until she released it when Jewel reached into her pocket, withdrew the derringer, then took a few steps into the room to shove it underneath a bed pillow and said, "Are you happy now?"

A smile her only response, Rosie picked up her torn tablet and broken pencil, and turned toward the door.

Scully awakened abruptly from his sleep. He glanced at the bright sunlight against the window shade of his bedroom, then at the clock on the wall. It was almost noon. He had slept for a few hours and had awakened automatically as if his inner clock, always so dependable in the past, was telling him he had an appointment with Lacey for their noon meal.

But he didn't.

Scully slid his arm underneath his head in a deceivingly casual pose that did not reflect the many conflicting thoughts that had plagued him since his conversation with Lacey that morning. He remembered the moment she had walked out of the boarding house door into his view. Her startling beauty had been luminous even in the limited light of morning, but the true significance of the moment had come when she heard his voice and turned toward him with true joy in her smile. That moment of reality had hit him hard. He hadn't realized how much he had been depending on her reaction to seeing him there that morning.

Scully shook his head. Lacey's attempt to distance herself from him had been more obvious to him than she'd realized, and whether he cared to admit it or not, the thought had tormented him. He'd been determined to discover why—for many reasons. He had told himself that Lacey was too beautiful, too honest and trusting for her own good. He had reminded himself of the many dangers she would face because of that potent combination of attributes—dangers she was unprepared to handle. He had purposely recalled to mind that

Charlie had entrusted him with her future, and that he had a right to his intense interest in her welfare. Keeping all those thoughts in mind, he had deliberately ignored the deadening ache that had twisted tight inside him when he became certain she was avoiding him.

But that was all changed now.

Almost.

It was now clear that for some reason he could not fathom, someone was trying to turn Lacey against him. He would be able to understand it, if not condone it, if that person had been Todd. Yet Lacey's instinctive reaction had dismissed that possibility. Was it Reverend Sykes or Doc Mayberry? He'd had difficult conflicts of opinions with both those men in the past, and they didn't especially approve of him. He wondered if, possibly, Janine Parker was spreading harmful gossip at the mercantile these days, or if Rita Johnson or Noelle Leach had made that untrue comment to Lacey about his preference for redheads—a remark he wouldn't have given a moment's thought to, if not for Lacey's reaction to it.

He had scrutinized Sadie's customers as he had eaten breakfast in the restaurant that morning. He had searched his memory for those who had become regulars since Lacey had begun working there. He'd thought of Hiram Watts, Jerry Livingston and Mitch Carter, all bachelors who hadn't disguised their interest in Lacey. He'd remembered Barret Gould, who had paid her special attention. He had searched his memory for the faces of Weaver residents who had expressed disapproval of him at any point in the past, and had considered the possibility of their interference. Lastly, he had then recalled the reaction of the Gold Nugget girls to

Lacey. He'd known that "preference for redheads" comment had been a direct reference to Charlotte, but he'd dismissed Charlotte's possible involvement. That wasn't Charlotte's way.

No…male or female, this person was sly. Scully couldn't figure out his or her agenda, and that worried him.

His discomfort dismissing any further thought of sleep, Scully threw back the coverlet and walked to the washstand. He splashed cold water against his face in an attempt to clear his mind, rubbed his hand against the shadow of a beard on his chin, then stared at his reflection as he dried his face. He wondered what Lacey saw when she looked at him.

She'd said he was handsome. He considered himself in the mirror more closely.

His hair was thick and dark, but he'd recently seen a gray hair or two at his temple.

His features were passably regular, but he'd been told his frown was too harsh and his smile too infrequent. He supposed there was truth in that.

In examining his broad-shouldered, tightly knit frame, he saw only hard muscle and sinew.

Lacey had said she had come back to Weaver expecting him to be an old man, that she had been surprised to find him so young. He supposed that comment had come back to roost uncomfortably with her when the person who had made the "redhead" comment made her consider everything that remark entailed.

Then Lacey had said she loved him.

Loved him.

She'd said it so easily, with an affection so obviously heartfelt that he'd been left momentarily speechless. He remembered the totally innocent touch of her lips against his cheek, the warmth of her arms around his neck, the sweet contact of her body pressed to his. It had seemed so right when he had closed his arms around her and held her close. And when he had kissed her cheek, he remembered the fleeting thought again returning, that her lips had been only a hairsbreadth away.

He had said he loved her, too.

The words had come easily, he supposed because, in a way, he had loved her from the first moment he had seen her as a sick, injured child.

But Lacey wasn't a child anymore.

That last thought the only clear reflection in his mind at that moment, Scully turned away from the washstand and reached for his clothes. He was too restless to sleep any longer, and he was hungry.

Scully glanced at the clock again. Lacey would be at the church by now. He was glad she was making a life for herself in Weaver.

Yes, he was.

Scully forced himself to retain that thought as he dressed and turned toward the door. But he had things to do.

"Oh, I see you've brought a friend."

Lacey glanced between Rosie and Jewel as the youthful saloon girl entered the silent church anteroom. She took another backward step to allow Jewel to enter as Rosie responded, "I hope you don't mind that Jewel came with me. We figured it would be just as easy to teach two of us as it was one." Rosie added, "You don't have to worry, you know. Jewel's smart. She learns fast, and I'll share my tablet with her."

"Of course, I don't mind." She looked down at the broken pencil and damaged tablet Rosie clutched and asked with concern, "What happened? Did you have an accident?"

Lacey saw the tense breath Rosie took before she responded, "I fell. I told you, I'm clumsy—but I saved all the pages that got torn out of the tablet and I'll still be able to use them."

Lacey scrutinized Rosie's flushed expression, then said, "I know there's more to it than that."

"It's nothing you have to worry about," Jewel responded in Rosie's stead, her expression void of emotion. "We can handle it."

We.

Meaning the two of them.

Saddened to be excluded, Lacey was silent for a few moments before she said, "I need to know, Rosie, does it have anything to do with your association with me?"

"Oh, no! He doesn't know about you. I mean…he…"

Rosie halted abruptly, her face flaming. With a concerned glance at her friend, Jewel repeated, "We can handle it."

Her expression unexpectedly softening, Jewel then said, "I'd like to stay if you don't mind, Lacey."

"Of course you may stay. I'm truly happy to welcome you." Lacey offered, "You can use my pencil while we practice."

"No."

"Please. I have others."

Jewel reluctantly nodded.

With those words meant to lessen Jewel's discomfort fresh on her lips, Lacey picked up her slate and chalk. She'd replace the pencil at the mercantile after the lesson was over. She hoped the Lord would forgive her stretch of the truth meant to alleviate Jewel's hesitation, then dismissed the thought from her mind.

Lacey glanced at the broken pencil Rosie clutched. She looked at the fading bruise on her cheek.

Despite Jewel's protestations, she could ignore the obvious no longer.

"Is that all you have to tell me?" Barret's narrow nostrils twitched as Larry stood a few feet across from his desk, his report completed. The odor of unwashed body permeated the distance between them as Barret said, "So you're telling me Lacey is now meeting with *two* saloon girls at the church—but you don't know why."

"How are Blackie and me supposed to know why? We ain't mind readers."

"But you do have eyes, don't you?"

"Yeah…so?"

"And ears."

"What are you getting at?"

"You couldn't get close enough to *see* what they were doing through a window, or possibly to *hear* what they were discussing?"

"You didn't say nothin' about that. You just told Blackie and me to follow Lacey and report back to you."

Barret's smile was cold. "But you aren't reporting anything."

"I told you that Jewel woman's with them other two now, didn't I?"

Barret took a secure hold on his patience. "Yes, but I don't know much more than I did before about the reason they're there. So now I'm telling you to find out what they're *doing* in that church."

Larry shrugged. "It can't be nothin' too bad. It is a church, after all."

His forbearance snapping, Barret ordered, "Find out!"

Larry responded defensively, "Me and Blackie always do the best we can."

"So far it hasn't been good enough. Get back there, and don't let Lacey out of your sight."

"Right."

"And take a bath!"

Larry scowled. He was about to respond when Barret ordered, "Go. We're done talking."

His eyes trained on the door through which Larry had disappeared, Barret paused to consider his situation coldly. He could not be truly certain how much ground he had gained in turning Lacey against Scully, and the reason for Lacey's association with the Gold Nugget women was a total mystery. If things did not change, Blackie and Larry's ineptitude would force him into a premature move that would not be totally wise. Yet impatience was tearing at his innards.

Barret took a deep breath and made the only wise decision available to him. He needed more time to assess the situation. He needed to be certain what he was walking into before he took any drastic steps.

That decision made, Barret growled a soft warning into the silence of the room.

"But don't waste too much time in making your move, Lacey, or...I'll make it for you."

"I don't want to bring trouble to the church, Reverend."

Her smooth brow knit with concern, Lacey looked at Reverend Sykes with uncertainty. She had waited patiently until Jewel and Rosie had left the church at the end of their lesson and had walked out of sight before seeking out the reverend where he was working in the small church garden.

Responding to her statement in his typically soothing manner, Reverend Sykes said, "You're not bringing trouble to the church. You're doing the Lord's work. That's what the church is here for."

Lacey hesitated, then said, "Rosie's beau beats her, Reverend. She doesn't want to admit it, but most everybody who knows her realizes it by now. Jewel came with Rosie to her lessons today. She said she needs to learn how to read and write, too, but I think there's more to it than that. She's so protective of Rosie. I have the feeling she's thinks Rosie's beau will be a problem if he finds out the reason she's coming here every day."

"You're doing the Lord's work, Lacey."

"But—"

"You're taking Rosie a step in the right direction, and Jewel is following, whatever her reason. You're succeeding."

"But—"

"Don't be concerned about anything else. Things will work out. And don't worry about the church. It will continue to stand. Just remember, in the short time you've been back in Weaver, you've given more thought to the future of those two women than anyone in this town ever has."

"That can't be true."

Reverend Sykes did not reply.

"What about Rosie, Reverend? Her beau—"

"The situation is longstanding, isn't it?" At Lacey's nod, the reverend continued, "You know Rosie will most likely retreat from you, that you'll probably lose her and Jewel, too, if you attempt to speak to Rosie about her beau at this early stage. It's probably taken all the courage she could muster to make this first attempt at improving herself. A step at a time, Lacey."

"But—"

"You'll be in a better position to have her listen to what you're saying if you wait."

"But—"

"You can't expect fast progress when attempting to reverse the conduct of years." He added with a smile, "*Let us not be weary in doing good—for at the proper time, we will reap the harvest.*"

Lacey sighed.

Patience.

Yet somehow she had to do more.

"We'd better hurry. We're going to be late for work."

Jewel turned toward Rosie as they rounded the corner and approached their boarding house. Rosie had been scanning the street nervously since they had emerged from the church. It was obvious that she was worried Riley might be lurking somewhere nearby, but they had also stayed at their lesson longer than they should because things had been going so well. With a day's head start on her, Rosie had actually begun printing her name so that the letters were recognizable. She'd never seen her friend so excited.

Jewel gave a mental shrug. She had no doubt she'd soon be writing her own name, too, but Rosie had been correct in her assumption that the lessons didn't mean as much to her. Rosie's sense of self-esteem was somehow tied to her progress. She was happy to see Rosie's enthusiasm, but she didn't fool herself that paper and pencil could change their lives.

Rosie was breathless from hurrying, and Jewel urged, "Slow down, Rosie. The Gold Nugget won't shut down if we get there a few minutes late."

Rosie nodded, her chestnut curls bobbing.

Chestnut curls.

A familiar knot of pain clenched tight in Jewel's gut. Cynthia's hair had been that same color. Her baby sister had also been small and slender like Rosie, and had had brown eyes so similar to Rosie's that she had caught her breath the first time she met Rosie a few years earlier.

Rosie and Cynthia were similar in so many other ways, too. Both were honest and totally forthright, with a way of looking directly into a person's eyes that elicited from Jewel a strong need to protect the trusting nature that in Rosie's case had been so badly abused.

Jewel fought back a familiar distress. Cynthia, her baby sister—dead at the age of twelve. Cynthia and both their parents had been victims of the fever that had swept through their small cabin. Jewel still could not comprehend why she had been spared. Alone and devastated afterward, she had fervently wished she had been taken, too. Yet it was later that she realized fully how merciful that would've been.

She had been orphaned at fourteen.

A trace of innocence had still remained at fifteen.

By the age of sixteen, however, she'd fully absorbed some of life's most painful lessons.

Those lessons had changed her.

It had stunned Jewel—and made her sad—to realize, when she met Rosie a few years earlier, that despite all that had happened to her, Rosie was still trusting at heart. Anybody with half an eye could've recognized Riley for what he was when he cozied up to Rosie with flattery and promises that first day, but he had said all the things Rosie wanted to hear, and Rosie had told herself she was "in love."

Jewel looked at Rosie's bruised face. That's what "love" had gotten her.

Jewel was determined that she'd never let herself be that kind of a fool.

Jewel's step slowed when the boarding house came into view and she saw the slim, dark-haired man leaning against the wall beside the door. She did not smile when his face brightened at the sight of her and he started toward them.

"Buddy's been waiting for you, Jewel."

Jewel nodded. "That's what it looks like."

Buddy reached her side and tipped his hat to Rosie as she hurried past with a nod. Then, turning his attention fully toward Jewel, he said, "I'm glad you got back. The boss sent me into town for some supplies, so I figured I'd use the time to see you while old man Parker was filling the order at the mercantile. I was starting to worry you wouldn't get back before I had to leave. Where've you been, darlin'?"

"That's my business, Buddy."

Buddy's smile faltered. "Yeah, I know. I didn't mean nothing by it." He hesitated, then said, "But it could be my business, too, if you'd let it be."

"That would be a mistake."

"Not for me, it wouldn't." Suddenly solemn, Buddy looked directly into her eyes and said, "I don't mean to blow my own horn, Jewel, honey, but I need to tell you again—I'm honest, loyal and a hard worker, and I'd never look at another woman if you'd say the word. I could make a good life for us."

"Like I said before, that would be a mistake."

"Why?"

Jewel forced a hard smile. "You know that old saying, 'Too much water has passed under that bridge.' Like I told you, right now I'm just floating with the current, and that's the way I like it."

Momentarily silent, Buddy responded, "That isn't the way it seemed when we was together a few nights ago."

Jewel's smile twitched. "That was then. This is now."

"Is that right?"

"Why would I say it if I didn't mean it?"

"I don't rightly know, but I don't intend to quit until I find out."

"You're a fool, Buddy Cross."

"A fool who loves you."

Love.

Jewel responded coldly, "I'll be late for work if I waste any more time here."

"You wouldn't want that."

Jewel did not reply.

"I'll see you tonight. Save the last dance for me. I'll take you home."

Jewel turned toward the boarding house door without responding. She looked up at Buddy when he stayed her with a touch on her shoulder.

Despite herself, her throat tightened when Buddy whispered, "I love you, darlin'. I'll put that ring on your finger yet."

Jewel shrugged off his touch and walked away without looking back.

The evening was balmy, and Lacey's hand on his arm felt right as Scully and she walked toward the livery stable after their evening meal.

Scully looked down at Lacey as she maintained her silence. She had been preoccupied throughout their meal. Something was bothering her. She had mentioned she hadn't stopped off to see Careful that morning and he had suggested they visit the feisty little critter after they finished eating. She had easily agreed, but her still diverted gaze spoke volumes.

Yet Scully was unprepared when Lacey looked up at him unexpectedly and asked, "How long has Rosie Burns been working for you?"

Scully was suddenly wary. He had spent a long, tedious day indulging town gossips and making inquiries that had led him nowhere. There had been nothing but sincere greeting in Janine Parker's expression when he had entered the mercantile. Their conversation had been open and friendly, and it had taken him no more than a few minutes to decide she wasn't responsible for the talk that had reached Lacey's ears. He'd met Jerry Livingston on the street a little later and had just as quickly dismissed him and his friends from his list of possible rumormongers. He had then visited Doc Mayberry and waited a half hour for him to finish with another patient before seeing him. The doc had appeared honestly concerned about his feigned complaint. The doc had prescribed an Epsom salt bath, which Scully had no intention of taking, and he had left the doc's office certain he'd have to look further for the culprit. He had already cancelled out Reverend Sykes, knowing Lacey wouldn't have gone back to the church if the reverend had been the one who had tried to poison her mind against him. He intended to talk to his Gold Nugget girls later that evening, but he didn't really expect any one of them to be guilty of carrying tales.

That left Barret Gould. He had never liked or trusted that

man. Neither did he like the two men Barret employed to do odd chores for him. He did not believe that dishonest men could be honestly employed by a man with as questionable a character as Barret Gould's. He supposed it was for those reasons that he had preferred to eliminate all the possible gossipmongers from his mind before considering him. Unfortunately, his opinion of Barret's character and choice of employees was not shared by the majority of Weaver's more respectable citizens.

He had been considering Barret's possible complicity more closely before picking up Lacey for supper, but all thought was presently struck from his mind by Lacey's question.

Scully thought back. "How long has Rosie been working for me? About two years, I guess."

Scully saw the effort Lacey expended to hold back her response before she blurted, "You know her that well, yet you didn't notice the bruises she's worked so hard to cover up since she met Riley Martin?"

Scully frowned. "I saw them, all right."

"And you didn't try to help her?"

"How would I do that?"

Lacey's astounding eyes widened with incredulity and her flawless skin flushed. Scully noted absentmindedly that she was somehow even more beautiful in the throes of her sudden anger as she replied hotly, "How? Are you asking me how you could've helped her?"

"That's right. I'm asking how I could've helped Rosie when each time she showed up with a split lip or a black eye, she told me and everybody else who asked that she had fallen, or walked into a door, or she had just made the mistake of applying too much makeup that night."

"But you knew Riley was responsible."

"Did I? Rosie denied it, and when Riley came to the Gold Nugget a few nights after she showed up with new bruises, they looked even cozier than before."

"She's afraid of him!"

"You wouldn't think so if you saw them together."

Lacey blushed.

Aware that he had embarrassed her, Scully said more kindly than before, "If I've learned nothing else while running the Gold Nugget, Lacey, I've learned to let the girls who work there handle their own problems unless it interferes with their work."

"But Rosie is being physically abused."

"She chose Riley. I didn't."

"She made a mistake."

"Maybe she did, but it's her life, and I'm not responsible for it."

Lacey's step slowed. Her face paled as she looked up at him solemnly and said, "I suppose you would've felt the same way about me, then, if you hadn't owed my grandfather a debt of gratitude."

They were beginning to draw the attention of passersby, and Scully urged Lacey forward into the livery stable. Breaking his silence when they finally emerged through the back door at the corral where Careful was confined, he responded quietly, "Don't compare yourself with Rosie, Lacey. You would never have turned out to be a Gold Nugget girl, whether your grandfather had sent you to me or not."

Scully noted the shaky breath Lacey took before she said, "not so sure about that." And she added, "But you didn't question."

"tion…meaning would I have seen to your needs

all these years if I hadn't owed Charlie a debt of gratitude?"
Scully stared down into Lacey's expectant expression. He responded truthfully, "It took only one look when you wandered into my saloon all those years ago, and I knew I could never have turned my back on you, whether you were Charlie's granddaughter or not."

"Why, Scully?"

Why, indeed?

Scully responded, "I can't tell you why. I can only tell you the way it was."

"Scully…"

Uncomfortable, Scully said gruffly, "I don't want you getting involved with Rosie's problems, Lacey. I told you before, and although the reality of it doesn't seem to have sunk into your mind yet, this is the Wild West and all that goes along with it. That means there are men and women out here who handle their problems with a gun rather than go to any authority—whether it's personal or business problems they intend to solve."

"Because people don't help them."

"Because they don't *want* anybody to help them."

"That's not true."

"True or not, Lacey, how the girls at the Gold Nugget handle their lives is none of your business."

"Why?"

"That should be obvious."

"It isn't, to me."

Scully said flatly, "I don't want you getting involved with Rosie or any of the other girls at the Nugget."

"Too late."

"What's that supposed to mean?"

Lacey turned away without responding.

"Lacey…"

"I don't want to discuss it anymore."

"I told you—"

"I said…I don't want to talk about it anymore."

A welcoming bray turned Lacey toward the corral fence as Careful slid his head through the bars and nudged Lacey's hand. Lacey frowned as she stroked Careful's muzzle.

Silence reigned heavily between them before Lacey turned back toward Scully with a shaky smile that tore at his heart and said, "I'm sorry. It's my fault. I made a mistake bringing the whole thing up. Please, let's not argue anymore, all right?"

"All right."

It was a long moment before Scully realized that whatever Lacey wanted, whatever she said, would ultimately be all right with him.

It was a wonder to him.

A wonder *why*.

Chapter Nine

The evening shadows filled Weaver's main street as Jewel stood in the doorway of the Gold Nugget Saloon. She turned her back on the heat and din within and walked out onto the boardwalk outside as the noise began overwhelming her. She nodded with a smile at the wranglers lounging there, her composure gradually returning.

She had dressed in a scarlet gown that was her favorite that evening because of the way it complemented her brunette coloring. She had used that dress to bolster her morale many times when it was faltering—and she needed it badly this night.

Jewel joked briefly with a smiling wrangler as he pushed his way through the swinging doors. She employed a facade she had perfected over a period of years, a facade that had hidden a multitude of emotions. She glanced at Rosie where her friend stood a few feet down the boardwalk. Rosie was smiling, her expression open as she laughed and conversed with the men on either side of her. That was Rosie's gift, the ability to keep her fears at bay for short periods of time, but Jewel did not possess that skill.

Jewel slipped her hand into the pocket of her dress that allowed her access to the derringer holstered in her garter. Small and potent, the gun was a reassurance that gave her confidence. She was especially in need of that confidence tonight because she had just learned Riley was back in the area.

Jewel laughed encouragingly at a comment made by the fellow at her elbow, then looked offhandedly down the street. Billy Watts had mentioned seeing Riley outside town a few hours earlier. Billy had remarked that Riley wouldn't like seeing Rosie enjoying herself with those two friendly customers when he came back to see her.

She had hidden her reaction with an expert smile and a wink, but her heart had begun a nervous thudding. She had sworn to herself the last time Rosie had come home beaten and bruised at Riley's hands that she would not let it happen again. She had not been able to save Cynthia, but Rosie—as dear and innocent at heart as her baby sister—was not beyond her help.

Jewel took a breath and responded appropriately to the man who walked up beside her. She breathed in the fresh air, grateful for a moment to think after speaking to Billy. She had the feeling she would especially need a clear head tonight.

Three days had passed since she and Rosie had returned from their lesson and found Buddy waiting at her boarding house door.

Three days…

So much had happened since then. Rosie's and her lessons had continued, and they were both advancing rapidly under Lacey's patient tutelage. She could already print her name as well as Rosie could, and both Rosie and she were working successfully on the alphabet. Lacey concluded each session by reading a chapter from the Bible at Rosie's request, and while peering over Lacey's shoulder, she had already become familiar with a few of the words.

Trust in the Lord with all your heart...He will direct your path.

Rosie had received more comfort from those words than she had, but the passage lingered in her mind. Perhaps it was easier for Rosie to trust in the Lord than it was for her, but she didn't understand how that was possible with all that Rosie had suffered. The only thing she knew for certain was that she would not allow Rosie to leave the Nugget with Riley that night if there was fear in her eyes.

As for Buddy...

Jewel smiled more broadly to conceal a surge of emotion. Buddy had come to the Nugget that evening three days previously as he had promised. She had been unable to deny her spontaneous joy at seeing him when he walked through the doorway, or the way she had warmed to his touch when he slipped his arm around her. She had saved the last dance for him. She hadn't been able to help herself.

Jewel swallowed against the lump that choked her throat. Buddy said he loved her, but he was a fool. Only a fool could love a woman who had so little love left in her. Only a fool would believe a woman like her could change her past simply by changing her future.

Only a fool believed in redemption.

As if bidden by her thoughts, Riley rode into view at the end of the street, and Jewel tensed. She watched as he rode gradually closer.

Slight, with curly hair, warm brown eyes and a youthful appearance, Riley looked deceivingly harmless. No one would initially believe he was capable of the cruelty hidden behind that benign exterior. Neither would anyone see through him as quickly as she had.

Experience was an unforgiving teacher.

Jewel noted the moment when Riley spotted Rosie standing between the two friendly wranglers a few feet away. She saw his mouth twitch into a hard smile as he drew his horse up to the hitching rail.

Scully briefly scanned the activity in the saloon as he walked down the stairs from his room. The clamor of merry-making was increasing as the hours progressed, but he somehow had little patience for it all. He hadn't finished dinner that evening and he was hungry. He needed to get to the restaurant before it closed for the night.

Scully acknowledged the greetings of Joe Mullens, a graying cowman, as he made his way across the crowded floor toward the swinging doors. He joked briefly with Harve Stone as he passed. He responded with a short comment to Willie Johnson as the wiry fellow looked up with a greeting, and he reacted with a laugh to Ness Green's quip before emerging out onto the street. His expression changed when he saw Riley Martin dismounting.

One glance, and Scully knew the reason for Riley's rigid posture. Rosie was standing farther down the walk with two wranglers who were obviously enjoying her conversation. She hadn't seen him yet, and she was laughing at a comment one of them made.

Scully saw the twist of Riley's lips as he started toward her.

Scully paused to scrutinize the men standing with Rosie. They were both wranglers from the Diamond R ranch. Both of them were decent men, and Rosie knew enough not to cause trouble when she was working. She'd handle it. She always did.

Turning his back on the scene unfolding, Scully continued on down the street.

Rosie gasped as Riley turned her roughly toward him. His hand still on her shoulder, he said, "You didn't see me, huh? You wasn't expecting me, neither, or you wouldn't be out here with these two fellas."

"What's your problem, boy?" The bearded fellow on Rosie's right eyed Riley more closely, then said, "The lady and me are just having some fine conversation."

"She doesn't need your conversation, do you, Rosie?" Riley's hand tightened on her shoulder as he repeated, "Do you, Rosie?"

Fear choked Rosie's throat. She needed no one to tell her that Riley was looking for trouble. She had been warned about him causing a ruckus at the Nugget. He knew it, too. He also knew how much she needed her job, and he was counting on it.

Despising him more at that moment than ever before, Rosie smiled at the cowpoke beside her and said, "It's all right, Johnny. Riley and me are…good friends. He gets mad sometimes when I enjoy myself too much with other fellas."

"That's too bad for him, ain't it?"

Riley looked at Rosie, his gaze menacing. "Tell him, Rosie. Tell him you don't want him hanging around you anymore."

"Johnny's a nice fella. We were only talking."

"Yeah, only talking. I know you better than that."

Johnny's expression hardened as he warned, "I'd watch what I said, if I was you, fella."

Rosie saw Jewel advancing toward them out of the corner

of her eye. Jewel had a strange look on her face. It frightened her, and she said in an attempt to placate Riley, "Johnny won't mind if I spend the rest of my time with you while I'm here tonight, will you, Johnny?" She looked at the frowning cowpoke almost pleadingly and said, "There's not a girl in the Nugget who won't be happy to take my place beside you once you walk back through those doors."

Rosie gasped as Riley's grip twisted painfully tight and he said, "You don't need *his* permission. You don't need anybody's permission but mine—'cause you know what'll happen to you if you don't listen to what I say."

Jewel was coming closer. Rosie felt a trembling begin somewhere in the pit of her stomach when she saw Jewel slide her hand into the pocket of her dress. So intent was she on Jewel's advance that she gasped aloud when Scully appeared unexpectedly behind them and jerked Riley around to face him.

Rosie felt the color drain from her face at Scully's tight expression. His tone was all the more compelling for its softness when he said in a voice barely audible over the din of the saloon behind them, "It's time for you to leave, Riley."

Bold in his arrogance, Riley replied, "I ain't leaving unless Rosie leaves with me."

Scully looked at Rosie, his expression cold. Rosie took a backward step at the intensity of Scully's gaze when he asked, "Do you want to go with him?"

Somehow frozen, Rosie was unable to respond. She heard Jewel answer in her stead, "Rosie doesn't want to leave with him. She doesn't want any part of him!"

Ignoring Jewel's interjection, Scully asked again, "Do you want to go with him or not, Rosie?"

Rosie shook her head.

Scully pressed, "Answer yes or no. Riley needs to hear you say it."

"No…I don't want to go with him."

"You heard her, Riley." Directing the full weight of his threatening stare at Riley, Scully said, "Either you leave now under your own power, or I'll personally escort you out of town."

"No, you won't."

"Try me."

Rosie recognized the rage burning in Riley's gaze. She saw his hand twitch the second before it moved toward the gun at his hip, then heard Riley's startled grunt of pain when Scully jammed his fist into Riley's ribs, halting him. She was breathless as Scully drew Riley's gun from his holster with a quick twist of his other hand and tossed it to the wrangler beside them, saying "Give this to Bill at the bar. He'll know what to do with it." Turning back to Riley, who was still gasping for air, Scully then said, "Let's go."

Incredibly, the activity on the boardwalk continued unaffected around them as Scully pulled Riley into the shadows of the alleyway between the buildings.

Rosie turned back to the wranglers beside her with a start when Johnny said, "I guess we don't have to worry about that fella no more with Scully taking care of things. What do you say we go back inside?"

Rosie nodded. Shaken, she started toward the swinging doors with as steady a step as she could manage.

Jewel hesitated and glanced toward the alleyway where Riley and Scully had disappeared. She looked again at Rosie, who was doing her best to appear as unaffected by the episode as the two wranglers beside her.

Never more conscious of the small gun holstered on her thigh, Jewel did not choose to consider how close she had come to using it this time. She would not have hesitated, and if not for Scully's intervention—

Jewel preferred not to take that thought any further. Scully had taken over, and he would set Riley straight for the time being. His warning wouldn't last long, but Rosie would be free of the threat Riley presented for a few more days.

And so would she.

Jewel turned toward the cowboy who had stepped up beside her. She smiled as he accompanied her back into the Nugget. Standing companionably beside Rosie a few minutes later, she squeezed Rosie's arm in a comradely gesture before joining in the easy banter around her.

Scully stood in the shadows of the alleyway with Riley still breathing raggedly beside him. Speaking in a cold tone that did not reflect the heat of his stare, he said, "Before you leave, I want to make sure you understand you're not welcome at the Nugget anymore, Riley. Don't…come…back."

Riley's response was a muttered expletive that caused Scully to respond more forcefully, "There's nothing more to say about it, so just get on your horse and git!"

"I want my gun!"

"You can pick it up at the sheriff's office tomorrow morning, after you tell him what you tried to do with it here."

"I didn't do nothin'!"

"Tell it to the sheriff."

Still mumbling as Scully escorted him forcefully to his horse, Riley mounted up. His boyish face was dark with fury when he turned back to say, "You think you won, but you made a mistake tonight, Scully. This ain't the end of it."

Scully stood fast as Riley kicked his horse into a gallop and thundered down the street. He waited until Riley disappeared from sight before turning determinedly back in the direction of the restaurant. In truth, he had lost his appetite just about the time the image of Rosie's terrified expression had forced him to retrace his steps and face Riley down.

Scully was nearing the restaurant when he finally acknowledged despite himself that his conversation with Lacey had probably influenced the action he had taken a few minutes previously, that she would probably approve of the way he had defended Rosie. Admittedly, he felt better knowing Rosie wouldn't have to fear Riley that evening; yet it troubled him to realize—where Lacey would not—that the effort had most likely been a waste of time.

Rosie and Riley would probably be back together before the week was out. That was the way of things—the way it had always been, and the way it would remain.

Scully paused at the restaurant doorway to look back at the brightly lit Nugget. He had no doubt that Rosie and Jewel were laughing and talking inside, continuing on as if the scene on the boardwalk with Riley had never happened.

Yes, that was the way of things, too.

Music and laughter from the Nugget reverberated on the street around Scully as he then glanced up at the starlit night sky overhead, knowing Lacey's room was silent and peaceful, that she was probably sleeping soundly, her beautiful face composed serenely in sleep.

The sleep of the innocent.

Scully pushed open the restaurant door and walked inside.

* * *

"Help me! Help me!"

The cabin was burning behind her. She had escaped from the flames, but she still struggled to breathe.

There was blood on Grandpa's chest. He was dying!

"Take the Bible, Lacey. Let it show you the way."

The shadows surrounding her began moving.

They started toward her, and she ran.

She heard pounding, footsteps following her.

She heard ragged breathing coming closer.

They were right behind her!

"Help me! Help me!"

"Wake up, Lacey!"

Lacey awakened with a start. She gasped at the shadow leaning over her bed, her heart pounding.

"Are you all right, dear?"

Lacey attempted a calming breath. She recognized the soft voice even before she her gaze penetrated the flickering light. It was Mary.

"I heard you calling for help. I thought you were sick, but you were having a nightmare."

"I know." Lacey breathed more deeply. "I'm sorry if I woke you up."

"No, that's all right. I'm here whenever you need me." Mary's tone was motherly as she probed gently, "You seem so restless at night. Are you bothered often by those frightening dreams?"

"Just sometimes, but I'll be fine, now. Please, go back to bed. I'm sorry I disturbed you."

"It isn't because you don't feel safe in this house...I mean, you do know no one can hurt you here, don't you? Scully was concerned how you'd do here, but I reassured him that you'd be fine, that I'd look out for you."

"I *am* fine. These are just dreams left over from my childhood. Scully understands that, but please don't mention it to him. I don't want him to worry."

Mary's face moved into lines of concern. "I think I know Scully better than most of the people in town because I've known him since he came here with only a few dollars in his pocket and a sack full of determination. He was living in this boarding house when my husband died. He helped me in so many ways, although he wouldn't especially like it if he knew I'd told anyone about it. He's a fine man, even if there are some in town who wouldn't agree."

"I agree."

"I know you do, dear." Mary smiled, then said, "Would you like me to get you anything before I go back to bed…some tea, perhaps?"

"I'm fine, really."

"Well, if there's nothing else I can do for you now, just call me if you should need me."

"Thank you."

Lacey closed her eyes when Mary pulled the door shut, taking the flickering light with her. She let out a shaken breath. The nightmares were worsening, becoming more frequent and more terrifying. They were changing in ways that she couldn't quite define.

She didn't understand the reason they continued to plague her.

She didn't know how to handle the panic they stirred.

Lacey brushed away the tear that squeezed out from underneath her closed eyelids.

And she didn't know how to make them stop.

* * *

"You're looking mighty pretty this morning, Lacey."

Lacey forced a smile for Todd's benefit. He had been sitting at a corner table waiting for her to make her way across the crowded restaurant floor toward him. She had not been particularly efficient at her job after the sleepless night past, and he had been extremely patient, as had Sadie's other customers. But she was not patient with herself.

Lacey withheld the sudden rush of tears. She was a fraud. She had taken on adult responsibilities, but it was all a pretense. She couldn't even defend herself against her own childish dreams.

"Lacey…?"

Lacey snapped back to the present. "I'm sorry, Todd. What can I get for you this morning?"

"The usual."

"Bacon, eggs, some of Sadie's fine biscuits and coffee."

"Right." Todd reached for the hand Lacey rested on his table. He held it lightly for a moment, his expression earnest. "I've been missing you these past few days, Lacey. I was wondering when we would get to spend some time together again—maybe a picnic. The stage won't be running this Saturday and my boss won't need me."

"Saturday…" Lacey raised her palm to her forehead. She was perspiring. It was so warm. She shook her head. "I can't really say. I have some things to do."

"Maybe if I talk to you later on in the week."

"Yes, maybe then."

Lacey made a fast retreat to the counter where Sadie seemed to be laying out filled plates with astonishing speed. She placed Todd's order there, then glanced at the door and heaved a sigh of relief when Scully walked in and sat at his customary table. The sight of him somehow calmed her.

"Lacey…"

Lacey turned at Sadie's summons.

"Jack's steak, and Shorty's ham and eggs are ready."

Lacey delivered them to the waiting customers. Endless moments passed before she reached Scully's table, but he wasn't smiling. His expression spoke for itself.

Anticipating his comment, she said, "Good morning, but don't say what you're thinking. You don't have to."

"You don't look rested."

He had said it.

Ignoring him, she asked, "What do you want for breakfast?"

"Didn't you sleep well last night?"

"Hotcakes and eggs? Do you want ham, too?"

Scully glanced at Todd's table and frowned.

"Don't look at Todd like that. He certainly isn't the one who's exhausting me." Realizing she had made an admission she hadn't wanted to make, Lacey said, "All right, so I'm tired. Maybe I just work too hard."

"Maybe."

Scully was still searching her face with his sober, gray-eyed stare. Its touch was almost palpable as it brushed her forehead, her eyes, her cheek. She felt a sudden rush of heat as it halted briefly on her lips.

"I'll get you your breakfast."

Lacey beat a hasty retreat from Scully's table. He was going to ask questions again, questions she didn't want to answer.

But questions or not, Lacey's heart was pounds lighter when she reached the counter. Scully was there. That meant everything would be all right.

* * *

She had deliberately ignored his questions. She was telling him in so many words he didn't have the right to ask them.

She was slipping away from him.

Scully sat at the table as Lacey hurried back to the counter at Sadie's summons. He glanced at Todd. There was no mutual exchange of friendly greetings when their glances met. Todd resented his association with Lacey. He admitted to himself for the first time that the feeling was mutual.

Scully considered that spontaneous thought. Actually, he had always considered Todd Fulton a nice fellow, but it bothered him that Todd might be the reason Lacey had begun shutting him out. He also knew it was unrealistic of him to think Lacey would always remain as close to him as she had been that first week after she arrived in Weaver. While living upstairs in the room near his at the Nugget, his had been the first face she had seen upon awakening, and the last face she had seen at night. It hadn't mattered to him that the reverse hadn't been true for him. As many familiar faces, both male and female, that he had seen before his long night was over, Lacey's was always the last face he saw before closing his eyes at night.

It was a beautiful face, all the more endearing for the unspoken bond that had existed between them from virtually the first moment she had returned home.

Yet although he still saw Lacey every morning and they were again eating their evening meals together, he still sensed a subtle distance between them. Lacey was holding something back. He didn't know what it was, but he knew it weighed heavily on her mind. He felt it. It was part of the bond they shared…innate…a part of him, just like Lacey, herself.

Those thoughts remained on Scully's mind as he finished

his breakfast. Without any further reason to remain, he placed his coins on the table and left with a tip of his hat to Lacey and Sadie alike.

He had been late arriving at the restaurant. He had stopped at Sheriff Connolly's office to drop off Riley Martin's gun and tell him what to expect. Riley was no stranger to the sheriff. Scully's mouth twitched wryly with the admission that he wasn't, either.

"Scully, wait a moment!"

The familiar voice turned Scully toward Mary McInnes as she hurried toward him. She glanced at the restaurant, then drew him out of its view and away from the early morning sidewalk traffic as she said softly, "I wouldn't want Lacey to see me talking to you."

Scully went still at Mary's anxious expression. His heart began a sudden pounding.

"What happened?"

"Nothing happened. I didn't mean to frighten you, Scully." Mary hesitated, then continued in a rush, "I've been debating whether I should talk to you about this for days, but last night—"

"What happened last night?"

Mary's lined face grew earnest. "I suppose you know about Lacey's nightmares."

Scully did not reply.

"They're probably nothing new to you, since Lacey's obviously been having them for a long time. The only thing is…"

Scully waited with growing impatience as Mary floundered. He prompted, "Lacey's always had the nightmares, since early childhood."

"They're getting worse. She cried out so loudly in her sleep last night that I went in to make sure she was all right.

I don't think anyone heard her but me, since her room is on the first floor close to mine, but she was terrified, Scully."

"What did she say?"

"She said the nightmares weren't a problem. She was fine." Of course.

"But she isn't fine. She's reliving that night when her grandfather was killed, and the dreams are becoming more intense. I could tell by her reaction to them. Something's bothering her, something she doesn't quite understand herself. She won't talk to me, Scully, but she trusts you implicitly. I think she'll talk to you if you try."

"I've tried, Mary."

"Then maybe there's something else you can do. She's a lovely girl, but she needs help." Mary hesitated again. "I didn't want to burden you with this. I know Lacey is close to the scriptures and she depends on them to console and guide her. I know for a fact that she's spent time talking to Reverend Sykes, but I don't think she feels as close to him as she does to you."

Scully said abruptly, "I'll take care of it, Mary."

"I hope you're not angry."

"No."

"If you choose to tell Lacey that I spoke to you, please tell her it was because I was concerned for her welfare."

"Lacey knows that. I know it, too. Thanks, Mary."

Scully watched as Mary returned to the boarding house. When he turned back toward the Nugget, his decision was made.

Blackie grasped Barret's arm, halting Barret on the street as he returned from his afternoon meal at home, and Barret struggled with soaring anger. His housekeeper had been particularly friendly upon his noontime arrival—her first offense. He had fought to conceal his contempt for her pride in the unimpressive dessert she claimed to have prepared especially for him.

The woman was as common as everyone else in Weaver, as were her culinary efforts. They would not have been considered fare fit for pack beasts at the gourmet restaurants he had frequented in San Francisco—restaurants he was *determined* he would patronize frequently again.

He had emerged back out into the afternoon sunshine and started toward his office with that resolution fresh in his mind. Blackie's unexpected appearance had not improved his disposition, and the touch of the fellow's less-than-clean hand on his arm had soured his disposition further.

Barret snapped, "Take you hand off me, Blackie. This isn't the place for us to discuss business."

Blackie's hand fell back to his side. Barret did not miss the dark look the man shot him when he said, "I went to your office, but you wasn't there. You wanted Larry and me to tell you more about what Lacey Stewart was doing at that church—"

"Be quiet, you fool!" Barret glanced around them, then continued, "Wait until we get back into the office."

Barret's lips twitched with anger at the sound of Blackie's footsteps following him on the boardwalk. He turned toward Blackie the moment the office door closed behind them and warned, "Don't ever do that again."

"Do what?"

"Accost me on the street."

"Accost…what are you talking about? I was just doing what you pay Larry and me for."

"I don't pay you to announce to the world that you're watching Lacey Stewart for me."

"Nobody heard me because nobody was listening."

Barret ground his teeth with frustration, then repeated, "Don't ever do that again, do you understand?"

"Yeah, I understand."

"So?"

"So, what?"

"What did you come to tell me?"

Blackie's bearded face darkened. "You wanted to know what Lacey was doing with those two saloon women at the church."

"So?"

"She's teaching them to read."

Barret did not immediately respond.

"And write."

Barret shook his head. "There has to be more to it than that."

"She reads the Bible to them, too."

"How do you know that?"

"Because Larry sneaked up to the window and peeked inside while I watched to make sure nobody saw him. He listened long enough to get a good idea what they was doing."

"Larry is stupid. He isn't capable of understanding the subtleties of situations. He's missing something."

"No, he ain't. He said those saloon women was working hard trying to write, even if he figured they was wasting their time."

"Wasting their time?"

"Like they need to know how to read or write with the kind of work they do. Besides, Larry and me don't know how to read or write, and we're doing fine."

Barret stared. Blackie truly was an imbecile.

Barret questioned, "When Larry was listening, did he hear Lacey ask the women any questions, or tell them she wanted them to find out anything for her?"

"No."

"How can you be so sure? Did you ask him?"

"Larry said they was learning to read and write. That was all."

Struggling to retain his patience, Barret asked, "Why didn't Larry come here himself and tell me what he heard?"

"He's watching Lacey, like you said—not letting her get out of our sight."

"You could've remained behind to watch Lacey so he could come."

"Yeah," Blackie sneered, "but Larry didn't take a bath yet, so he sent me."

Really. As if Blackie smelled any better.

Choosing to keep that thought to himself, Barret instructed, "She's up to something. She'll be ready to make her move, soon. Keep your eyes on her."

"Yeah…anything you say."

His temper exploding at Blackie's mocking tone, Barret retorted, "You and Larry are involved as deeply in this whole situation as I am, so watching Lacey Stewart should be as important to you as it is to me!"

"Sure."

Imbecile was too generous a description.

Barret strove to control his anger as he repeated, "Don't let her out of your sight."

"How many times are you going to say the same thing?"

"As many times as I have to in order to make you understand."

"Larry and me understand. We ain't dummies."

Sure.

Barret watched as Blackie walked out onto the street, slamming the office door behind him.

One thought remained in Barret's mind. He would soon have no recourse in what he must do.

* * *

Lacey glanced up at the position of the sun as it dropped past the midpoint in the clear sky. As she made her way back from the church at the conclusion of Rosie and Jewel's lesson, it occurred to her that she'd seen nothing but clear skies since she had returned to Weaver. She had somehow forgotten that detail during the long years spent at school in New York. A rainy spring and fall was more the norm in that city, with undependable weather in between. Somehow she'd forgotten how bright the Arizona sun was, how vast the sky could be, and how blue.

Careful's welcoming bray brought a smile to Lacey's lips as she turned into sight of the livery corral. The dear burro had been expecting her. It hadn't taken him long to become accustomed to her routine and to expect her visit on her way back to the boarding house each afternoon. However, Careful's uncanny comprehension of human activity had turned out to be a drawback for her in this particular case. She had known he would be waiting and had not wanted to disappoint him, even though she was exhausted after her sleepless night and wanted nothing more than to go back to her room to rest before she met Scully for supper.

Scully…so intent on her welfare, so perceptive, and so *annoyingly* outspoken in his observances. Lacey scratched Careful's muzzle and the patient animal practically smiled. The unusual attachment between them had resumed as if her ten-year absence did not exist for the burro. She could not express how much that simple continuity meant to her. It was a link to the past that she treasured and she—

"Lacey."

Lacey jumped with surprise when Scully walked out of the livery stable into her view. She gasped, "You startled me!"

"Did I?"

"You walk as silently as a cat. You'd make anybody jump."

"You're on edge because you're tired."

Lacey did not reply.

"Your nightmares are getting worse, aren't they?"

"Mary told you."

Scully did not confirm or deny.

"I frightened her, Scully. I'm sorry about that."

"There's only one way to stop those dreams. You know that as well as I do."

"I'm not ready, yet."

"You're as ready as you'll ever be."

"Besides, I don't have time. Sadie needs me at the restaurant."

"She can get Millie to replace you for a day."

"I have…things to do at the church."

"They can wait."

"No."

"Listen to me, Lacey. You won't be free of your nightmares until you face them head-on."

Lacey felt panic rising. "I won't go."

Scully's voice softened. "You don't have to be afraid. I'll be there."

"No, I can't."

"You have to face the shadows in your dreams sooner or later."

The sudden fear in Lacey's expression stopped Scully cold.

"What wrong, Lacey?"

"Nothing."

"Tell me."

"It's just…I don't know if I want to face them. The shadows scare me, Scully. I don't want to remember anything about them."

"Shadows can't hurt you."

"I know, but—"

"But what?"

Lacey's eyes filled. "You won't always be there for me, Scully. What will I do then?"

The question suddenly more than he could bear, Scully slid his arms around Lacey and drew her close. She trembled as he stroked her hair and said, "Who said I wouldn't always be there for you? That might be wishful thinking on the part of some young fellas in Weaver, but I expect to be around as long as you need me."

Lacey drew back from him. Suddenly embarrassed, she said, "Are you disgusted with me, Scully?"

"Disgusted?"

"I keep telling you I'm an adult and I'm responsible for myself, then I end up shaking like a child because of a dream."

Scully gripped her shoulders, forcing her gaze up to his when she looked away. He said, "Those nightmares aren't simple bad dreams. They're memories that have been lurking in the back of your mind for ten years, waiting to be finally put to rest. You have to remember whatever it is that's frightening you, or you'll never be free."

Lacey did not reply.

"I'll get the supplies together and tell Sadie to talk to Millie."

"I didn't say I'd go."

"We'll go tomorrow."

Silence.

"Tomorrow, Lacey."

Scully watched as Lacey turned and walked away. She did not look back.

Chapter Ten

She couldn't believe she was doing this. She didn't want to believe it.

Lacey glanced at Scully as he rode beside her on the trail lit by early morning sun. Scully sat his mount easily, his weathered hat pulled down low on his forehead to shade those sober gray eyes; his broad shoulders erect; his boots fitted firmly, but naturally, into the stirrups as his long legs hugged his mount's sides with instinctive skill.

It occurred to her that no one would believe this fit, alert cowboy was the same man whose dark, custom-tailored suit, brocade vest and dark Stetson normally marked him the owner of the area's largest and most successful saloon. Nor would they believe that the strong, callused hands presently holding the reins also dealt cards with consummate skill.

The truth was, Scully was at ease in whatever setting he chose, with a competence and self-confidence he had earned the hard way while overcoming difficult years.

Self-confidence in which Lacey was presently, sadly, lacking.

The day had barely dawned before Scully was at the boarding

house door with the day's supplies carefully packed on his saddle, and with Careful trailing behind. They had stopped only for breakfast before mounting up and leaving town. They had eaten breakfast in virtual silence, the same condition that had existed between them since Scully had insisted on the journey they were presently taking. They had been on the trail for hours with hardly a word spoken between them.

In thinking back, Lacey didn't remember actually agreeing to Scully's plan. He had merely announced during their supper meal the previous evening that the supplies would be ready for their journey in the morning, that Millie White would replace her at the restaurant while she was gone and they would be leaving at dawn.

She supposed her consent had come when she had slipped out of the boarding house after Scully left her there and had gone to the church to leave the day's lesson for Rosie and Jewel with Reverend Sykes.

She had returned to her room afterward and retired to her bed with true trepidation for the night to come. Yet, surprisingly enough, she had slept nightmare-free.

Lacey's mount moved relentlessly forward, appearing unaffected by the heat of the day even as perspiration beaded her forehead and upper lip. Scully looked her way unexpectedly. Their eyes met, and her throat choked tight.

That observant gaze.

Scully said, "We'll be stopping soon. There's a stream not far from here where the horses can drink and we can rest for a few minutes."

Lacey nodded, then looked away. She felt the weight of Scully's stare, but she refused to look back. Her eyes were still averted when they stopped and Scully dismounted.

Dismounting as well, Lacey walked to the narrow rivulet sparkling in the afternoon sunlight. She leaned down and splashed her face, then looked up to see Scully crouched beside her.

She was unprepared when Scully asked softly, "Are you still mad at me, Lacey?"

Mad at him?

Was she?

"I'm not angry, Scully. I'm just…" She took a breath. "I'm just *afraid*."

Her emotions bursting free with that admission, Lacey began sobbing in earnest. How could she make him understand that as much as she wanted to remember every detail of the time her grandfather and she had spent together, she feared remembering the night she had lost him?

But Scully's arms were around her. He was murmuring soft reassurances against her hair, and the realization belatedly dawned that she had no need for explanations, or the attempt to make Scully understand.

Because he understood instinctively—without any explanations at all.

"What's going on down there?"

Larry adjusted his spyglass and studied the shaded spot where Scully and Lacey had paused at the stream. His view was partially blocked by low-lying bushes thickly shielding the area, but that did not halt his response as he turned to his cohort and said, "What do you think's going on, Blackie? They're cooling off at the stream while we're baking out here in the hot sun."

Blackie grabbed the spyglass from his hand and focused it

carefully. He heard Blackie's low curse as he studied the scene, then lowered the glass and said, "It don't seem like they're going to be stopping there very long—just to water the horses and wet down a bit. I expect they'll be moving on soon."

"To find her grandfather's strike." Larry gave a harsh laugh. "You know what I think? I think there ain't no strike at all. I think that old coot Charlie Pratt never did strike it rich like the boss thinks. I think it was all in Pratt's head, and now it's stuck in the boss's head, too!"

"You're crazy."

"No, it's the boss who's crazy." When Blackie shook his head, negating his statement, Larry continued hotly, "If there was gold out there, how come we couldn't find it?"

"Because we didn't know where to look, that's why."

"We checked every inch of ground for weeks after we killed that old man. No, we couldn't find that gold because there wasn't any to find."

"That isn't what the boss thinks."

"He's crazy, I tell you! And since Lacey Stewart came back, he's been getting crazier."

"Maybe." Blackie lifted his hat and wiped his arm across his forehead. "And maybe not. All I know is that he puts money in my pocket, and that suits me fine."

"It don't suit me too fine. I don't like it out here, sizzling my heels in the sun while he sits back in his office, all cool and fine, waiting to tell us how dumb we are for not being able to find a claim that don't exist."

Blackie responded, "Did you ever stop to think that woman down there wouldn't be so determined to go back to a burned-out cabin in the middle of nowhere unless there was a good reason?"

"Her grandpa's buried out there."

Blackie's expression was skeptical. "Would you ride all the way out here just to look at a grave?"

Larry did not reply.

"And if you'd been living in a big city for ten years, and you grew up to look half as good as she does, would you come back to Weaver just to work in a restaurant?"

Still no reply.

"So maybe the boss ain't so crazy after all."

Larry's tight expression did not change as he replied, "All I know is that I'm getting tired of doing *hoity-toity* Gould's dirty work."

"But here you are, ain't you?"

Larry took an aggressive step. "You ain't thinking this whole thing through. What do you think the boss is going to do if he finds out there ain't no gold strike out there for him to cash in on?"

"I don't know, and I don't care. It's no skin off my nose either way."

"He ain't going to take it kindly, I'm telling you."

"Yeah…sure."

"There ain't no telling which way he'll jump when that happens."

"*If* it happens." Blackie raised the glass back to his eye, then reported, "They're leaving. Get yourself ready."

"For what?"

"We're going to sit ourselves down by that stream when they get far enough away, and we're going to cool ourselves off for a while."

"But I thought—"

"You thought, what—that I'd say we'd better keep on their

tails? What for? We know where them two are heading. We can catch up with them anytime we want. They won't get away from us."

Larry considered that thought, then grabbed the spyglass from Blackie's hand and raised it back to his eye. "Yeah, there they go, all right, traveling at a snail's pace. We can be right behind them when they get to the grave with no trouble at all."

Larry turned back to Blackie, smiling for the first time as he said, "Now, that's using your head."

He must've been imagining things.

Scully scrutinized the terrain around him cautiously as the sun burned hotly on his shoulders. The first portion of Lacey's and his journey had been fraught with tension, a part of it of his own making. He'd been unable to pinpoint the source of his discomfort, but a sense of being watched had plagued him, setting him on edge. The sensation had waned inexplicably as they neared their destination.

He had begun wondering if the heat had been getting to him, and had then dismissed the thought, grateful that the former strain that had existed between Lacey and him earlier had also dissipated.

I'm afraid.

With those two words, the dam had broken, releasing Lacey's fears. The truth was, he had known it would be difficult for her to return to the site of her grandfather's grave, yet he had not realized the depth of her misgivings.

Nor had he realized how difficult it would be to release Lacey after he had held her comfortingly close again in his arms.

Emotion twisted tight inside Scully. He was disturbingly affected by Lacey's distress, so much so that he knew he would gladly have assumed her fears if he could, no matter how great their proportions, but that would've been too easy. Instead, he was forced to watch while she suffered through her terrors.

He was beginning to learn it was the hardest thing he had ever done.

Scully glanced at the mountains in the distance. They were drawing closer. They'd be arriving at the site of Charlie's cabin soon. He looked at Lacey where she rode silently beside him. She would soon be faced with memories she had avoided for years.

How would they affect her?

What would she do?

Scully knew only one thing for sure. He would take care of her—and, yes, he would protect her with his life.

Rosie's forced smile began failing as the sun fell from its apex. She had started work early at the Nugget, only a few hours after Jewel and she had gone to the church and found Reverend Sykes waiting to tell them Lacey couldn't make their lesson that day, but that she had prepared some work for them to do. They had accepted the paperwork Lacey had left and had departed immediately, uncomfortable in the pastor's presence.

They had been stopped by Bill, the bartender, on the way back to their boarding house. He had notified them that in Scully's absence, he needed them to come in to work a little early.

The realization that both Lacey and Scully were gone had momentarily panicked her. The safety that the Nugget afforded had relieved that anxiety temporarily. However, the extended hours spent there had come back to haunt her.

The surrounding din rebounded, and Rosie's head pounded in time with the sound. She took an unsteady breath as she looked out at lengthening afternoon shadows on the street, then stood stock-still as her stomach lurched perilously close to revolting.

Rosie attempted to steady the queasy waves engulfing her. She was more upset than she realized, and her stomach was paying the price. The problem was, she had just begun believing things could change.

It had been incredible to her that she could actually write her name. She had also been touched in a way she had never been before when she realized that Lacey was almost as excited as she at her progress.

Then Scully had stood up for her, and when he had sent Riley packing, she had felt almost *worthy*.

Now they were both gone.

Rosie glanced to where Jewel was talking with a bearded, smiling wrangler. She knew Jewel felt somehow responsible for her welfare. She wasn't quite sure how that had come about, except that Jewel and she had become closer than most sisters she knew. Yet, if only for that reason, she didn't want Jewel taking the risk of getting involved in her problems.

Her stomach lurched, and Rosie hastened out through the swinging doors onto the street. She took a few unsteady steps toward the alleyway and gulped in fresh air free of the smoke and closeness of the saloon. She caught her breath when she was jerked unexpectedly backward, then dragged into the shadows between the buildings. She shuddered when a familiar voice whispered into her ear, "You ain't too smart, are you, Rosie?"

Riley.

Riley turned her around to face him as he said, "Did you

think your protector would spend all his time looking out for you? No, he's got better things to do, and you ain't one of them."

Rosie struggled to free herself from his painful grip as she said, "What are you doing here, Riley? Scully's inside right now. If I call him—"

"He ain't in town, and you know it!"

Rosie's blood went cold.

"Did you think I wouldn't hear about how he's out somewhere having fun with that fancy woman he's been supporting all these years? He chose her over you, Rosie, and he left you for me."

"It's not like that—none of it! You're twisting things like you always do."

"But he's not here now, is he?"

Failing to free herself, Rosie asked abruptly, "What do you want from me, Riley? Everything you said to me about how much you love me was a lie. You know it, and I know it."

"No, it wasn't. You're just saying that now because somebody made you think you can do better than me." Riley crushed her closer. "You need to get it through your head that there ain't nobody who'll ever treat a Nugget woman any better than I treat you."

"Let me go." Rosie refused to listen. "Let me go!"

"I ain't letting you go, and there's no way you can make me." Still holding her cruelly tight, he said, "Set your mind to it. You're *my* girl, Rosie. You're going to stay *my* girl until I'm ready to let you go."

"No, she isn't."

Rosie gasped at the unexpected sound of Jewel's voice.

Her expression emotionless, Jewel entered the alleyway and advanced toward them. Her hand closed around the handle of her concealed derringer as she walked closer. She had known it would come to this sooner or later, just as she had known what she would do when it did.

"Get back into the saloon, Jewel." Rosie's voice shook revealingly. "Riley and me are just talking."

The panic in Rosie's tone was obvious as Jewel continued her approach, ordering softly, "Let Rosie go, Riley."

"Sure—like I'm going to take orders from a Nugget woman like you."

Jewel's finger curled around the trigger of her derringer. The metal had warmed to her skin. It felt strangely comfortable in her hand, as if it were a part of her.

She repeated more softly than before, "Let her go."

"I told you I ain't letting her—"

Riley's reply was cut short when Buddy slipped unexpectedly into the alleyway beside him and ripped Rosie from his arms. Thrust back against the Nugget wall, Riley stared, aghast, gasping as the lean cowpoke glared at him warningly with his gun drawn.

Jewel held her breath as Buddy directed, "You and Rosie, get back into the saloon—now. I'll take care of this."

Jewel shook her head. "I'm not going anywhere."

"Get out of this alleyway, both of you."

Jewel stared at Buddy. She had never seen him like this before, so cold, so…determined. She said abruptly, "Let's go, Rosie."

"No! I want to—"

"Let's go!"

Ignoring her protest, Jewel pushed Rosie out onto the boardwalk ahead of her. Time stood still as Rosie and she stood rigidly inside the swinging doors, waiting. Jewel released a pent-up breath just short of a sob when Buddy finally nudged his way through the swinging doors into sight.

Jewel searched Buddy's expression, inwardly trembling. She hardly breathed when he directed his first comment to Rosie, saying, "You don't have to worry about Riley anymore."

Jewel saw the relief that flickered across Rosie's face as she mumbled her thanks. Buddy then walked to the bar, tossed Riley's gun to the startled bartender and said, "Get rid of that for me, will you, Bill?"

Jewel asked shakily when he turned back toward her, "What happened?"

"Riley's gone."

"Gone?"

"I told him not to come back again…not if he expects to keep breathing."

Rosie gasped.

Jewel remained silent.

His expression pure ice in the brief silence that followed, Buddy then said, "It's over."

The desert landscape slipped into afternoon shadows as Lacey turned a shaken glance toward the remains of her grandfather's cabin a distance away. She clutched the Bible to her heart.

I can do everything through Christ, who strengthens me.

Lacey had read that passage often. She believed it sincerely, yet as the area became more familiar, trepidation had made persistent inroads into her mind. She searched out Scully's figure as he tended to the horses, then glanced away.

The landscape—barrel, cholla and prickly pear cactus; giant saguaros outlined against purple-tinted mountains; with palo verde and mesquite trees in between—all had gained gradual familiarity as they had continued their steady approach to this spot. Yet her first view of the charred debris of her grandfather's cabin earlier had sliced open old wounds that had begun bleeding profusely.

Memories had returned in a swelling rush, reviving the beauty of long days spent under Grandpa's loving care: hours passed wandering the desolate terrain as she followed her grandfather on his prospecting excursions into the brush; leisurely moments spent while Grandpa wielded his pick and shovel with relentless determination; the discovery of shaded places where she would close her eyes and rest through the heat of the day with Careful at her side.

The trickle of a narrow stream nearby had stirred recollections of wading delightedly as Careful drank, of Grandpa's voice calling her back to the cabin and the sound of Careful's hoofbeats behind her as she returned. She had remembered simple but joyful celebrations, while Grandpa played his fiddle and she sang loudly and enthusiastically, songs ranging from "Oh, Susannah" to "Amazing Grace." Then, best of all, she had recalled the quiet times as twilight changed into night, when she would sit on Grandpa's lap and he would read to her from the Bible—familiar passages, precious words on which he had based the conduct of his life.

But Grandpa was gone. His voice had stilled, and the music was silent. All that remained were shadows.

Lacey turned abruptly toward the grave marked by a simple, wooden cross. The shadow enveloping it was somehow symbolic. Her recollection of that fiery night still limited, she remembered the roaring flames, her grandfather's whispered words and a pain that was more than physical as she had watched him breathe his last breath.

Would she ever remember more?

Did she truly *want* to remember?

Unaware that she was trembling until Scully's strong arm slipped around her, Lacey melted into his strength. She could feel Scully's breath against her hair as she whispered against his chest, "Why would anyone want to kill my grandfather, Scully?"

"I don't know." Scully's husky whisper rang with frustration. "Nobody could figure that out. Your grandfather wasn't rich in much of anything except his faith and his belief in the future."

"It's funny...all the happy memories flooded back at first, but now everything's changing."

"There's nothing to worry about here, Lacey." Scully's deep voice was earnest. "You know I wouldn't let anything hurt you."

Lacey drew back with an effort at a smile. "When will we be leaving?"

"We'll leave anytime you want to—sooner or later. It's up to you."

Lacey began slowly, "I know why we came, and I appreciate all you've done." Lacey could not restrain an apprehensive glance around her. "I've remembered so much already, and I—"

Somehow unable to finish that statement, Lacey said simply, "Thank you, for helping me remember so many of the good memories, but I'd like to go back now."

"All right, just as soon as we have something to eat."

Scully slipped his arm around her as they walked back to the horses. Lacey tried to relax. She had forgotten how bright the desert sun could be, how hot it could get...and how desolate this location was.

She had forgotten so many things…just as she had forgotten the memories that still lurked in the shadows of her mind.

"Warm water and jerky." Larry turned and spat on the ground in contempt. He looked back up at Blackie and motioned toward the campfire in the distance. "But they're down at that stream refreshing themselves in the water and eating like they're out on a picnic."

"Stop complaining, will you, Larry? We can't afford to go nowheres near that stream and chance them seeing us, and you know it." Blackie tossed away his last bite of jerky and stood up in exasperation. "You ain't been the same since that day the boss told you to take a bath."

"That don't have nothing to do with it!"

"Don't it? You ain't had a good word for anything he's told us to do since."

"Are you telling me this whole trip isn't a waste of time? Scully and the woman ain't doing nothing down there but walking around, staring at that charred wood for a while, then going back to look at that grave. From the way Scully was packing up a while ago, they're not going to be staying much longer, neither."

"You should be happy about that."

"I ain't, because the boss ain't going to be happy when we tell him Lacey didn't even make an attempt to locate that strike."

"Maybe she saw more than she's letting on."

"It didn't look like it to me."

"Maybe she don't want to share that strike with Scully, no matter what he did for her."

"That don't seem likely, either."

"Likely or not, you don't know nothing more than I do!"

His patience short, Blackie said, "I don't want to hear nothing more about it. The boss said to follow them, so we followed them. He said to report back to him, and we'll report back to him what we saw—which was nothing. And that's the end of it."

"He's not going to let it go, I tell you."

"I don't care if he does or not."

"He's crazy. There's no telling what he'll do."

"You're the one who's crazy."

"Yeah...sure." Larry turned his back on his cohort, then muttered into the silence that followed, "He's crazy, I'm telling you. We're going to have to watch our step."

The shadows of the endless day were lengthening and the streets of Weaver would soon be brightly lit. The Gold Nugget was already ablaze with light and merriment, but the atmosphere between the three sitting at a table in the corner was restrained after the tense confrontation with Riley earlier.

All three turned toward the smiling cowpoke who unexpectedly tapped Rosie's shoulder and said, "How about a dance, Rosie?"

Rosie nodded. She turned with a forced smile toward Jewel and Buddy as she took the cowboy's arm and said, "I'll see you later."

Jewel swallowed a strange sadness as Rosie walked away. Rosie was Rosie. She'd make the best of things, if only to alleviate their concern.

Jewel looked up at Buddy as he moved his chair closer. She felt the press of his warmth against her and her heart skipped a beat as she forced herself to say, "Thank you, Buddy."

"For what?"

"You know the answer to that question. If you hadn't showed up when you did, things might be a lot different right now."

Buddy whispered soberly, "You're thanking me for stopping you from what you intended to do to Riley out there, so I'm telling you not to thank me for it. I didn't do it for you, or for Rosie, either. I did it for myself."

"Buddy—"

"You would've shot him."

"I just—"

"Don't deny it. I know about that hidden gun you carry, remember? But I don't understand how you got it into your head that it's your job to fight Rosie's battles for her."

"Rosie made a mistake trusting Riley, and I'm not going to watch Riley make her pay over and over for it. She doesn't deserve that."

"You don't deserve a lifetime of paying for Rosie's mistakes, either. That's what would happen if you did what you intended to do out there."

"She's my friend, Buddy. I won't desert her."

"So, Rosie's your friend. What am I to you, Jewel?"

Jewel averted her gaze.

"Look at me, Jewel." Buddy's gaze grew intense. "I want to know."

"You're my...friend."

"What else?"

"What else is there?"

"Don't pretend."

"I'm not pretending. I'm accepting a truth that you won't face. There *is* nothing else—there *can't be* anything else between you and me."

"I don't believe that."

"I told you, what you want and what I want are different."

"I don't believe that, either."

Jewel took a shaky breath, then continued in a voice barely audible over the surrounding din, "I appreciate what you did, Buddy, more than you know, but it doesn't change anything. What I said may not be true for you, but it's true for me. If you can't accept that we already have all there can ever be between us, then you're wasting your time with the wrong woman."

"Are you telling me to find somebody else?"

A breathtaking pain stabbed sharply inside Jewel, so deeply that she was momentarily unable to respond. Regaining control, she whispered, "You're the only one who can answer that question."

Buddy's gaze lingered in the extended silence that followed Jewel's response. She saw his expression tighten as he drew himself slowly erect. She watched his gaze go cold. She felt a moment coming that she had always anticipated, yet now dreaded more than she had believed possible.

A voice at her elbow shattered the silence of the moment as a man interrupted to ask, "Hey, Jewel, Buddy's been monopolizing you long enough. How about a dance?"

Jewel glanced up at the grinning cowpoke. Willie Johnson was a nice fella, and dancing with the customers was her job.

Intensely aware that Buddy had remained silent, Jewel stood up, only to feel Buddy's touch restrain her as he stood up beside her. Her throat choked with emotion as Buddy responded softly in her stead, "Find yourself another girl, Willie. This one's mine."

Scully worked with the horses as they prepared to leave. Lacey scanned the landscape around her for a lingering look at the remains of the cabin that had once been her home and the lonely grave nearby. The shadows were lengthening too quickly to suit her and a strange agitation was expanding inside her at the thought of all that the darkness at this location might bring.

Lacey turned abruptly at the sound of Careful's bray and Scully's annoyed response to see the determined burro break unexpectedly away from his tether to start back toward the cabin debris.

Starting after him instinctively, Lacey reached the burro as he stopped beside the charred timbers. She reached for his broken tether only to freeze into motionlessness as familiar images began inundating her mind....

Flickering shadows and darkness...she needed to cover Grandpa. She couldn't leave him lying cold and alone.

But the shadows were moving. They were coming closer. She yelled at them to stay back, but fear gripped her throat and no sound emerged.

She started to run, then tripped and fell.

She got up to run again.

Grandpa, help me!

No, he was dead.

The shadows were right behind her.

They caught her by the hair!

Help me! Somebody, help me!

"Lacey, what's wrong?"

Breathless, shaking with terror, Lacey stirred from the on-slaught of the paralyzing images as Scully grasped her shoulders.

"What happened, Lacey?"

Lacey struggled for breath. She strained to focus on the

features of the man supporting her with his grip. It was Scully, and the threatening darkness had evaporated into the brightness of day.

"Are you all right, darlin'?"

Scully's rough palm stroked her cheek. He drew her closer as Lacey whispered, "The shadows almost caught up to me, Scully. I could feel their hands on my hair."

"You're safe now." Regret rang in his tone as he said, "I shouldn't have brought you here. Coming has only made things worse."

"No, I'm all right now." Lacey tried to smile. "It was only a flash of memory—something I have to learn to face."

"Not *only* a memory, Lacey."

Scully brushed her mouth unexpectedly with his, then whispered, "You don't have to be afraid anymore, not with me beside you. Remember that, darlin'. Keep it close to you."

Slipping his arm around her as he picked up Careful's tether, Scully urged Lacey back toward the horses.

Lacey felt no need to respond as they reached their mounts and Scully swung her up into the saddle. No words were necessary. She'd be all right now. Nothing could happen to her with Scully so near.

Besides, he had kissed her.

And…he had called her "darlin'."

Lacey had stopped shaking.

As they rode, Scully looked at Lacey. She had not spoken a word since they started back toward Weaver. Nor had she taken her eyes from the trail ahead.

Scully remembered with a tight knot deep inside him the way Lacey had turned to him in her fear. She had looked up at him with the same trust in her eyes that he had seen that first day so many years ago.

And he had drawn her close instinctively.

He recalled the brush of her fair hair against his chin as he had held her against him. The memory of her sweet scent stirred him, as did recalling the warmth of her lips as he had brushed them with his own.

She was so beautiful and so innocent…and so terrified of shadows that stalked her darkness.

Scully unconsciously touched the gun on his hip. He looked at the Bible that Lacey gripped tightly as they rode.

A potent combination.

Scully admitted to himself with sudden, silent candor that there was nothing or no one who meant more to him than Lacey did.

"They didn't do nothing, I tell you!"

Incredulous, Barret stared at his two hirelings. He attempted to read their expressions as shadows held them in dark relief in the doorway of his home, but it was to no avail.

Both frustrated and grateful that his housekeeper had left for the day, Barret ushered the two men inside. He glanced at their grimy boots as they carelessly tracked residue from the livery stable across his spotless hallway floor.

Unable to bear another step, Barret slammed the front door closed behind them and ordered, "That's far enough. Now repeat what you just said."

Blackie spoke up, his weak grin displaying an uneven row of yellow teeth as he said, "How many ways do we have to say it, boss? Scully and his girlfriend just got back to Weaver from the old man's burned-out cabin. We came back a safe distance behind them. We didn't let them out of our sight for a minute, like you said, but we ain't got nothing to tell you. Them two didn't do nothing at the cabin but stand around."

"Impossible. They didn't go there without a reason."

"Well, that's all they did. The woman and Scully went to stand beside the old man's grave for a bit, then they wandered around what was left of the cabin."

"They didn't check a map…search out the nearby terrain…trek up farther into the wilderness."

"No."

"Tell me exactly what they did from the moment they got there."

Blackie shot Larry a glance before replying, "Like I said, they looked at what was left of the cabin, then they looked at the grave."

"And? And?"

"They talked. They went to get water from the stream. They made their camp. They ate. Then they packed up and left."

"You weren't watching closely enough."

"We didn't miss nothing."

"They must've seen you watching them."

"They didn't see nothing. We was too careful."

"The woman was the one you needed to watch closely. What did she do?"

"She didn't do nothing but hold onto that Bible every minute she was there. She hardly let it out of her hand, even when she took that burro to the stream to drink…even when she walked around the grave, and all the while Scully was sticking to her like glue."

"What do you mean?"

"They was talking to each other all the time, and Scully didn't let her out of his sight."

"Even when she was reading the Bible?"

"I told you—"

"That's it!" Barret felt a surge of pure jubilation as the thought struck him. "The secret is in the Bible. The old man must've drawn a map to his claim in it, and his grand-daughter was doing her best to coordinate the direction without letting Scully see what she was up to."

"No, I don't think so, she—"

"I'm not paying either of you to think." Barret's glance was scathing. "I'm the one who does the thinking, and I'm telling you the secret to that old man's claim is in that Bible."

Barret paused. His heart was racing. Ten long years of staring at that gold nugget in his drawer was about to come to fruition.

He declared, "I want that Bible."

Speaking up for the first time, Larry said, "And we're supposed to get it for you? How're we supposed to do that? She always has it with her."

"Always? She doesn't take it with her when she goes to work at the restaurant in the morning, does she?"

"No, but—"

"Get it then."

"That won't be so easy. She—"

"I didn't say it would be easy. I just told you to get it."

Barret noted the glances the two men exchanged, and his temper flared. "Is that so hard to understand? Go to the boarding house when she leaves, find the Bible, and bring it to me!"

"What about Old Lady McInnes?"

"That's your problem. I want that Bible in my hands tomorrow."

"But—"

"Tomorrow."

Barely in control of his agitation, Barret watched as Blackie and Larry walked out. His patrician face flushed, he told himself he need be patient only a little longer. His hirelings were dolts, but they were more than capable of the task he had set for them. They were also necessary for the manual labor that would be needed to verify the strike before he could register it in his name. He'd dispense with them when they weren't needed any longer.

And good riddance.

Barret smiled at the thought. Yes, a very good riddance.

It was night when Scully faced Lacey beside her boarding house door. They had returned to Weaver and had gone to the restaurant for a warm meal, which Lacey had picked at sparingly. It was now time to say good-night.

But Lacey was frowning when she looked up at him. Her gaze lingered on his face and Scully felt the knot inside him tighten. The distance they had covered and Lacey's confrontation with the past had been emotionally exhausting, but, strangely, he had treasured every moment. He didn't want to leave her to go alone to her room where the demons of her dreams might haunt her again. He wanted to keep her close to him, to know that she'd always be near.

The direction of his thoughts brought a frown to Scully's brow as well. He said gruffly, "You should go right to bed. You're tired and you're going to have to be up early in the morning."

"I suppose." Lacey hesitated. She glanced in the direction of the Gold Nugget. Music and laughter spilled out through its portals, echoing on the night breeze as she said with a forced smile, "I guess you'll be busy for a while though."

Scully shrugged. "Maybe."

Lacey said unexpectedly, "I'm sorry for all the problems I caused you out there today."

"You'll never be a problem to me."

Scully noted the uncertainty in Lacey's expression when she nodded and looked away. He said, "About your nightmares, Lacey—"

Lacey's gaze snapped back up to his.

"If you'd feel better sleeping at the Gold Nugget until they fade, I could ask Helen to come back to stay for a while."

"No." Lacey shook her head emphatically. "I'm responsible for handling my nightmares."

He asked softly, "Is it because you couldn't be comfortable at the Nugget anymore?"

"I didn't say that!" Lacey gasped. "I'd *never* say that."

"But…?"

"It would be taking a step backward when I'm supposed to be an adult."

"Don't make the mistake of thinking your behavior is immature, Lacey. Your nightmares are a small price to pay for survival."

"I should have them under control by now." Lacey paused. "I *will* get them under control."

"The nightmares are growing clearer because you're getting closer to remembering everything your mind couldn't face when you were a child. They'll end when your memory of that night fully returns."

Lacey replied, "Even if I'm not sure I want to remember it all?"

"I don't think you have a choice." Scully paused, then said, "I wish I could help you, darlin'. The only thing I can say is that I'll always be close by if you need me."

"I know."

Scully stroked a pale wisp of hair back from Lacey's cheek. He ached to hold her again in his arms, to feel her close against him. He lowered his head to brush her mouth lightly with his.

The brief, sweet taste of her…

Scully jerked back, then said gruffly, "Go to bed, Lacey." And when she hesitated, he added, "Go ahead. I don't want to leave until you're safely inside."

His heart was pounding when Lacey closed the boarding house door behind her, and Scully struggled to regain stability. What had he been thinking? It could never work…a man like him who had strayed so far from The Word during his lifetime, and a young woman who believed in every syllable that was written, and who lived her life accordingly.

Scully turned back toward the Gold Nugget with long, determined strides. No, it would never work.

"I told you he's crazy."

Blackie rubbed his stubbled jaw at Larry's comment and glanced back briefly in the direction of Barret's house as the two men turned onto Weaver's main street. He shrugged as he responded, "Maybe you're right, after all. The boss sure is acting crazy enough with all that talk about Lacey Stewart's Bible—"

"As if he's going to find a map to the old man's strike in it, even if we do get it for him."

"What do you mean, 'if'?"

Larry gave an amused snort. "So you're telling me you want to follow through on his orders?"

"Is there any reason we shouldn't?"

"Because he's crazy!"

"So?"

"What's going to happen when he gets that Bible and doesn't find what he wants in it?"

"That's his problem, not ours."

"I'm telling you, he's like a powder keg waiting to go off."

"I don't think so."

"I do."

"What's that supposed to mean?" Blackie halted abruptly on the walk. He turned to glare at the cowpokes behind them who had walked up their heels, then looked back at Larry and lowered his voice as the cowpokes walked past. "Are you telling me you don't want any part of getting that Bible for him?"

"I don't know."

"Well, I do. I'm going to get it for the boss *because* he's been the boss for the last ten years, his money's good and even when things didn't go as planned, he handled it. Yeah, he might be slipping toward the edge with the way he's talking, but it'll be simple enough to walk away without nobody even giving us a thought if it all turns out to be a problem. In the meantime, I'm going to ride this gravy train as long as I can. If that means getting him that Bible, that's all right with me."

Larry shrugged.

"What're you saying now?"

"I guess you're right. Getting that Bible ain't the hardest thing he ever asked us to do."

"As a matter of fact, it'll be easy—especially since we know Lacey's room is nice and handy on the first floor of the boarding house."

"With Old Lady McInnes standing watch."

"I can take care of that."

"You can?"

"Just watch me."

Yea, though I walk through the valley of the shadow of death, I shall fear no evil: for thou art with me; thy rod and thy staff, they comfort me.

Lacey raised her head from her Bible and glanced out into the darkness through the window of her room. The day of Scully's and her trek into the wilderness was coming to an end as she read the 23rd Psalm. She had read it countless times before, but the words had never struck as close to her heart as they did that night.

Music from the Gold Nugget wafted in on the night breeze, and her mind wandered.

Thy rod and thy staff, they comfort me.

Scully's and her visit to the devastating terror of her childhood had resulted in the return of memories, both good and bad. Although shadows still remained, the experience had also proved to her beyond doubt that the Lord had chosen Scully to be the unlikely *rod and staff* to guide and comfort her. She was grateful—but she was keenly aware that her feelings for Scully were rapidly surpassing ordinary gratitude.

Lacey raised trembling fingers to her lips. The touch of Scully's kiss was still vividly real, raising a desire within her that was just as vivid and real. She had wanted to slide her arms around Scully's neck and draw him closer, to feel his mouth press more tightly to hers. Yet Scully had drawn back from their kiss so abruptly.

When she had previously declared her platonic love for him, he had responded in kind, and she had known he spoke truthfully. That bond remained firm and unbreakable—but this was more.

Uncertain, Lacey clutched her Bible more tightly. As always, when she did, it was as if she could feel Grandpa's presence, as if his gnarled hand again held hers. She treasured that link to the dear man she had lost in the violence of that fiery night.

She missed his counsel.

She missed his solace.

She missed...him.

Scully's image returned at that moment, so intensely bright in her mind's eye that Lacey caught her breath. Yes, she had lost Grandpa, but Scully now stood stalwart at her side. He would never desert her.

That thought a somehow aching consolation, Lacey stood up and walked to her bed. She placed her Bible on the night-stand. She then lowered the lamp, lay down, and drew the coverlet up across her shoulders as music from the Gold Nugget echoed through her room.

"He loves you, Jewel."

Jewel paused in the doorway of her room. She had come in late after spending some private time with Buddy after her work at the Nugget was done—private hours that she told herself meant nothing more to her than those she had spent with other men before him. But it had been harder than usual to part from Buddy after his tenderness, after his loving words—words she had heard before and would not allow herself to make the mistake of believing.

Rosie had been waiting for her in her room. Rosie had greeted her with the words she had just spoken so solemnly.

Jewel pushed her bedroom door closed behind her and

said, "Buddy loves me, huh? Didn't you learn anything with Riley? How many times did he say he loved you? How many times did he say he needed you?"

"That's different. Riley's a liar. He doesn't love anybody but himself. I didn't know it then, but I know it now. Besides, Riley never said he wanted to marry me."

Jewel went still. "How'd you know Buddy wants to marry me?"

"So he *did* ask you."

"So you were guessing."

"Yeah, but it wasn't hard to figure out. It's easy to see the kind of fella Buddy is, and nobody can miss the way he looks at you." Rosie paused. "He risked his life when he faced Riley down, Jewel. He did it for you—not for me."

Jewel did not respond, allowing Rosie to say, "Buddy saw the look on your face, and he heard the threat in Riley's voice. He stepped in before you could get hurt. I'm telling you, if I had a man like that wanting to marry me—"

"What Buddy and I do is none of your business, Rosie."

"Just like what Riley and I do is none of *your* business, you mean?"

When Jewel did not answer, Rosie stood up and said, "I don't mean to seem ungrateful, Jewel. You got in the middle of things for me, and if you didn't and Buddy hadn't interfered, I don't know what would've happened."

"Riley's not a fool. Scully backed him off the first time, and Buddy took care of the rest. Riley won't be back because he knows what'll be waiting for him if he does."

"That's right, Buddy took care of the rest—and he'd take care of you, too, if you'd let him."

"I don't need anybody to take care of me."

"Why are you so stubborn, Jewel? Buddy loves you!"

"I don't believe in love."

Silent for a moment, Rosie said, "I don't think I could live with believing that."

"So you're telling me *you* believe in love after you've been lied to and tossed aside by every man who ever said those words to you?"

"Those words do mean something to some people."

"Oh, I forgot. You're the expert."

Rosie glanced away and Jewel took a conciliatory step toward her. "I'm sorry. I shouldn't have said that. It's just that no man I've ever trusted has proved worth his salt, so I've learned to depend only on myself."

"Buddy's not like that."

"No, I don't really think he is." Startling Rosie with those words, Jewel blinked back the moisture that had sprung into her eyes and said, "But if he isn't, he deserves better than getting stuck with a Gold Nugget woman for the rest of his life." Jewel forced an expression of emotionless acceptance as she continued, "Buddy will get tired of waiting when he figures out I'm not what he thinks I am. Then he'll find himself a woman who's everything that I'm not. Until then, whether it's right or wrong, I'll enjoy things as they are. Can you understand that, Rosie?"

Her eyes moist, Rosie rasped, "I can understand it, but I don't think—"

"Don't think, Rosie. Just let me be. Will you do that for me?"

"Jewel…"

Jewel waited for Rosie to continue. She stood still as a tear slipped down Rosie's cheek. She remained silent as Rosie hugged her tightly, then slipped out of the room without another word.

Chapter Eleven

Mary McInnes looked at the disreputable-looking fellow standing on her doorstep, then at the sun that had barely risen in the morning sky. It was early…too early to open the door to an unwashed undesirable like Blackie Oaks, and *far* too early to be subjected to his overwhelmingly unpleasant body odor.

Mary's lips tightened. She could never understand the tolerance the good people of Weaver had for this man and his partner. Nor, for that matter, could she understand the respect most townsfolk had for Barret Gould, the man who "so generously" employed Blackie and his partner at odd jobs. As far as she was concerned, the town of Weaver would be better off without the three of them. For that reason, she had never been overly friendly with any of them—and for that reason she had been surprised to find Blackie standing at her door so early in the morning. She had been even more stunned at his question.

Somehow incredulous, Mary shook her head. "You're asking me if I have a room to let to you in my boarding house, Mr. Oaks?"

"My name is Blackie, ma'am." Blackie's mouth widened

in an unappealing smile as he continued, "I heard in town that you had a room available, and I rushed right over here to see if I could get it."

"There must be some mistake. I don't have any empty rooms. Almost all my boarders are of long standing."

"You're sure…I mean, maybe somebody told you they might be moving, or maybe—"

"Nobody's moving out of my boarding house at this time. You were misinformed." Mary took a backward step in an attempt to avoid the man's aroma. Unable to escape it, she brought the conversation to a quick halt by saying, "I'm sorry you wasted your time. Good day."

"Wait a minute, ma'am!" Blackie jammed his foot onto the doorway, preventing Mary from closing the door. He smiled at her annoyance as he said, "I've been hearing about the great meals you serve your boarders. Even if you don't have a room to let, I was wondering if you'd have room at your table for me and my partner on a regular basis. We ain't been getting too many decent meals lately, and we'd be willing to pay any reasonable price you'd set."

"That's out of the question."

"Why? I mean, couldn't I talk you in to it?"

"No, definitely not. Sadie serves very good meals at her restaurant, and she serves everyone. You should have no complaints if you go there. Now, if you wouldn't mind taking your foot out of my door…"

"Oh, sorry, ma'am." Blackie smiled again. Mary cringed at the sight as he continued, "I just want to say that I hope you'll keep Larry and me in mind if things should change here."

"Yes…of course."

Mary closed the door with a firm click, and Blackie's smile

sagged into a sneer as he turned away. He wondered what the old lady would say if she knew that he wouldn't take a room in her old rattletrap of a house even if *she* paid *him*.

Still mumbling under his breath, Blackie turned the corner of the street and waited impatiently for the sound of a familiar footstep. As Larry came into view, he whispered, "Did you get it?"

"Yeah, I got it." Larry tapped the sack he held in his hand. "But I barely got in and out of the boarding house before the old lady came back into the hallway. It's a good thing that Bible was in clear view or by the time I found it, she might've seen me climbing back out through that window. Then I would've had to fix her good, and the boss wouldn't have liked that too much."

"The boss is going to be happy about this."

Larry gave him a look. "I wouldn't count on it. He ain't going to be too happy if he doesn't find the old man's map in there."

"And if he does find what he's looking for?"

Larry did not bother to reply.

Barret paced his office floor, then glanced out the window at the sunlit morning street beyond. He was perspiring profusely. He glanced at the small wall mirror in passing, and noted that sweat was leeching through the underarms of his custom-fitted jacket in the most common way.

With a grunt of disgust, he pulled off his jacket and tossed it onto the chair, then pushed back a straying strand of dark hair and mopped his handkerchief across his brow. Work was piling up on his desk...mundane work, boring work, in a town that was just as mundane and boring, and which he had barely tolerated for the past ten, endless years. He had come

to his office without stopping to eat the breakfast his housekeeper had prepared, and had been forced to suffer her disapproving glances as he left. He had been waiting for what
seemed an eternity for his hirelings to bring him the small
volume that would eliminate his present torment forever.

They still had not arrived.

Barret looked again out his office window, then stopped
dead in his tracks. He did not move until the door opened and
two unkempt figures pushed their way into the room. He
glanced down at the small sack Blackie carried, then asked,
"Did you get it?"

"Of course." Blackie's smile was cocky. "Did you think
we wouldn't?"

Barret snatched the sack from Blackie's hand with a sound
that clearly bespoke the response he had not needed to utter.
He looked into the sack and took a relieved breath. It was
there. He had it in his hands. The waiting would soon be over.

"Get out."

Blackie and Larry both frowned at Barret's tone, but they
did not move. He repeated, "You heard me."

Blackie blustered, "We thought you'd be—"

"I don't know what you both thought, and neither do I care.
I intend to examine this prize you've brought me *privately,*
without interruption. That means, I will do it behind closed
doors with the drapes drawn. Do you understand?"

"Yeah, but—"

"Privately means without either of you present."

"But—"

"I'll call you when I need you. Get out."

Blackie stumbled backward at Barret's admonition.
Tripping over Larry behind him, Blackie hardly waited for his

cohort to clear the doorway before pulling the door shut behind him.

Barret shook his head with disgust. Their behavior was so typical of their limited mentality that it was not even amusing.

Barret took the few steps to the door in an expectant rush. He turned the key in the lock and pulled the heavy drapes closed over the windows before returning to his desk.

His heart pounding, Barret withdrew the Bible from the sack with an extravagantly ceremonious gesture.

His moment had come.

"It's gone, just like I told you. It's just…gone!"

Lacey took a breath and swallowed against encroaching tears as she faced Scully solemnly in the silence of her room. She had come back to the boarding house after finishing work at the restaurant. Her intention had been to pick up her Bible and the next lesson she had prepared for Rosie and Jewel. The papers had been where she'd left them, but the Bible was not. She had searched the entire room, but it was nowhere to be found.

Panicking when she realized further effort would be wasted, she had left her room and asked Mary if she had seen her Bible, only to remember belatedly that Rosie and Jewel were waiting for her at the church. She had then returned swiftly to her room, snatched up the written lesson and dropped off the papers for the two women with a brief explanation before rushing back to search her room again.

Lacey attempted to swallow the lump in her throat. She wasn't certain when Mary had sent for Scully, but he had arrived at the door of her room a few minutes previously. Relaxing her rules as she had once before, Mary had again allowed him inside to help with the search, leaving the door open at her silent exit.

They had not found her Bible.

Lacey fought to control her trembling. "Where could it be, Scully? I left it on my nightstand. I always leave it there."

Scully did not reply.

"Do you think somebody took it?" Immediately she countered, "But that doesn't make sense. Why would anybody steal an old Bible? It isn't worth much to anybody but me."

"Somebody obviously took a fancy to it."

"Who would want a Bible enough to steal it, especially since Reverend Sykes would gladly provide one for anybody who asked? And how would somebody get into my room? Mary has been home all morning."

"Was your window locked?"

"It was when I left."

"Your door?"

"I don't have a key, just a latch on the inside, but Mary said her boarders are totally dependable. She's never had a problem with anything being missing."

Scully walked out into the hallway, then returned to the room, his expression dark. "The hallway window is open."

"Mary always leaves it open. She says it's cooler that way."

Scully did not comment. He asked, "Has anybody shown an interest in your Bible lately?"

"No, nobody except—" Lacey halted abruptly. Rosie had remarked several times how fortunate she was to have something so precious, but Rosie was too sweet and sincere to be at fault.

Scully pinned her with his gaze. "What were you going to say?"

"Nothing…except some people at the church have remarked about the care I take with it."

Scully remained silent and Lacey took a shuddering breath. With an attempt to face reality head-on, she said, "It's gone, Scully. I'll never get it back."

That thought suddenly more than she could bear, Lacey collapsed against Scully. She pressed herself instinctively tight against him as she whispered, "I know it's only an old Bible, but it's important to me. It's taken me through so many difficult times, and it's all I had...all that's left of my grand-father...of my past."

Scully clutched her close. Tilting her chin up toward him, the sincerity in his gaze clearly visible, he whispered huskily, "That's where you're wrong. You have me, Lacey. You'll always have me."

She had known that, just as she suddenly knew, as Scully lowered his mouth toward hers, that he was going to kiss her again.

But Scully's kiss was different this time. He kissed her slowly, gently, with a tenderness that continued when he finally drew his mouth from hers and pressed his lips to her eyelids, her cheek, the curve of her jaw. Held breathless by the soaring emotion he evoked inside her, Lacey encircled Scully's neck with her arms to draw him closer. She was lost in the glory of the moment when Scully pulled back from her with startling abruptness. She was unprepared when he said, "I'm sorry. That was...a mistake."

Lacey shook her head, uncomprehending. How could it be a mistake when being in Scully's arms felt so right? Surely he—

"Don't look at me like that, Lacey. You're upset. I shouldn't have taken advantage of you."

"You didn't. I—"

Scully took a backward step. "You're feeling lost and vulnerable right now. You aren't thinking rationally, or you'd be telling me to get out of your room."

"Why? I don't want you to leave."

"You don't know what you're saying, Lacey."

"I'm saying that something bad has happened. Someone came into my room. Someone stole my Bible. I don't know who would do such a thing, or why, but the only person I really trust is you."

"Maybe you shouldn't trust me too much right now."

Lacey took a forward step. She whispered, "Why, because you kissed me? I'm glad you kissed me, Scully."

"This is wrong, Lacey, more wrong than you realize. Your grandfather wouldn't have wanted…he didn't expect…" Scully shook his head. "It's time for me to leave."

"No."

"I'll get your Bible back for you. That's a promise."

"But—"

"Keep your window locked. I'll tell Mary to lock the hallway window, too." He paused. "I'm sorry."

"Don't go yet, Scully!"

Lacey watched as Scully walked out the doorway and disappeared from sight.

Stunned, she stood motionless. She had never felt more alone.

I don't want you to leave.

Lacey's simple statement rang over again in Scully's mind as he exited the boarding house. Out on the street at last, he took a deep breath. He had come so close to losing control when Lacey was in his arms.

Scully forced himself to face a truth he had so diligently avoided. He loved her. Not in the way he had always loved

Lacey, as he loved a dear, young girl left in his care; or in a way he might've thought he had loved any woman before her—but as a man truly loves a woman.

I'm glad you kissed me, Scully.

She shouldn't have been.

Don't go.

He hadn't wanted to, but the truth had never been more evident than when he had drawn back from kissing Lacey, barely in control of the emotion building inside him, and had seen the innocence in her eyes.

He wasn't the man for Lacey. Too many years had passed in between, with too many nights for him to ever hope to erase. He had slipped into a lifestyle that was in too great a conflict with hers. Lacey didn't realize that now because her thoughts were in a turmoil, but when her life was back on an even keel, she'd begin looking at him differently. She'd see him for the man he was—a saloonkeeper, a gambler, a man who took his pleasures at will, while giving little thought to the Book she cherished or its message. No, he was not the man she imagined him to be.

Lacey needed him right now, but when a decent young fellow like Todd Fulton decided to make his move—

Scully forced that painful thought from his mind. He filled the aching void with details that he needed to examine more closely.

He had no doubt that Lacey's Bible had been stolen. She would never have misplaced it. Accepting that conclusion then shed a different light on the sensation he had had of being watched as Lacey and he had traveled to the remains of Charlie's cabin.

Were the two incidents related?

If so, who was behind it all, and why?

Possibilities sprang to mind, but Scully was certain of only one thing.

Someone would pay.

"It's not here!" Barret glared at Blackie, then flashed a similarly heated glance at Larry before continuing, "There's no map in this Bible. What did you do with it?"

Momentarily speechless as he faced Barret across the still darkened office to which he and his cohort had been summoned, Blackie replied, "We didn't do nothing with it, boss."

Barret shuddered with wrath. He had spent the greater part of the morning going through the pages of Lacey Stewart's Bible—and he had found *nothing*. In frustration, he had shaken out the aged volume, checked the binding and gone so far as to rip some of the binding loose with the thought that the map might be concealed inside. As a last resort, he had tried to discover a pattern in the crude, faded illustrations Charlie had drawn in the margins of some pages, obviously for Lacey's benefit when she was a child, but he'd been unable to make sense of the birds, angels and trumpets randomly sketched.

He had almost begun believing that his dream had ended. He had then withdrawn the small sack from his drawer and removed the gold nugget Charlie had left with him, and his dream had been restored anew.

The nugget was real, and so was the strike.

Barret insisted with growing vehemence, "The map was in the Bible. It had to have been."

"If it was, somebody took it out before we got there, boss." Larry continued defensively, "Blackie and me never saw it.

We ain't dumb enough to try to cross you. Even if we did, we'd be long gone by now."

His chest heaving, Barret considered Larry's response. Neither of the two were smart enough to get away with stealing that map from him, and they knew it. They'd have to kill him first. Of course, they had killed before, but he prided himself on the fact that they had become too subservient to him to give even a moment's thought to the possibility of slaying him.

Barret gradually drew his breathing under control. So, if the map hadn't been in the Bible, it had to be somewhere else. Old Charlie had to have left some kind of signs leading to the location of the strike. The old man wasn't a novice. He knew even the most experienced prospector could become confused in the wilderness without leaving some kind of markings behind him.

Lacey was the only person who could possibly know what those signs were. Since she hadn't made a move toward the strike, she'd obviously gone out with Scully only with the intention of refamiliarizing herself with the territory. Now that she had gotten her bearings, she would make a move on her own soon.

Barret muttered a soft curse. Stealing the Bible had been a mistake. Lacey was now alerted to the fact that someone might be on to her plans. It might cause her to be more careful…to take her time.

Barret took a firm hold on his frustration. All right, he'd waited ten years. He could wait a little longer.

Barret looked again at his henchmen, then said, "I believe you. You didn't take the map, but if the map wasn't in the Bible, it's in Lacey Stewart's head."

Barret almost laughed at the startled expressions his statement evoked. He saw the wary glances Blackie and Larry exchanged when he said, "Lacey Stewart has waited as long as I have to claim this strike. Her deviousness proves she's as determined as I am to get it. Unfortunately for her, she's not as smart as I am. I'll win out in the end."

Barret added more intently, "She's nervous, but she'll make her move sooner or later, so don't let her out of your sight."

"What about Jake Scully?" Blackie grumbled. "I ain't too anxious to come up against him."

"You don't have to worry about Scully. It should be obvious to you that if Lacey was going to cut him in on the claim, she would've done it already. No, she's going after it by herself."

Barret was momentarily, perversely amused as he added, "Under different circumstances, I might even be tempted to say Lacey Stewart's a woman after my own heart."

Sobering abruptly, he continued, "But right now I'm telling you both that whatever happens, one thing is certain. That claim is mine."

Chapter Twelve

"*The Lord is my shepherd: I shall not want. He maketh me to lie down in green pastures. He leadeth me beside the still waters.*"

Lacey halted at that point in her reading. She glanced at Rosie and Jewel as they waited for her to continue, but she was suddenly unable to speak past the thickness in her throat.

The lessons had been going well. She had been stunned at both women's quick grasp of every advance in learning she had attempted. The full depth of their desire to learn was never more evident, however, than when they requested that she read to them from the Bible Reverend Sykes had given her. Their questions were quick and instinctive as they peered over her shoulders, following her finger as she pointed at every word.

Lacey swallowed again. Rosie had requested that she read this particular psalm. Rosie had remembered abstract portions of it from her childhood, portions that had remained with her through the years. Lacey had recognized the lines immediately when Rosie had quoted them, but it was more difficult for her to read the psalm than she had ever imagined it would be.

Because of Scully.

Because he was slipping away from her.

Lacey breathed deeply to stabilize her emotions. Two weeks had passed since her Bible was stolen…since Scully had kissed her and stirred her so deeply. She had wanted to talk to Scully about the moment. She had regretted telling him that she was glad he had kissed her, because she had realized belatedly that Scully was not.

She had recalled, just as belatedly, beautiful, red-haired Charlotte's easy manner with Scully as they had walked back into the Gold Nugget that night. There had been no tension between them. Charlotte obviously asked for no promises from Scully, and Scully appeared to prefer things that way. She had told herself in retrospect that she needed to accept Scully's apology for those brief moments she had spent in his arms. She had told herself that if he wanted it that way, she would accept his apology—but Scully didn't seem willing to give her the chance. He had forced a painful distance between them since that morning, which he began by skipping breakfast at the restaurant while she was working there, by not appearing until evening, when he spoke to her briefly, often with an excuse why they couldn't have supper together.

Her Bible was lost to her.

Her nightmares continued.

And she had lost her best friend.

"Lacey, are you all right?"

Lacey looked up into Rosie's querulous expression, then back down at the Bible in her hand. She replied past the lump in her throat, "I'm sorry. My mind must've drifted."

Aware that they were waiting, she continued softly and sincerely, *"He restoreth my soul."*

* * *

Scully walked solemnly up the street, his expression forbidding. It had been a long two weeks since he had last held Lacey in his arms, and he ached inside. He wasn't sure when it had happened, when his feelings had slipped past protectiveness and friendship. Yet he knew the distance he had put between them was not only necessary. It was urgent.

Urgent, because he did not want to make the mistake of telling Lacey he loved her.

Scully lengthened his stride as the storefront he sought came into view. He needed no one to tell him that more had to have been at stake than an old Bible in order for someone to secretly follow Lacey and him on their long, tedious journey into the wilderness. During the week past, he had discreetly talked to everyone who could've been on the street the day Lacey's Bible was stolen, but no one had noticed anything unusual. Then he had gone back to talk to Mary.

Scully remembered Mary's annoyance at her off-handed recollection of Blackie Oaks's visit to her front door. She had said, "His inquiry was a complete waste of time, and what irritated me most was the half smile on his face that made me think he was aware of it. All that talk about rushing right over to talk to me when he heard a room might be available in my house—then all that hogwash about how he and that other ruffian friend of his wanted to pay to eat at my table every night because they hadn't been eating well lately…as if I'd ever allow it!" She had shuddered. "That Blackie fella actually had the nerve to stick his foot in my doorway so I couldn't close it on him!"

With those comments under his belt, Scully had then talked to Harry Rice, who usually ate breakfast at the restaurant at that time of day. Harry had nodded and said, "I did see Blackie and Larry on the street when I left Sadie's that morning. I remember thinking they must've fallen out of bed to be up and out on the street so early, but then when they went into Barret Gould's office, I figured he must've sent for them."

Blackie Oaks *and* Larry Hayes...

Yes, there had to be more to the theft of the Bible than was obviously apparent.

Scully had strained to remember that last day when Charlie and he had talked. Strangely, what he remembered most was the way Charlie had smiled when they had reminisced about the time they had spent working together years earlier. In retrospect, however, it seemed they had passed the greatest portion of the time discussing how Scully had come into the unexpected ownership of the Gold Nugget. He remembered his surprise when Charlie mentioned his granddaughter, saying she was a gift in his old age, and that he treasured her more than he could ever treasure the gold strike he had prospected for all his life. He had said he'd left her behind at the cabin to take care of Careful, who had seemed to be ailing, but he'd bring her in to meet Scully the next time he was in town—which would probably be soon.

Scully wondered why he hadn't asked what would be bringing Charlie into town again so soon, especially when he knew Charlie spent as many hours as he could squeeze into the day prospecting for the gold that he always expected he'd find in the next shovelful of dirt to be turned over.

He now wished he had.

Scully halted outside Barret Gould's office, his expression grim. He pushed open the door and walked inside.

Scully fixed his gaze on Barret's neatly shaven face as

Barret stood up behind his great mahogany desk. He noted the fellow's forced smile as Barret said, "Well, well...if it isn't Jake Scully. How may I help you?"

Silent, Scully remembered the day that impressive mahogany desk arrived in town. The outlandish scene Barret had made as he had directed the unloading of that prestigious piece of furniture from the delivery wagon had amused some onlookers, but it hadn't amused him. The true nature of the man had been revealed that day, and he hadn't liked when he had seen.

He still didn't.

Scully responded, "I can't rightly say if you can help me, but maybe you can answer a few questions that have been bothering me of late."

"Questions?" Barret's smile froze.

Scully pressed, "You know Lacey Stewart, of course."

Barret shrugged. "Yes, I do. She's a lovely young woman."

"You also know she's Charlie Pratt's granddaughter."

"I assume that's general knowledge in Weaver."

"Nobody ever did find out who killed Charlie."

"So?"

"Or why."

"What does that have to do with me?"

"I was wondering if you had any business with Charlie Pratt years back."

"Charlie? No, not that I recall. Why do you ask?"

"Charlie never did say why he came into town that last day."

"I should think you'd know better than anyone else in this town the answer to that question. Like all the other prospectors who frequent your establishment, Charlie was most likely hot, thirsty and in need of a break from prospecting. A visit to your saloon was a natural choice."

"Charlie wasn't like 'all the other prospectors.'"

"I didn't know the man well enough, so I can't comment on that."

In order to see the lawyer's reaction, Scully prevaricated, "There are some folks in Weaver who seem to remember Charlie paying a visit to your office when he was in town."

"They'd be mistaken."

Noting Barret's instinctively defensive posture, Scully added, "There's been more than a usual interest in Lacey's comings and goings lately."

"That's understandable, don't you think? She's quite a beauty."

"She's also had something very important stolen from her recently—something old Charlie gave her."

"So?"

"Aren't you curious about what was stolen?"

Barret shrugged again. "Not really. I can't imagine that old man would have left his granddaughter anything that could possibly be of interest to me."

"Really?"

Barret's posture grew rigid. "Are you accusing me of theft?"

Scully did not reply.

"You're insane. I don't have the slightest interest in Lacey Stewart's meager possessions."

Scully pinned him with his gaze. "Maybe. Maybe not."

"It's time for you to leave."

Scully paused, then added, "Charlie put Lacey in my care. I want you to know that I take that charge very seriously. Anybody who tries to harm her in any way will answer to me."

"You're wasting your time and mine. Please leave."

"I'll leave in my own time, Barret, but first I want to make something very clear. If you have any intentions toward Lacey Stewart, back off. Otherwise, you'll end up a sorry man."

"Is that a threat?"

"If the shoe fits…"

"Get out."

Scully allowed his gaze to linger for a few tense moments before he turned slowly toward the exit. He did not bother to look back as he pulled the door closed behind him and started back down the street.

He had seen what he had wanted to see.

Barret Gould had the look of a guilty man.

The office door closed behind Scully, and Barret felt a flush of pure fury.

The gall of the man, to approach a respectable citizen in his own quarters and accuse him of petty thievery when Scully, himself, was nothing more than a barkeep!

Barret took a shuddering breath and walked to the window to watch Scully as he strode down the street. The man was a fool for warning him, but now that he had, it appeared Scully would have to be taken care of when everything came to a close. That's where Blackie and Larry would again earn their keep. A bullet in the man's back wouldn't cause either one of them much stress.

Or him, either.

Scully turned the corner of the street and Barret whispered into the silence, "You came here to give me warning, Scully, but you succeeded in doing only one thing. Fool. You've signed your own death warrant."

"You look like a man on a mission."

Scully turned at the sound of the familiar, throaty voice.

He paused, his hand on the Gold Nugget's swinging door, and looked down into Charlotte's smile.

"Can't manage a smile for an old friend, Scully?" Charlotte chided him softly as she ran a dainty hand against the upward sweep of her blazing red hair. "I must be losing my touch."

Scully swept her with a glance. Charlotte was wearing a small straw hat and a simple green gown that emphasized her natural assets clearly. Scully smiled. Even in her street clothes, Charlotte dressed to be noticed, a fact that she never denied. He had always admired her candor.

Scully had the feeling he would be subjected to her candor in another way when Charlotte began, "I've been missing you more than ever, Scully. I was expecting I'd start seeing more of you when things started cooling down between you and Lacey."

"I'm Lacey's guardian, Charlotte. That's all I've ever been to her."

"Right, and like my mama told me, the moon is made of green cheese." Charlotte slanted him a half smile. "You used to be one of my biggest admirers, Scully."

Scully reluctantly returned her smile. "I still admire you, Charlotte."

"So, what's going on?"

"I've been busy."

Charlotte's smile faded. "Have you and Lacey had a falling out?"

"No, I told you—"

"I know what you told me, and I know what I see." Charlotte moved a step closer. "You're a man in a million, Scully. I don't expect to give up on you easily."

"Give up on me?"

"Let me clarify…turn you over to another woman."

"Like I said, there's no 'other woman' involved. I've been busy."

"And like I said, I know what I see. Scully…" Charlotte's voice dropped a note softer as she said, "I've always been a woman who said what she thinks. As you know, I have no shortage of admirers, but I've been missing you—because you make me smile inside. It's a good thing to smile inside. I miss that, too."

"Charlotte…"

"Give what I'm saying a little thought…and remember that I'll be there for you."

"Charlotte…"

"I said, think about it." Charlotte suddenly laughed. "And don't look so serious."

Standing on tiptoe, Charlotte brushed Scully's mouth with hers and whispered with a wink, "There's more where that came from, darlin'." She walked off down the street with a practiced sway. Scully stared after her for an extended moment, then turned back to push his way through the swinging doors. He did not stop until he reached his office at the rear, then closed the door behind him.

Charlotte dismissed from his mind, Scully stood still in the silence, recalling the look on Barret's face when he left. Yes, Barret had the look of a guilty man…an *impatient*, guilty man.

If he was right, Barret would make things start happening soon.

Lacey stood, shaken, in the shadows of the mercantile doorway. Her new Bible in hand, Rosie and Jewel's paperwork under her arm, she had been making her way back to the boarding house when she had seen *them*.

Her breathing uneven, her throat tight, Lacey struggled against tears. She had seen the kiss Charlotte and Scully had exchanged. She had also seen the expression on Charlotte's face when she had turned to walk back down the street, and the way Scully's gaze had followed her. Their short conversation and that kiss had been laced with a history between the two of them that could not be denied.

Lacey could avoid the truth no longer. Scully was a man of the world. The kiss he had given her had been merely an expression of affection and an appreciation of her distress. By reading more into it, she had made him uncomfortable, and the former ease that had been between them had disappeared in an instant, never to be reclaimed.

Lacey forced up her chin and started toward the boarding house. She was such a fool. In his mind, Scully was still her guardian and nothing more.

Lacey brushed away the tear that slipped down her cheek, then raised her chin higher. Another truth that she could deny no longer was that she loved Scully in a way that surpassed friendship. She could think of no greater joy than that of spending the rest of her life in his arms as his wife and the mother of his children. But he regarded *her* as a child.

That thought doused Lacey with sudden, cold reality. Scully thought of her as a child because she had been behaving like a child—dependent, needy, uncertain. Her dependency was a disservice to Scully, to the man who had cared for her for the greater portion of her life. He deserved to be set free of the responsibility that had been fostered upon him by her well-meaning grandfather. He needed to be freed to take steps toward settling his own future—a future held in abeyance because of her; a future that included a woman who would love him the way he was meant to be loved, and who would bring him back to a more stable way of life.

Sadly, that woman would not be she.

Still struggling for control of her emotions as she reached her boarding house door, Lacey was about to push it open when a slim, dark-haired cowpoke stepped unexpectedly into view.

Lacey gasped with a start, and the fellow said politely, "I'm sorry if I frightened you, ma'am, but we have a mutual friend, and I'd like to talk to you a moment if I can."

Lacey struggled to regain her composure as she responded, "A mutual friend?"

"Jewel Nichols. My name's Buddy Cross."

"Oh, yes, I remember." He had appeared with Jewel at the boarding house door that early morning after Riley struck Rosie. Lacey managed an uncertain smile. "You wanted to talk to me?"

"Yes, ma'am." Buddy continued soberly, "I wanted to make sure you knew how much the lessons you're giving Jewel and Rosie mean to them."

Lacey was momentarily startled. "You know about the lessons?"

Smiling for the first time, Buddy said shyly, "Yes, ma'am. Jewel doesn't keep too much a secret from me." His smile faded as he continued earnestly, "But Jewel does hide her feelings from most folks. She's not like Rosie, who wears the way she feels out in the open, so I figured it was important to let you know, in case she didn't, how much the lessons mean to Jewel, too."

"I—I'm glad to hear that, Buddy."

"I wanted to make sure you knew that Rosie and Jewel both consider you a friend."

"I *am* their friend."

"Ma'am..." Buddy hesitated as he searched for the right words. He continued, "I needed to tell you that being Jewel's friend makes you my friend, and you can call on me if there's anything I can ever do for you."

"Thank you, Buddy."

"No, I'm the one who's thanking you, ma'am. You're the only person besides me who's ever given a thought to making Jewel's life better, and I appreciate that...a lot."

Lacey was momentarily unable to reply.

His face flushing, the slender cowhand continued, "You see, I'm Jewel's friend, but I also hope to make her my missus someday."

His words causing a lump to tighten in her throat, Lacey extended her hand and said, with true warmth, "Buddy Cross, I'm so pleased to meet you."

Buddy's heartfelt declaration lingered in Lacey's mind as Buddy tipped his hat with a polite goodbye and walked back to the horse he had tethered nearby.

Pushing open the door to her room with a determined hand moments later, Lacey felt the weight of her former decision returning. It was time to take adult steps to correct the situation between Scully and her...to relieve him of the responsibility that was weighing him down.

Her decision steadfast, she knew she could do that in only one way.

"Lacey's upset." Rosie shook her head as she and Jewel walked down Main Street. They had finished their lesson a short time earlier, had waited the required minutes after Lacey left the church before leaving behind her so no one would suspect that they had been working together. Silent since Lacey closed the church door behind her, Rosie had then stated the obvious as a way of breaking the silence. She continued with a glance at her friend, "She's trying to hide it, but Lacey's miserable."

"You don't need to be a mind reader to see that."

"We need to help her, Jewel."

Jewel's quick glance was sharp. "It's none of our business, Rosie."

"Like it was none of Lacey's business that we couldn't read or write, you mean?"

"Don't start that again. It's not the same thing."

"Isn't it?"

"Rosie…" Jewel stopped dead in her tracks and turned to face her friend, "You can't fix everybody's life, especially when you can't even fix your own."

Sobering, Rosie replied, "You're right. I couldn't fix my own life, but Riley's been out of it for more than two weeks now. He won't be coming back this time, all because a couple of friends helped me out. I'm also learning to read and write because another friend is taking the time to teach me, so I figure I owe something in return."

"Rosie…"

"I know having her Bible stolen was hard for Lacey. I still can't imagine why anyone would take it, but I don't think that's all that's bothering her. Maybe I should tell Scully and he can—"

"No!"

Rosie's pale eyes narrowed. "Why?"

Jewel shook her head.

She repeated, "Why?"

"Haven't you noticed that Scully and Lacey haven't been seen around together very much lately…that Scully's been spending more time at the Nugget than before…that Charlotte's been sashaying around him again?"

"Yes, but—"

Jewel looked at her pointedly.

"Oh, no, that can't be it!"

"Maybe not, but it's obvious that Lacey and Scully have had some kind of a falling out. The only thing I don't know is what Lacey's thinking."

Her eyes filling with sudden tears, Rosie whispered, "She must feel so alone. What can we do to help her?"

No response.

"Jewel?"

Jewel sighed. "We can't change Scully's preference for redheads, if that's the problem. I suppose we can only watch and wait, and be there if Lacey needs us."

Rosie nodded. She supposed Jewel was right. What other strategy could two women employ to help a friend when their own lives were too far from perfect to enable them to give advice?

Yes, they'd just have to watch and wait.

Yes, she could relieve Scully of the responsibility he felt for her in only one way.

The dawn sky was still streaked with night as Lacey, dressed in riding clothes, made her way toward the livery stable with that thought foremost in mind.

Lacey reviewed her decision as she neared the dimly lit

stable. As painful as it was, the message from Scully the previous day, saying he'd again be unable to meet her for supper, had been a clear confirmation of the conclusion she had forced herself to face. She had taken a job at the restaurant and attempted to face her fears when she went to the site of her grandfather's cabin to see his grave, but she had continued to lean on Scully by refusing to face those fears. She needed to eliminate her nightmares forever by forcing herself to remember the lost details of the night her grandfather was killed.

She needed to do that for herself; but mostly, she needed to do that for Scully—to set him free.

It was the least she could do.

Because she loved him.

Resolved, she had taken immediate steps toward that goal. She had made arrangements with Sadie to have Millie replace her at the restaurant until she returned. She had prepared Rosie and Jewel's lessons for a few days and had delivered them to their door. She had bought the necessary supplies at the mercantile store and had arranged to have them packed on the mount that would be ready for her when she reached the livery stable that morning. She would be on her way within minutes—a step she hadn't had the courage to take until now.

Her heart pounding as she entered the stable, Lacey met Barney Pettit's concerned glance. She returned it with a forced smile at the livery stable proprietor as he said, "You're sure you want to do this, ma'am? Riding out alone in this country is dangerous for a young woman like you."

"I won't be alone...not really." She patted the new Bible Reverend Sykes had given her before slipping it into her saddle bag. Touched by the old man's concern, she continued, "Besides, it's no more dangerous now than it was for an eight-year-old girl who made it to Weaver alone ten years ago. I did it then without supplies, and by walking a good part of the way. Surely I can do it now, as prepared as I am, and with a good, strong horse under me."

"I don't know…"

"Don't worry, Barney. I traveled this country with my grandfather when he was prospecting, remember? I know it quite well." Aware that her statement was a stretch of the truth, Lacey patted Barney's arm reassuringly. "I'll be fine."

A sudden braying from the corral in the rear turned Lacey in its direction. "And you don't have to worry about my getting lost, since I'm taking Careful with me. He knows these trails better than most people in these parts do. He'll get me back."

"Well, he's as ready to go as he'll ever be."

Like her.

Mounted within minutes, Lacey turned her horse out onto the street with Careful trotting behind.

"Lacey Stewart isn't working in the restaurant this morning, and do you know why?" Barret glared at his sleep-drugged hirelings as he harangued, "Because she left town at dawn…while you both were sleeping!"

Barret was apoplectic as he faced the two men in the cabin they shared at the edge of town. He had arrived at their quarters moments earlier as the morning sun began rising, and had found both Larry and Blackie asleep in unclean bunks unfit for man or beast. Infuriated almost as much by being subjected to the rank odor of the cabin as he was by their ineptitude, he said, "I told you she'd make her move soon. I told you to watch her…not to let her out of your sight!"

"You didn't say nothing about watching her all night long."

"Do I have to spell everything out for you? Anyone with half a brain—anyone who was doing his job and watching her closely enough—would've realized what she was planning and would have been prepared."

Barret continued, "You know as well as I do where Lacey's headed. I want you to catch up with her and follow her covertly. That shouldn't be hard for you to do. She'll lead you right to the strike."

"What if she don't?"

Turning on Larry with sudden venom, Barret said, "Then do what you must to *make* her tell you where the strike is located. I'm tired of waiting."

"That's easy for you to say, but if Scully—"

"She rode out *alone,* you fool, just as I said she would! You'll never have a better chance."

"Alone…" Blackie exchanged a glance with his partner. "Where's Scully?"

"Who cares? Scully obviously doesn't even know she left. He hasn't been meeting her for breakfast lately, and if the rumors around town are correct, he won't miss her until suppertime tonight. That should give you enough time to accomplish what you need to do."

"But when Scully finds out—"

"He's going to have to be taken care of eventually anyway." Barret's expression hardened. "You might even be able to kill two birds with one stone if you're smart enough."

"Two birds with one stone." Blackie grinned unexpectedly. "That sounds fine to me."

But Barret did not smile in return. Instead, he warned, "I'm telling you now—I expect results. I don't expect to have waited ten years in vain."

"We'll find that strike for you, boss."

"Yeah, we'll make her talk. You can bet on it."

Barret paused for a last, lingering stare at the two men before he turned toward the door.

That sounded right to him. He *would* bet on it, too. What they did not know was, at stake would be their lives.

"When did she leave, Barney?"

Tension twisted tight inside Scully as he stood in the livery stable awaiting Barney Pettit's response. He still couldn't believe it. He had gone to the restaurant at midmorning expecting to get a glimpse of Lacey while she worked. He had wanted to make sure she was all right, as he had done countless times during the past two weeks without her knowledge. Startled this time to find Millie replacing her, he had spoken to Sadie and had then gone directly to the boarding house, hoping to find Lacey there.

Trepidation had expanded inside him as he tried to convince himself that Lacey wouldn't be foolish enough to venture out into the rough, dangerous country surrounding Weaver alone, that she was too smart for that. One look at Mary when she opened the boarding house door, however, and he knew he had only been fooling himself.

"She left at dawn." Replying to his question, Barney eyed Scully's stiff expression with a frown. "I figured it was kinda strange that Lacey would be going out to visit her grandfather's grave alone, being's you was looking after her and all, but she said she'd be fine because she knew her way around these parts."

Scully glanced toward the rear of the stable. Anticipating his question, Barney said, "Yeah, she took Careful with her. She said she didn't have to worry about getting lost as long as that old burro was along."

Dreading Barney's response, Scully questioned tightly, "Did you see anybody else leave town after she did…anybody you didn't expect to see?"

"Funny you should ask." Barney shook his head. "I was tending to one of the mounts a fella left for me at the hitching post out front when Larry Hayes went running into the blacksmith's shop next door a little while after Lacey left. Noah told me Larry was in such a rush that he didn't even wait for Noah to reshoe his horse before riding off like a bat out of you-know-where, heading for parts unknown."

Scully went cold. He had no doubt where that degenerate had been heading. He instructed tensely, "Get my horse ready for the trail, Barney. I'll be right back to pick him up."

Cold fear expanded inside Scully as he pushed open the door to his room minutes later and changed into his riding clothes.

You'll never be free of those nightmares until you face them down, Lacey, and there's only one way to do it.

Scully shuddered as his words returned to taunt him. Lacey had gone back to old Charlie's cabin because of him. Because of his feelings for her and emotions he was unable to control, he had abandoned her to her fears and left her with no recourse but to meet them alone.

He should've known. He should've realized what he was forcing her to do.

His hands shaking as myriad images flashed across his mind, Scully drew open his dresser drawer. He hadn't warned Lacey of his suspicions about Barret because he hadn't wanted to frighten her. She had no idea of the possible danger she faced. She was vulnerable and alone, and hours ahead of him on the trail.

Scully reached for the gun belt in his drawer, fear for the

woman he loved shaking him to the core. Lacey was at the mercy of men who had no mercy at all, yet he could not help her unless he could reach her in time.

His need profound, Scully felt the desperate stirring of a part of him that he had thought long dismissed. He sank slowly to his knees and raised his eyes toward the God so familiar to him in his youth, the supreme power with whom he had become estranged. His throat tight, he reminded himself that Lacey was unlike him, that this same God was the source of her strength, that she was devoted to His Son's teachings and had charted the course of her life accordingly. He began earnestly, "I've strayed from you, dear Jesus. I've done my share of sinning. I've done little to deserve your love or intercession, but I'm not asking for your help for myself. I'm asking for you to help Lacey. She's familiar to you, I know, and far more worthy of your protection than I ever was. I'm asking you…pleading for you to find a way to keep her safe from whatever bad intentions are stalking her until I can reach her. I'm asking you to keep watch over her and hold all evil at bay until I stand at her side. I'll take it from there, Lord. I'll fulfill the promise I made to Lacey's grandfather at any price that's asked of me. That's my promise to you, Lord Jesus, and it's a promise I will not break."

Pausing for a stabilizing breath, his eyes brimming with the power of his plea, Scully added hoarsely, "I beg you to answer this prayer, my dear Lord Jesus, not for my sake, but for Lacey, who is so worthy of your love."

Shaken by his heartfelt appeal, Scully stood up and strapped his gun belt around his hips. He would honor his promise to Charlie, and he would fulfill the sacred promise he had just made. He would do it, at any price.

* * *

The day had turned hot and bright. Lacey glanced at the position of the sun in the cloudless sky as she followed the dusty trail at a steady pace. Her expression sober, she ignored the perspiration trailing down her cheek from underneath the damp band of her hat. She scrutinized her mount, then looked back at Careful as he trotted behind. Like her, both animals were thirsty and tired, but they'd reach her grandfather's gravesite soon.

Lacey paused at that thought as her mount continued dutifully forward. Strangely, the same terrain that had seemed so foreign to her previously had now become familiar. She took each turn in the trail instinctively, with certainty in her direction. She was able to calculate the time it would take for her to reach her grandfather's cabin easily when she had been formerly at a loss. She sensed this change in her had no relationship to her previous journey with Scully. Instead, it was as if a part of her was gradually returning to life—a part that had been asleep, or had been paralyzed by the terror of a fateful night.

More certain than ever before of the necessity of the journey she had undertaken, Lacey glanced at the emptiness surrounding her as her thirsty mount increased his pace. The emptiness stirred memories…painful memories of a long, exhausting walk while her head had throbbed incessantly and her weakened legs had seemed ready to fail her. She recalled her fading consciousness and the echo of her grandfather's gruff, beloved voice that had urged her on. She remembered the name of the man he had sent her to seek with his dying breath.

The name rebounded again inside her.

Jake Scully.

It seemed ironic that years earlier she had walked this same trail hoping to find Scully, while she was now making this journey hoping to find the courage to leave him.

That thought raised the mist of tears to Lacey's eyes as the remains of the cabin came into view. Somehow unwilling to immediately face the blackened timbers and the small mounded spot a short distance from it, she headed to the stream to water her animals. Dismounting, she released Careful so he might drink more easily. She then kneeled at the stream's edge to cup the water in her palms and splash it against her face.

Refreshed and resolute, she stood up and looked back at the cabin debris. She had come to confront her past and to face her future. She would not leave until she met them both.

Chapter Thirteen

The sun dipped slowly toward the horizon with colors expanding brilliantly against the darkening sky. Immune to the glorious display, Lacey struggled to subdue the trembling that had begun inside her with the advent of twilight shadows.

Feeling an overwhelming sense of dread, she looked at the charred remains of her childhood and gathered her strength as she determinedly kneeled to set up her bedroll. She glanced back at the mound marked with a simple wooden cross. The lonesome sight revealed none of the goodness of the old man who had lived and worked nearby. It reflected nothing of the generous nature and loving qualities that compounded the tragedy of his death, and Lacey was suddenly alone—more alone than she wished to be.

Her skin was burning hot, and choking smoke filled her lungs. She was afraid, but Grandpa held her hand tightly as he dragged her from the flames.

Disoriented, she looked up at Grandpa. Her head hurt. She

wasn't sure what had happened, why the cabin was burning, why Grandpa was looking at her so strangely.

She gasped as Grandpa fell to the ground clutching his chest, and she saw the bloody wound there.

Grandpa!

She was trembling so hard that she could hardly talk when Grandpa clutched her hand and started to speak. She—

A playful tug on her hair snapped Lacey back to the present with a gasp. Her heart pounding, she looked up into Careful's expectant expression, then raised a shaky hand to stroke his graying muzzle. With supreme strength of will, she shook off the images that had made determined inroads into her consciousness and stood up. She was an adult now, not a child. She could not afford to surrender to her fears.

Lacey surveyed her camp, then turned her attention back to the patient burro, still feeling truly alone.

"The boss ain't going to like this."

Blackie's mumbled words ended the silence that had prevailed between Larry and him as he watched Lacey's camp through his spyglass. It hadn't taken them long to find Lacey on the trail, but that's where the problems had begun.

Blackie adjusted his spyglass and studied the scene more carefully. Something was wrong. Lacey Stewart had made her way directly to her grandfather's old cabin site as expected, but that's where the expected had ended. In the time since, she had done nothing but water her animals and walk around the camp she had set up. She had shown no interest in the surrounding terrain, had made no attempt to forage out into the wilderness for old trails or possible signs her grandfather might have left indicating the direction of his strike. In fact, she had shown no interest at all in anything but the old man's mounded grave. What was she up to?

"What do you mean the boss ain't going to like this? Give me that glass!"

"Hey!" Protesting when Larry snatched the spyglass out of his hand to survey the scene for himself, Blackie added, "You ain't going to see nothing more than I did, no matter how hard you try, 'cause there ain't nothing to see."

A low growl his only comment, Larry watched the camp a few moments longer, before lowering the spyglass and replying, "I'm not going through this again, you know—watching and waiting who knows how long for that woman to make a move. I'm tired of the boss making out like I'm dumb, and I'm tired of taking his guff. I *ain't* dumb, and I ain't letting no woman lead me around in circles. I'm telling you now, Lacey Stewart's going to point out where that strike is located, and I ain't going to take no for an answer."

"I know what you mean." Blackie studied his cohort's flushed expression. "But you know what'll happen then. Scully will be on us faster than chain lightning."

"You heard what the boss said about him."

"Yeah, but I'm thinking taking care of Scully will be easier said than done."

"The boss don't care about what you think! All he wants is for us to come back with a map of that strike, and that's what's going to happen."

"But—"

"He wants what he wants, and I'm going to make sure he gets it."

Blackie did not immediately respond to Larry's unexpected turnabout in attitude. He supposed Larry was thinking differently now because the boss had been so mad that they'd let Lacey get a head start on them, and because, like Larry said, the boss was crazy when he was mad. The truth was, like Larry, he didn't fancy the thought of the boss getting any madder at them than he already was.

Blackie said belatedly, "We told the boss we'd get him what he wanted, one way or another."

Larry stared at Blackie malevolently, then demanded, "Say it again, Blackie…like you mean it, or I'll take care of both of them by myself, if I have to."

"Don't worry about that." Embarrassed to be reprimanded by his cohort, Blackie repeated with conviction, "We'll get the boss what he wants together." He hesitated, then questioned, "How do you think we should do it?"

"It ain't going to be as easy as the boss said it would be, that's for sure. I don't fancy waiting for that Stewart gal to make her move. If she don't show me something soon, I'm going to move first."

"What are you saying?"

"You'll see."

"Larry…"

"I told you, you'll see!"

Blackie took a backward step, then turned toward his horse. As far as he was concerned, Larry was beginning to act as crazy as the boss he was always complaining about.

And he wasn't sure he liked it.

Lacey forced herself to finish her meager supper as the wilderness shadows darkened into night. Her hands trembling, she dropped her canteen, then stood abruptly still in an effort to bring her emotions under control. She despised her realization that her courage had seemed to dissipate along with the waning light. She had striven to keep foremost in her mind the reasons she had made her expedition into the wilderness and the memories she hoped to revive. In that effort, she had stood at her grandfather's graveside and had talked to the dear old man buried there, but while tears had welled, the blank spots in her memory had prevailed. She had missed the solace of holding her old, worn Bible and knowing her grandfather's gnarled hands had turned those same pages so many years ago. But most of all, she had longed for Scully's presence beside her, and the loving warmth of looking up into sober gray eyes that seemed able to read her heart.

Lacey blinked back the persistent tears, knowing the worst was yet to come. She would not wait for sleep knowing that Scully was nearby. She would not close her eyes knowing he cared. She would not hear the echo of his whispered reassurances or feel his comforting touch. She had lost those moments forever.

Lacey glanced back toward her horse at the sound of his nervous whinny to see that Careful had disappeared into the shadows. She heard him bray abruptly, and she frowned. She had not bothered to tether the faithful burro, but neither had she expected that he would wander from her sight in a darkness that held possible danger for him.

Myriad thoughts filled her mind when Careful brayed again. Lacey started spontaneously toward the sound. Her mount was moving restlessly at his tether when she paused at the edge of the campfire's light and called out, "Careful...come here, old fella. Come on."

Silence.

Lacey swallowed against a gradually expanding fear. She

remembered the ancient six-shooter her grandpa had kept handy for varmints that foraged in the night. She had not thought to carry a similar reassurance, and she repeated tentatively, "Careful…?"

When no response was forthcoming, she walked tentatively into the shadows, only to stumble and fall to her knees over an unexpected obstacle on the path. She reached out and gasped when she touched a male figure lying on the ground. The sound choked in her throat when a shaft of moonlight illuminated the face of a man whose forehead was streaked with blood.

It was Buddy Cross!

The sound of footsteps in the darkness behind her brought Lacey to her feet with a jolt of terror. Somehow mesmerized, she watched as dark shadows materialized into hulking, male forms moving rapidly toward her….

Grandpa lay motionless on the ground as their cabin collapsed into a flaming heap behind them.

He wasn't talking. He wasn't breathing.

She stood up, staring transfixed with horror as the flickering shadows came to life in the silhouettes of two men.

She fled blindly as the men started toward her at a run. Slipping and falling, she got up to run again as the heavy footsteps drew closer.

They were directly behind her when a rough hand grabbed her by the hair and jerked her backward. She glimpsed the faces of the men then—terrifying, vicious faces—the second before a brief, shattering burst of pain brought darkness closing down around her….

Lacey returned to the present with a start as the advancing shadows neared. Terror shot up her spine when the faces of the men became visible at last.

It was they, the same men, with the same, deadly intent in their eyes!

Somehow unwilling to move, Lacey demanded, "Who are you? What do you want?"

"You know what we want!" The men halted a few feet away. The smaller of the two glared as he said, "We want the same thing we wanted all them years ago, and you're the only one who knows where it is."

"I don't know what you're talking about!" Lacey's heart pounded as she said, "All I know is that you killed my grandfather and tried to kill me. And now you killed Buddy."

"We spotted him out there watching your camp. We couldn't take any chances with what he was doing there, so you can thank him for what's happening now, not us." The taller fellow continued hotly, "Just like your grandpa pulled a switch on us when we tried to find out where his strike was all them years ago. He sneaked up on us with a gun when we was watching the cabin. He made us shoot him."

"No!"

"We didn't have no choice. We threw his body into the cabin and set it on fire so's it would look like an accident. We didn't know there was anybody else in there, and we figured we'd find his strike sooner or later without him."

"What strike?"

"Don't act like you don't know what we're talking about."

"You're crazy…both of you! My grandfather never struck it rich. You killed him for nothing."

"No, you're the crazy one if you think we're going to believe you came all the way back here from that fancy school in New York just to see your grandfather's grave."

The smaller of the two men advanced menacingly closer

as he said, "All the trouble can stop here if you want it to, you know. Just tell us where your grandpa made his strike, and we'll let you live."

Lacey glanced down at Buddy's still body, then replied with shaken conviction, "No, you won't, but you won't get rich by killing me, either, because my grandpa never made a strike."

"Yes, he did."

"He didn't."

"Liar!" The smaller of the two men raised his fist threateningly. "I'll teach you to—"

"Don't try it!" Scully's deep, familiar voice sounded from the shadows, stunning the scene into motionlessness as he stepped forward into view with his gun drawn.

Incredulous at the sight of him, Lacey watched as Scully ordered, "Drop your guns, both of you."

"No." The smaller of the two men almost grinned. "You ain't got the guts to shoot us head-on, Scully. You're just a cardsharp...a gambler. There ain't nothing in your veins but—"

A sudden blaze of gunfire shattered the silence of the clearing as the taller of the two men snapped his gun from his holster and fired—as Scully and the second man fired simultaneously, and the campsite was suddenly filled with gunshots that left only Lacey standing.

Stunned, Lacey was momentarily unable to react. She gasped with horror as the gun smoke cleared and she saw Scully lying on the ground, a bloody wound on his chest.

She rushed to his side, a voice inside her mind screaming, no, not again!

She could not lose Scully for the same, senseless reason that she had lost her grandfather.

Determined that she would not, Lacey untied her neckerchief and pressed it tight to his wound with trembling hands, hoping to stanch the flow of blood. She pleaded, "Talk to me, Scully. Please talk to me."

Panic made inroads into Lacey's mind when Scully's eyes remained closed. His chest moved shallowly underneath her palm and she leaned closer to rasp, "Don't leave me, Scully. I need to know you'll be all right. Please tell me you'll be all right."

Buddy staggered into the circle of the fire's light behind her. He brushed away the blood still streaming from his head wound as he checked the two lifeless men briefly, then came to crouch at her side.

Hardly aware of Buddy's presence, Lacey whispered again, "Please, Scully…open your eyes."

Scully heard her voice. He felt her touch. A teardrop fell on his cheek, and he realized Lacey was crying.

He struggled against the heavy weight of his eyelids. It hurt to move—to breathe—but Lacey was calling him.

His eyes opening into narrow slits, Scully saw her. She was beautiful, even in tears. He wanted to tell her that. He wanted to say he had never known any woman more beautiful than she, but he needed to tell her something more important, to warn her."

"Talk to me, Scully."

Scully struggled to speak. He needed to tell her it wasn't all over yet. She was still in danger.

"You're a part of me, Scully. If you die, a part of me will die, too."

No, he didn't want that! He wanted to protect her… keep her safe.

Buddy's face appeared in Scully's line of vision, and the

panic inside Scully lessened. Buddy was a good man. He'd do his best to protect Lacey for the present, but Buddy didn't know Barret was the man behind her grandfather's death, either.

"Scully, please…"

Lacey was pleading with him to talk to her, but his stiff lips were unable to form a response. He tried harder, but his strength was fading. He wouldn't last much longer.

He managed to say, "Lacey…"

Scully heard Lacey's intake of breath as he spoke her name. He felt the responsive tightening of her hand on his as she whispered, "We'll get you back to Weaver, Scully. You're going to be all right, you'll see."

He had to tell her about Barret first. She wouldn't be safe there unless she knew.

But consciousness was fading; Lacey's tears were still falling; the words were going unspoken.

And as the silent darkness closed in around him, Scully realized he had not even said he loved her.

Chapter Fourteen

The undertaker's wagon rolled almost ceremoniously slowly down Weaver's main street as it returned from the site of Charlie Pratt's burned-out cabin. The sky had turned suddenly as gray as the town's mood—as dark as Barret's disposition.

He glanced down the street at the many townsfolk who stood watching in their doorways. The unexpectedly violent turn of events at Charlie's cabin had elevated Lacey's story to the point of folklore in Weaver. He supposed it was to be expected in a town with so little to amuse it. After all, a child of eight had survived an attack from unknowns that had left her grandfather dead and their cabin burned. She had trekked through the wilderness to arrive in town wounded and dragging a limping burro behind her. She had gone to the saloon where her grandfather had sent her to be raised by a local barkeep, had been sent away to finishing school and had returned ten years later beautiful and cultured, only to be attacked again by the same men who had killed her grandfather.

And in the face of all odds, she had survived a second time.

Incredible.

And infuriating!

The wagon drew to a halt in front of the undertaker's parlor as Barret watched coldly. An unmarked hole in the ground was more well-deserved than the spot on Boot Hill that had already been marked for the burial. He had displayed the proper amount of shock at what had happened in order to satisfy the town, but he was yet incapable of feigning any other emotion.

The truth was, the way things now stood, he would be glad when the last shovelful of dirt covered the graves. As far as he was concerned—despite what anyone in Weaver might expect considering his former association with the deceased—the matter was cut and dried.

Goodbye, Blackie.

Goodbye, Larry.

And most definitely—good riddance.

It was time for him to take over.

He was hot, and the pain was deadening. Spiraling images filled Scully's mind. He saw Blackie's hand flash to his gun. He felt the bullets strike him as he returned fire.

Lacey's face materialized before him and he caught his breath. He had to tell her Barret was behind it all. She didn't know.

He called out, shouting Barret's name, but the words emerged cruelly distorted.

"Lacey…"

He said her name, but the sound was indiscernible to his own ears.

He could not protect her.

Consciousness again began fading and Scully mumbled the name of the only One to whom he could turn.

He whispered, "Jesus…"

"I don't know if he'll make it."

Lacey stood rigidly still outside Scully's bedroom doorway as sunset trailed into twilight on the street beyond. A burst of laughter resounded from the saloon below, the levity in sharp contrast with the dire circumstances in Scully's upstairs room.

Lacey stared at the elderly doctor's sober countenance. She told herself she hadn't heard him correctly. Scully had been gravely wounded in the gunfight that had brought about final justice for her grandfather's death. She remembered the moment when Buddy walked unsteadily into the circle of the fire's light. His head was still bleeding as he checked the two lifeless men lying a few feet away, then came to crouch at her side and whisper, "I'm sorry I let those two sneak up on me, ma'am. Jewel figured out where you were heading after you left the lessons for her and Rosie. She asked me to follow you and watch out for you, but I didn't see those two others until it was too late."

Buddy, sent by Jewel to watch over her. She knew if it hadn't been for him and the travois he had fashioned from two blackened cabin beams and the blankets from her bedroll, Scully would not have survived the long, grueling journey back to Weaver.

Her fears had heightened as Scully's fever rose, but she had truly believed the worst of it was over when he was carried through his bedroom doorway at last and Doc Mayberry walked into the room.

Yet Doc Mayberry's expression was now grave as he said,

"I'm sorry, Lacey. It just doesn't look good. Scully lost a lot of blood, he's having trouble breathing and his temperature is soaring."

Hysteria nudged at Lacey's mind as she replied, "Are you telling me he's going to die?"

"My dear…" Doc Mayberry took her hands gently in his. "I know how much this man means to you. He's the rock that has sustained you through difficult years, and he was willing to risk his life for you."

Lacey replied, "I just need to know how I can help him now that he needs me."

"You're doing all you can, Lacey."

"But it's not enough! You said it's not enough."

"We've both done all we can for him. I'll continue to care for him, of course, but the rest is out of my hands. All you can do for him is to make sure he gets the medicine I left for him every hour. Otherwise…" He shook his head, "I'm very sorry, dear."

Silent as Doc Mayberry walked down the staircase toward the saloon floor, Lacey turned abruptly and walked back into Scully's room.

Out of his hands.

The phrase Doc Mayberry had spoken reverberated in Lacey's mind as she looked down into Scully's tormented expression. His eyes were closed, but despite his weakness, he hadn't been still for a moment. He continued to writhe in the throes of an inner tribulation she did not understand. He called out sharply in his delirium, his voice sometimes raised to a shout, but his words were unclear. She had strained to understand him in the hope of offering him reassurance that would allay his torment, but she had failed.

Lacey brushed away the tears that slipped down her cheeks,

despising their weakness. She had no time for tears. Doc Mayberry had said it clearly. He had done all he could for Scully. The rest was out of his hands.

Lacey briefly closed her eyes. She knew in whose hands Scully's life now rested. She had always known, and she had prayed. Now looking down at Scully's pale, fevered countenance, Doc Mayberry's dire words rang again in her mind.

Her heart full, Lacey kneeled beside Scully's bed. She closed her eyes and clasped her hands tightly together as she whispered, "Dear Heavenly Father, I beg You to shed Your healing power down on Scully now. You are his only hope. You know him well. He made his own way in a difficult world, and in doing so, he strayed from Your word at times, but his heart is good and his spirit generous. He risked his safety for me, and he now teeters between life and death. I can't understand why he would so easily trade off his own safety for mine, except that he can't accept that his word, once given, should ever be rescinded.

"My dear Father, since returning to Weaver, I have come to comprehend the true significance of Samuel's words when he said, *'For the Lord seeth not as man seeth—for man looketh on the outward appearance, but the Lord looketh on the heart.'* Those words have offered me understanding and consolation, and I pray that You will see in Scully not the man he has occasionally been, but the man of great potential that he is. My eyes and my heart see that man clearly. My faith is full and strong that his life will one day come to reflect Your Son's teachings in a way that will be apparent to all. I believe that in Your goodness, You watch over us all, and that Scully was 'the rod and staff that comforted me,' because You deigned it to be so.

"Heavenly Father, I now kneel at Scully's bedside in the hope of returning just a portion of all You have given me through Scully with Your blessings. I beg that You hear my prayer when I beseech Your aid for Scully, and ask that in Your benevolence You will look with favor on my plea and make Scully well and strong again. I ask this fervently, in the name of Your Son, the Lord Jesus Christ. Amen."

Lacey wiped the dampness from her cheeks as she drew herself slowly to her feet. Scully's restless contortions continued, and the ache inside her deepened.

Barret paused as he picked up his suitcoat from the chair. He looked out his bedroom window, anxious anticipation fluttering inside him as twilight began fading into night. He slipped on his suitcoat and turned to his dresser. He picked up the derringer lying there and slipped it into his breast pocket with a hard smile. He had waited ten years for the moment fast approaching.

Barret adjusted his collar and stepped back to scrutinize his appearance. His performance when he visited Mary McInnes at her boarding house that afternoon had been touched with genius. He had been so clearly affected when he admitted regretting that he hadn't been particularly friendly with Scully in the past. Properly contrite, he had then said he admired Scully for the sacrifice he had made for Lacey's safety, that he was pained at the thought of his former attitude toward him, but even more distressed that the men he had innocently employed for so many years had murdered Charlie Pratt. He had said he wanted to make amends by offering both Scully and Lacey his support.

It amused him to recall how taken the old woman had been with his sincerity. She had actually asked him into her parlor for tea. During the course of the following half hour, he had learned all he needed to know about the events that had taken place at the campsite. Mary had told him that Lacey was grateful it was finally over and the men who had killed her grandfather had paid for their crime at last. She claimed that Scully had ridden out after Lacey simply because he had feared for her safety in the wilderness—an act that had proved prophetic in the eyes of the town.

Regarding Scully's care, she said that Lacey hadn't left Scully's bedside since they had returned to town, but however conscientious her care, Scully was failing. She said she had delivered Lacey a tray each mealtime, only to take the previous tray back untouched; that she had begged Lacey to rest, but Lacey had ignored her pleas. She said she feared for Lacey's health and had made the decision that she would go to the sickroom that evening when her work was done at the boarding house, and would insist that Lacey return to her room for a little while, if only to refresh herself. She had said she would not allow Lacey to refuse this time.

When looking at the old woman's determined expression, he had been certain she would not…and the plan he now intended to carry through had been born.

Dear Lacey, sweet Lacey, so concerned about her guardian's welfare—*and so determined to keep the secret of her grandfather's strike to herself.*

He had waited too long. He would get the information he wanted from her tonight, without delay.

The sound of Scully's labored breathing filled the otherwise silent bedroom. Sitting on an upholstered chair beside the bed, Lacey watched the rise and fall of his chest, her gaze lingering on the bloodstained bandage wrapped across it. The stain was dry. The wound had stopped bleeding. She supposed that was a good sign, but she wanted so much more. She wanted to feel the fever leave his body and see his constant tossing become a restful sleep. She wanted to see him well and strong again. She prayed the Lord would answer her prayers and she—

Lacey stood up at the sound of a knock on the door. She managed a smile for Mary when she entered the room. Mary looked at Scully, then looked back at Lacey with a sad shake of her head.

Without spoken comment on Scully's condition, Mary addressed Lacey, saying in a motherly tone, "You look exhausted, dear." She added, "You'll notice I didn't bring you a tray this evening."

"That's fine, Mary. I'm really not hungry."

"I know you aren't, but that isn't the reason I've come empty-handed. You haven't left Scully's side since he was put into that bed. You've refused everyone's help, including Helen's and mine, but I won't let you refuse me any longer, dear. I know Scully. He wouldn't want you to wear yourself out the way you have been."

"I can't leave him, Mary."

"He'll be angry when his fever breaks and he sees you looking totally spent."

Lacey did not reply.

"I want you to go back to the boarding house—"

"No."

"Just for a little while, dear. I've left a tray for you on the kitchen table, and I want you to make yourself eat, if only to keep up your strength."

"No, Mary, I—"

"Listen to me, please, dear. Scully will be angry with me if I failed to look out for you while he was ill. I have great affection for the fellow, you know, and I certainly wouldn't want that to happen."

"I'm sorry. I'll explain it all to him when he recovers."

"You don't look well," Mary continued with determined bluntness. "You're pale, and your appearance is disheveled. You don't want Scully to see you that way when he wakes up."

"He won't care."

"But he will—for your sake! Please, dear, go back to the boarding house. Take an hour for yourself so you may return refreshed and renewed. That's what Scully would want."

"No, I—"

"You owe it to him, Lacey, to be your best when he opens his eyes."

Lacey looked into Mary's sweet countenance. The dear woman was so obviously sincere.

Lacey paused in reply, uncertain. Maybe Mary was right. She hadn't eaten or slept more than an hour or two in the last few days. Nor had she looked in the mirror. She couldn't go on this way, and she knew it. She needed to look strong and fresh in order to set Scully at ease while he recovered.

Those thoughts in mind, Lacey forced herself to say, "You're right, of course, Mary. I owe it to Scully to be the person he expects to see when he's lucid again." She swallowed against the tightening lump in her throat and continued, "I'll go back to my room and refresh myself, but I'll return in time to give Scully his medicine in an hour." She paused, then added, "You will send someone for me if…in case Scully…"

"Dear, please go. It's only an hour, after all."

With a lingering look at Scully, Lacey left the room. She avoided the saloon floor and turned toward the newly repaired rear staircase where she might exit into the alley and elude comment about her red-rimmed eyes.

Lacey emerged from the alleyway and kept to the shadowed building overhangs on the street in order to evade concerned questions for which she had no answers. Within minutes she had slipped through the boarding house door and was headed for her room.

Cursing low in his throat, Barret watched as Lacey turned the corner toward the boarding house and disappeared from view. He had been just a few minutes too late and had missed her. The old woman had obviously finished her work at the boarding house and had come to relieve Lacey earlier than he had expected.

Just his luck!

Barret tensed as music wafted out onto the night air through the Gold Nugget's swinging doors.

More waiting. More wasted time.

No. He would not wait another day. He would not return to his home without the information he sought, even if he had to wait all night for Lacey to return.

Determined, Barret glanced around him, then faded back into the shadows of the Gold Nugget's alleyway. The thought that he was above skulking like a thief in the night flashed briefly across his mind, but he forced back its taunting. He would be a rich thief—a *very* rich thief—before this night ended. And he would see to it that no one, including Lacey Stewart, got in his way.

* * *

A knock on the bedroom door turned Mary toward it with a frown. She looked back at Scully, uncertain. His fevered contortions had ceased abruptly a few minutes earlier. Frightened, she had rushed to his bedside to discover that his forehead was cool and his breathing even. Elation had brought momentary tears to her eyes.

The knock sounded again and Mary walked quickly toward the door. She drew it open to Rosie's surprised expression at seeing her there.

Fearing that the necessary explanations would disturb Scully's restful sleep, Mary slipped out into the hallway and drew the door closed behind her. Smiling, she drew Rosie a few steps away and started to speak.

Jewel looked up at the exposed portion of the Nugget's second floor where Rosie and Mary stood by the railing. Her stomach tense, she watched their faces as they talked, hardly conscious of the cowpoke who stood beside her.

A chill worked down Jewel's spine. The reported violence at Charlie's campsite days previously had left her shaken. She remembered Lacey and Buddy's entrance into town, dragging the travois on which Scully lay. She recalled the instant when she saw the gash on Buddy's forehead, then realized that except for a twist of fate, Buddy might have been the man at death's door on that travois—or worse, that he might be lying back at the campsite just as dead as the two men who had tried to kill him.

The realization that she had sent Buddy into harm's way to watch over Lacey, and that he had gone simply because he loved her, had twisted the knife of pain in her stomach even tighter.

Yes, she loved Buddy. That reality had never been clearer in her mind than at that moment, but neither had it ever been clearer to her that Buddy might have given his life to please her.

To please *her*—when she wasn't worth the sacrifice.

Her heart aching, she had known what she must do, and she had done it. She had sent Buddy away. She had told him it was over between them, as she should have done so many months earlier.

She supposed she would never forget the look on Buddy's face when she told him. She knew she would never forget the pain of the moment when he left.

The anguish was with her still.

But with Lacey, it was different. Lacey was good and kind. Lacey was worth any sacrifice Scully could make for her. She hoped Scully would recover, for his sake as well as for Lacey's. She knew how important it was to Lacey that he did get well. She knew Lacey would never forgive herself if he didn't.

As for herself, she only wished—

Suddenly unable to finish that thought…unable to bear the weight of her distress a moment longer, Jewel rushed toward the swinging doors. She needed air, and some time by herself. She needed to put her sadness behind her…if only she were able.

Familiar voices outside his bedroom door awoke Scully to the silence of his room. He raised a heavy hand to his chest and felt the bandage there, then closed his eyes.

He remembered gunfire at the cabin campsite…Larry's startled expression before he fell…the hard ground underneath his own back and the pain in his chest that stole his breath. Most vivid of all was his memory of Lacey's stricken expression as she looked down at him.

Blackie and Larry were dead. They couldn't hurt Lacey any longer.

Total recall flushed Scully's mind with sudden panic. But Lacey had not even an inkling of Barret's part in her grandfather's death, or the fact that she was still in danger!

The conversation outside his bedroom door caught Scully's ear as he heard Mary say, "Lacey isn't here right now. She hasn't left Scully's bedside for a minute since their return to Weaver, so I sent her back to the boarding house to take an hour for herself. She's exhausted."

"I know." It was Rosie. "That's why I came. I wanted to know if I could do anything to help. I figured nobody would miss me downstairs if I stayed here for a while so Lacey could rest."

"You are a dear, Rosie." Mary's voice deepened with sincerity. "So many people have offered their help... Sadie, Helen, Janine Parker, Millie White, Jewel and you. Even Barret Gould came to my door today to offer his services."

Scully tensed. Barret Gould.

"He feels so guilty that he had at times employed the men who killed Charlie and shot Scully."

Scully's heart pounded.

"I told Barret we appreciated his offer, but Lacey was taking care of Scully. I also told him that when I finished work at the boarding house, I would come here and *insist* that Lacey go back to her room to take some time for herself. He seemed happy to hear it."

Scully's mind raced. Barret had been asking about Lacey. He wanted something from her...something he was willing to kill to get.

"Lacey should be back any minute. To tell the truth, I expected her back before this, but I guess she took my advice and decided to rest up a bit."

Scully glanced at the bedroom window. It was dark, and Lacey was alone on the street. He needed to find her before Barret did.

A loud crash from the saloon floor rebounded in the room, startling Scully from his thoughts.

"What happened?" Mary's voice rose a frightened notch outside his door.

"It's a fight downstairs." Rosie gasped, "Old Pokey fell. He's going to get trampled down there!"

The sound of footsteps running away from the door signaled Mary and Rosie's departure down the staircase.

His mind racing, Scully threw back the coverlet and slung his legs over the side of the bed. One purpose in mind, he forced himself upright.

Pain slashed at his chest and his senses reeled. A new gush of blood heated the bandages there as he pulled his trousers from the chair and slipped them on. Staggering, he fell against the dresser drawer and pulled it open. He grasped the handgun inside and turned toward the door.

Hardly aware of the commotion continuing in the saloon below, Scully staggered toward the rear staircase. His strength was rapidly failing. He reached for the doorknob, but it eluded him. His focus blurred. His knees weakened. He railed silently against his infirmity as consciousness dimmed and he sank slowly to his knees.

Lacey walked back toward the Gold Nugget, inwardly trembling. More than an hour had passed since she had left

Scully's bedside. She hadn't intended to stay away from him so long; but she had been clumsy in her haste and everything had seemed to go wrong. She had finally managed to freshen up and was forcing herself to eat some of the food Mary had left for her when a full glass of milk slipped from her shaky fingers and spilled onto her skirt. Rushing to change for the second time, she had then snapped the bodice button off her only other cotton frock, and had been obliged to take the time to repair it.

The thought of Scully's fevered countenance driving her, Lacey turned into the Gold Nugget's alleyway and started toward the rear staircase at a run. Mary was taking good care of him, she was sure, but she needed to see Scully, to hear the sound of his breathing. She needed that visual proof, that assurance that he would survive.

She was also late in giving Scully his medicine. Doc Mayberry had not looked particularly encouraging when he had handed her the bottle, but she had—

"Lacey."

Lacey jumped with a start at the sound of her name. She squinted into the shadows of the dark alleyway and frowned as Barret emerged into view. She questioned, "Barret, what are you doing here?"

"I came to see you, Lacey."

Barret walked closer, and Lacey caught her breath when she glimpsed the gun in his hand.

"What do you want? I have to get back to Scully. He needs his medicine."

"No, he doesn't."

"Yes, he does. Doc Mayberry said—"

"Stop pretending, Lacey!" Barret interrupted her, his expression suddenly vicious. "You've fooled everyone else, but you can't fool me. I know why you came back to Weaver."

"Why I came back?" Momentarily at a loss, Lacey said, "What are you talking about?"

"You came back to claim your grandfather's strike."

"My grandfather's strike?" Incredulous, Lacey said, "That's crazy! I told those other two and I'm telling you, too—my grandfather never struck it rich."

"I know better."

"Then you know better than I do." Impatient, Lacey said, "I don't have time for this. Scully needs me, and I'm going to him."

"Try it, and you won't make it past your first step."

Barret spoke with icy control. The realization that he meant every word registered sharply inside Lacey as she said slowly, "Someone misled you, Barret. My grandfather never struck it rich out here. He died just as poor as he lived every day of his life."

"Did he? Maybe you need proof before you'll understand that you can't bluff me anymore." Barret pulled a small leather sack from his pocket and threw it toward Lacey with a sneer. Lacey caught it in her palm as he ordered, "Open it!"

Complying, Lacey shook a large gold nugget out into her hand. She looked back up at Barret.

"Beautiful, isn't it? Your grandfather gave it to me in payment of the legal work he wanted me to do for him. He wanted to make sure *his strike* would be legally registered in both your name and his. He left the nugget with me without disclosing the claim's location. He said he'd be back, expecting that I needed time to draw up the papers."

Barret continued harshly, "You thought it was a secret. You thought no one knew about your grandfather's strike.

You thought you'd be able to pull the wool over everybody's eyes with that act about coming back to Weaver to see your grandfather's grave, when you really came back for the gold. Well, you almost succeeded. Your grandfather didn't tell anyone about his strike—only me. But as it turned out, telling me was enough."

Barret sobered. "I never intended to kill him—not if he cooperated. He could've been alive today if he hadn't turned the tables on Blackie and Larry when I sent them out to follow him. Then those two fools foiled my plans by killing him before he could tell them the location of the strike."

Incredulous, Lacey said, "You sent Blackie and Larry out after my grandfather, and you sent them out after me."

"I did."

"And you waited all these years to find out where my grandfather's claim is?"

"Not really. I had written the entire episode off as a failure until you came back to Weaver and gave yourself away."

"I don't know what you mean."

"You should've been more careful. I heard you talking to Wilson Parker at the store shortly after you arrived. You said you had plans that didn't include Scully or waiting for the 'right fella' to turn up. You didn't think anyone would suspect what you really meant by that—but then, you didn't think anyone knew about your grandfather's strike, either."

"My grandfather never made a strike. This nugget…" She looked down to consider it again. "I don't know where it came from."

"Liar!"

"I'm not a liar. My grandfather would've told me if he had finally made a strike."

"You know where that strike is. You went back to the cabin to get your bearings. I want to know where it is—now. I've waited ten years to leave this miserable town in style, and I'm not going to wait any longer."

"I told you, you're mistaken. There is no strike."

"I'm warning you—"

"You can warn me all you want. My grandfather never struck it rich."

"That strike won't do you any good if you don't live to enjoy it."

"Can't you hear me? There is no gold. My grandfather never made a strike."

"Are you trying to make me believe—"

"How many times do I have to say it? There…is…no…strike!"

Suddenly shaken, Barret snapped, "Shut up!"

He stared at her for long, silent moments before saying, "Congratulations! You've convinced me that you're telling the truth and you don't know the location of your grandfather's strike—but that was a mistake. Do you want to know why? Because in doing so, you've just sealed your own fate."

"What are you saying?"

"Walk back farther into the alleyway, Lacey."

"Why?"

"Do it!"

"No."

"I'll shoot you right here, if that's what you want."

"If you shoot me here, somebody will hear the shot. You'll never get away with it."

"You're wrong. No one will challenge me." Barret suddenly smiled. "You see, I'm Barret Gould—educated, respected, the town's only attorney. I'm above reproach and above suspicion. Whatever story I make up will be accepted by the cretins that inhabit this town, simply because they know don't know any better."

Barret's expression sent a chill down Lacey's spine as he then added in a lifeless tone, "No one will *dare* to challenge me. Goodbye, Lacey."

Shots rang out in quick succession, and Lacey took a staggering step backward. She gasped for air. She was somehow unable to move as Barret slumped slowly to the ground with round circles of blood rapidly widening on his chest.

Lacey looked up at the Nugget's rear staircase where Scully stood halfway down, swaying weakly, a smoking gun in his hand. Beside him in a moment, she had slid her arms around him supportively. Only then did she see Jewel standing in the alleyway, the gun in her hand also smoking.

Clutching Scully close as he sagged down onto the step, she saw Jewel turn and walk back out onto the street—directly into Buddy's arms.

Struck with the determination to fight for the man she loved, Lacey separated herself far enough from Scully to whisper, "I love you, Scully. You're a part of me. You always have been. I want to be with you always. I know that now, just as I know we were meant to be together. Speak to me, Scully, tell me—"

Lacey looked up toward sounds on the staircase above them the moment before helpful hands lifted Scully to his feet and turned him back toward his room. Hardly aware of the scurrying footsteps and the mumbling of deep voices in the alleyway below as onlookers gathered around Barret's body, she remained close beside Scully, refusing to surrender his hand.

Lacey stood anxiously beside Scully's bed when Doc

Mayberry appeared in the doorway minutes later. She heard him mumble as he approached, "That fella down in the alleyway won't be needing my help, so let's see what I can do here."

Lacey said shakily, "Scully's going to be fine, doctor." She bent down toward Scully to conclude in a whisper, "Because we were meant for each other."

Startled when Scully's eyelids lifted and his sober gray eyes met hers, when he curled his palm unexpectedly around her head to press her mouth down to his, Lacey leaned into his brief kiss.

She was breathless at the love reflected clearly in his gaze when Scully released her and he said weakly, but with conviction that came clearly from the heart, "That's right, darlin', we were meant for each other...and I'll never let you go."

Chapter Fifteen

The ranch house bedroom was large and airy, with flowered wallpaper in pale shades of blue. The early morning sun shone on the large bed that dominated the center of the room—the bed where Lacey and Scully lingered with their infant son lying beside them.

Lacey looked down at her sleeping child, at the spiky lashes lying against his smooth cheeks, knowing that underneath his closed eyelids, Jacob Scully, Junior's eyes were a clear and sober gray like his father's.

Her heart was full.

At Scully's touch, Lacey looked up to find his gaze searching her face. He whispered, "Is something wrong, Lacey?"

Wrong?

The thickness in Lacey's throat briefly precluded speech. How could anything be wrong? She was lying beside her husband, the man she loved, the man who had recuperated fully from his grievous wounds more than a year earlier. He was the same man who had relinquished his former life at the Gold Nugget to become a rancher—not because she had demanded it of him, but because he had accepted a need to follow the Lord's word more closely...and because he loved her. In the time since, she had borne him a son, and the love between them had expanded in ways she had never even dreamed.

Yet there was more.

Lacey recalled the beautiful moment almost a year earlier when Jewel and Buddy came to Sunday church services; when afterward, they asked Reverend Sykes to marry them. It had never been determined whether it was Scully's or Jewel's bullet that ended Barret's life. She supposed it was better that way because both Scully and Jewel had made a difficult, split-second decision for which she would be forever grateful.

Jewel had confided that she hadn't expected to see Buddy on the street when she emerged from the dark alleyway that fateful night. Yet when he was there with his arms open and waiting, she had walked into them instinctively, suddenly sure his love was true and his fidelity would never fail her.

Jewel had also confided that in that moment, she had resolved she would become worthy of Buddy's love, and of God's love as well. In truth, that was all she had ever wanted.

Lacey remembered the day shortly after Jewel and Buddy's wedding when Rosie came to tell her she was quitting her job at the Gold Nugget, that she had saved up enough money to leave town for a job farther west where she would start over using her new skills at reading and writing to good advantage. Lacey knew Rosie would succeed because the dear girl's heart was pure and open to the Lord's word.

Lacey glanced at the night table where her grandfather's Bible lay. Scully had recovered it from Barret's office, further proof of Barret's guilt, although, in reality, no proof had been needed. She had been overjoyed to be able to touch it again with the feeling that Grandpa was always near. Scully had accomplished that for her, and in doing so, had ended her nightmares and rounded out her circle of love.

She was so blessed.

"Lacey?"

Lacey responded belatedly, "No, nothing is wrong, Scully. I was just thinking."

Anticipating her need to hold the precious volume in her hands, Scully took her Bible from the night table and handed it to her. She fingered it lightly, then turned to the page where her grandfather's simple drawing noted a familiar passage: *Thou will show me the path of life; in thy presence is fullness of joy; at thy right hand there are pleasures for evermore.*

She remembered the moment when it all came together in her mind. Her grandfather had read that passage to her often, but he had read it to her with particular significance while drawing a small critter resembling Careful beside it before he left for Weaver the day he was killed. The truth of that passage had guided him throughout his life, and she suddenly realized that he had meant for it to guide her in other ways as well.

Lacey stroked the miniature drawing with her finger. She and Scully had followed that thought to fruition so simply. They had returned to her grandfather's gravesite, had loaded prospector's tools on Careful's back as her grandfather had done countless times before. The loyal burro had then turned instinctively to follow a trail through the wilderness that he had walked with her grandfather. He had stopped automatically at the last location her grandfather had worked—*the site of his lost strike.*

Lacey remembered the moment when the first nugget was

uncovered. She had met that moment and her grandfather's legacy with tears of bittersweet joy.

So many good things had come from that legacy—improvements on the ranch where Scully and she would spend the rest of their lives, Weaver's newly repaired church, the clinic that Doc Mayberry had always wanted to found.

Scully drew Lacey from her meandering thoughts as he nudged, "You were just thinking—about what, Lacey?"

"Weaver already has a school, but I was thinking how fine it would be if Weaver had another kind of school." She looked up at him, her clear eyes suddenly intent. "For people like Rosie and Jewel who aren't able to read and write because they never had the chance to learn."

Scully responded, "That sounds like a fine idea to me. I could talk to Reverend Sykes about it if you want."

Lacey's eyes filled. "And maybe...possibly...Rosie could come back to teach others to read."

"Maybe she could."

Suddenly solemn, Scully took a silky lock of Lacey's pale, unbound hair in his hand as he whispered, "But I want you to know, darlin', that when all is said and done, this gold is my true treasure. You mean more to me than any other legacy Charlie could possibly have intended."

His voice growing hoarse with emotion, Scully continued more softly still, "Charlie meant you for me...I know that now. That was that old man's purpose in sending you to find me that last day. He meant to keep you safe, which you will always be in my arms. He also meant to turn my life back onto the right path with love—which he did." Pausing briefly, Scully said, "Because I love you, Lacey."

Lacey saw the truth of Scully's words reflected in the

planes of his handsome face. She felt it in the touch of his lips as they lingered on hers, then glimpsed it in his eyes as he looked down at their son when he stirred.

Lacey comforted their son softly. She then leaned back to luxuriate in Scully's embrace as she held close a truth that was etched into her heart. In sending her to Scully, her grandfather had left her the most precious legacy of all—a legacy of love more precious than gold. A legacy that would last a lifetime.

* * * * *

Dear Reader,

When I was first asked to write for Love Inspired Historicals, I was immediately certain that Lacey and Scully's story would be the perfect one to tell. I had kept the premise for *The Redemption of Jake Scully* tucked away in a folder just waiting for the opportunity to develop an outline that had come to my mind so many years previously that I can't truly remember when or how it did. I knew *The Redemption of Jake Scully* was perfect because it embodied all that I felt was true about romance.

So much is written and said about romance and true love. To my mind, nothing has truly changed about it over the years. Most men and women always have been—and always will be—looking for a sense of commitment that will make them feel complete. My feeling is that when all material elements are stripped away, it is how much a couple is willing to share with each other, to sacrifice in a way that proves not to be a sacrifice in the end, and how willing each is to participate in making themselves become *one* in God's eyes that defines the true meaning of love.

I cherished Lacey and Scully's story. I wanted to bring their characters to life in *The Redemption of Jake Scully*. Writing about them was a true joy, and I hope I shared that joy with you.

Sincerely,

Elaine Barbieri

QUESTIONS FOR DISCUSSION

1. In the beginning of the story, Lacey leaves her school and a potential position in New York to return to Weaver, a place she both fears and loves. Why do you think Lacey felt so driven to return to her beginnings when she had the potential for a good life in the East?

2. Aside from sympathy for the unusual circumstances under which Lacey first entered his life, why do you think Scully felt so great a commitment to a young girl he had never seen before? Was it guilt for the lifestyle he had developed or loyalty to his mentor? Or was there more to it?

3. How did the author bring the Old West to life? What do you remember most about the setting and the time period based on this story?

4. What mannerisms did the characters have that marked them as living in the Old West? How do they differ from people today, and how are they the same?

5. How did faith impact the plot of *The Redemption of Jake Scully*? Might everything have worked out differently had Lacey exhibited a different attitude toward the teachings in the Bible? How so?

6. The religious quotations that sprang to mind in different situations in her life guided Lacey. Which quotations

spoke particularly to you? Which do you feel best represented the messages in the story?

7. Do you think Lacey compromised her faith with her devotion to Scully when his lifestyle conflicted with that faith? Why or why not? Did Scully's actions to save Lacey at the end of the story redeem him, or does he need to do more?

8. Did Lacey make a mistake by becoming friends with two of society's outcasts? What did Jewel and Rosie bring to Lacey besides their friendship? How did the choices they made fit with the book's redemption theme?

9. Barret Gould and his henchmen act selfishly throughout the story. Did they get what they deserved in the end, or was there any hope of redeeming them?

10. Did Lacey's grandfather make a mistake by keeping his strike a secret from Lacey? Why do you think he kept that secret?

11. Burros like Careful were common in the Old West. They thrived in hot, dry environments and were popular for carrying supplies for miners. How did Careful's presence enhance the plot of the story? What did he symbolize to Lacey, and to the heart of the book?

REQUEST YOUR FREE BOOKS!

2 FREE INSPIRATIONAL NOVELS
PLUS 2
FREE
MYSTERY GIFTS

Love Inspired
HISTORICAL
INSPIRATIONAL HISTORICAL ROMANCE

YES! Please send me 2 FREE Love Inspired® Historical novels and my 2 FREE mystery gifts (gifts are worth about $10). After receiving them, if I don't wish to receive any more books, I can return the shipping statement marked "cancel". If I don't cancel, I will receive 4 brand-new novels every other month and be billed just $4.24 per book in the U.S. or $4.74 per book in Canada, plus 25¢ shipping and handling per book and applicable taxes, if any*. That's a savings of over 20% off the cover price! I understand that accepting the 2 free books and gifts places me under no obligation to buy anything. I can always return a shipment and cancel at any time. Even if I never buy another book, the two free books and gifts are mine to keep forever. 102 IDN ERYA 302 IDN ERYM

Name	(PLEASE PRINT)	
Address		Apt. #
City	State/Prov.	Zip/Postal Code

Signature (if under 18, a parent or guardian must sign)

Mail to Steeple Hill Reader Service:
IN U.S.A.: P.O. Box 1867, Buffalo, NY 14240-1867
IN CANADA: P.O. Box 609, Fort Erie, Ontario L2A 5X3

Not valid to current subscribers of Love Inspired Historical books.

Want to try two free books from another series?
Call 1-800-873-8635 or visit www.morefreebooks.com

* Terms and prices subject to change without notice. N.Y. residents add applicable sales tax. Canadian residents will be charged applicable provincial taxes and GST. This offer is limited to one order per household. All orders subject to approval. Credit or debit balances in a customer's account(s) may be offset by any other outstanding balance owed by or to the customer. Please allow 4 to 6 weeks for delivery. Offer available while quantities last.

Your Privacy: Steeple Hill Books is committed to protecting your privacy. Our Privacy Policy is available online at www.SteepleHill.com or upon request from the Reader Service. From time to time we make our lists of customers available to reputable third parties who have a product or service of interest to you. If you would prefer we not share your name and address, please check here. ☐

LIH08

HISTORICAL

TITLES AVAILABLE NEXT MONTH

Don't miss these two stories in July

HIGH COUNTRY BRIDE by Jillian Hart
For widow Joanna Nelson, life presented constant hardships. Evicted from her home, she and her two children sought refuge on rancher Aidan McKaslin's property. He sheltered her family, while she brought faith and a woman's touch back into his world. Could Aidan convince the special woman to bind herself to him permanently or would he drive her away forever?

SEASIDE CINDERELLA by Anna Schmidt
Nantucket Island offered Lucie McNeil a chance for a better life. But her quiet existence was thrown into chaos when her employers' handsome son stepped ashore. Their pasts were connected by tragedy. She knew she should hate Gabriel Hunter, yet she could not. Instead she was drawn to the caring soul she sensed behind the ruthless facade he showed the world.

LIHCNM0608